Eden Palms Murder

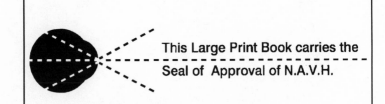

This Large Print Book carries the
Seal of Approval of N.A.V.H.

A KEY WEST MYSTERY

EDEN PALMS MURDER

DOROTHY FRANCIS

THORNDIKE PRESS
A part of Gale, Cengage Learning

GALE
CENGAGE Learning™

Detroit • New York • San Francisco • New Haven, Conn • Waterville, Maine • London

GALE
CENGAGE Learning·

LIBRARY OF CONGRESS CATALOGING-IN-PUBLICATION DATA

Francis, Dorothy Brenner.
    Eden Palms murder : a Key West mystery / by Dorothy
Francis.
      p. cm. — (Thorndike Press large print mystery)
    ISBN-13: 978-1-4104-1293-5 (alk. paper)
    ISBN-10: 1-4104-1293-8 (alk. paper)
    1. Single women—Fiction. 2. Homeless men—Fiction. 3.
Missing persons—Fiction. 4. Donation of organs, tissues,
etc.—Fiction. 5. Key West (Fla.)—Fiction. 6. Large type books I.
Title.
PS3556.R327E34 2009
813'.54—dc22   2008042535

Published in 2009 by arrangement with Tekno Books and Ed Gorman.

Printed in Mexico
2 3 4 5 6 7 12 11 10 09

For my family.

PROLOGUE

The mid-afternoon storm arrived without notice. Lightning slashed through black thunderheads, and wind screamed in from Hawk Channel, threatening Key West on this wintry day. Palms bent in the onslaught. Surprised gulls fluttered a moment then dropped like stones onto the beach where they huddled together for protection. The weather matched my mood. I turned my back to the wind and strode away from the sea, heading toward Eden Palms.

I had no trouble entering the Shipton mansion in Old Town. Locals throughout the island knew Francine Shipton as an outgoing hostess who welcomed friends and family whether or not they called ahead to announce their impending arrival. But gaining access to the upstairs, the home's second floor suite that Francine claimed as her private quarters, was sometimes difficult for some, but never for me.

"Hello, hello," Francine called through her front doorway when she saw me on her veranda. "Do come inside. I'm getting ready for this evening's meeting — plumping the pillows and all that. This cold snap's supposed to blow itself out quickly." She gave me a puzzled look. "Is there some problem?"

"Not at all." The wind slammed the screen door with a bang when I stepped into the spacious foyer and bent to kiss her cheek. "You've a big evening ahead of you and I wondered if you might need some help before your guests arrive." I glanced around, seeing nothing amiss. "Need chairs carried into the solarium? Extra ice toted to the freezer? How many people are you expecting?"

"Just a handful — my near neighbors. Of course they're among the strongest protestors. Want to convince them to see the situation from my viewpoint."

I looked up the curving stairway. On the balcony, I saw the thing I'd expected to see — the teakwood table Francine always used when she served coffee to a small group. The situation couldn't have been more perfect.

"I know you're counting on using that card table, Francine. You shouldn't try to carry something that heavy and awkward down the stairs. Let me give you a hand." Francine smiled and I started toward the second floor before she could argue. Counting each polished step from one to twenty-three helped divert my thoughts from the horror I knew was to come.

"That *would* be a help. You're such a dear friend."

Francine followed me up the steps. At the top of the staircase she picked up a blue cloth lying on the table.

"I started to dust, but I got sidetracked." She began swishing the cloth across the inlaid teak.

I took the cloth from her. "Let me do that for you, please." I took my time brushing nonexistent dust from the table legs, all the time nudging her ever so slightly to ease her in the best position possible.

"Oh, look, downstairs." I nodded toward the veranda doorway. "You have more guests."

She looked, and in that nanosecond I acted. Placing both my hands on her hipbones, I gave her a hard shove. Her scream gurgled into silence when her head cracked against the banister and her body thudded down, down, down the glossy steps. Now I clutched the pistol I'd hidden in my jacket pocket. I waited. Her head lay skewed at an impossible angle and she didn't move. Blood poured from her nose and trickled from her left ear. I wouldn't need the gun.

I dashed down the stairs, felt for her pulse, found none. Then reaching into my other pocket, I pulled out the dead blacksnake and smiled. The medical examiner would know she hadn't died from snakebite or suffocation, but the shock value of seeing the snake would give both the police and the town gossips much to speculate about in the days to come. Who hated socialite Francine Shipton enough to murder her? Who?

I wrapped the blacksnake around her neck twice before I pried her mouth open and stuffed the snake's head between her teeth and down her throat. The wind had died by the time I stepped back onto the veranda.

In an unusual stillness, I headed for home.

1

Later, I told myself that if I'd flown to Key West on a morning flight I might have saved everyone at Eden Palms a lot of trouble. But it didn't happen that way.

I'm Bailey Green, wannabe blues vocalist and songwriter. On this Monday night, I landed at Key West International at seven-thirty as scheduled, expecting our family friend, Francine Shipton, to meet me. She planned to drive me to her Eden Palms estate and the guest cottage that I'd rent for a nominal fee. I looked forward to working part-time as her secretary and gofer, helping her implement some project she'd devised to aid indigent people on the island. The rest of the time I'd be free to pursue my music career.

A couple of years ago I made a demo, and a little Internet record label wanted to sell my CD from their website. A nightclub owner in Des Moines heard it and hired me

11

for some singing gigs at his club. I retain ownership of the recording and the deal with the Internet people was strictly for distribution and sales. The CD sold fairly well for a while. But for the past two years I'd put my singing career on hold while I cared for my cancer-ridden mother — with little help from my brother, Chet.

When Mother passed away, grief almost overwhelmed me. Although Des Moines was only fifty miles from our small town, musicians in the city had forgotten about me, and I didn't have the moxie to pursue those former contacts. When Francine offered me a job in Key West and wouldn't take no for an answer, I wound up my affairs in Iowa and packed my things.

Goodbye depression. Goodbye snow. Hello trade winds. I'd hoped that leaving Iowa and living in the Keys would lighten my spirits, but no. Tonight, the memory of Mother's death left me with an inner chill I couldn't shake. I found it hard to believe that the locals called this island Paradise.

A flight attendant led me and the six other passengers on our feeder aircraft down a few precarious steps from the plane to the concrete runway.

"You'll find your luggage at the baggage claim area at the end of the terminal," she said, pointing. "Thank you for flying Air Sunshine. We've enjoyed having you aboard and wish you a pleasant stay on our island."

"Thank you," I murmured, then strolled toward the baggage claim area.

No point in hurrying. A ground crew would be loading our suitcases onto a cart for the next few minutes. My comfort-food gene kicked in and I pulled a miniature Reese's peanut butter cup from my pocket, unwrapped it, and savored its chocolate fragrance before popping it into my mouth. I wished government nutritionists would relieve my guilt by naming chocolate one of the four basic food groups.

Inhaling deeply, I hoped for a welcoming scent of night-blooming jasmine. Instead, I almost choked on a lungful of diesel exhaust. Once inside the terminal, I breathed the odor of stale cigarette smoke. I let others scramble to reclaim their bags while I scanned the waiting area and then the street outside looking for Francine.

Night blanketed the island. Overhead a skein of clouds half-masked an almost-full moon and a sprinkling of stars, and I caught the salt aroma of the sea. I stood for a moment enjoying the cool breeze as I peered at the almost-empty parking lot. No Francine. Drat. A few taxis waited at curbside near the baggage claim exit and I ducked back into the terminal to avoid a vendor with a tray of trinkets hanging from a strap around his scrawny neck.

I couldn't imagine Francine running late. She always prided herself on her promptness. *Others* ran late — never Francine Shipton. The baggage carousel began moving, groaning a bit under its load of suitcases, golf clubs, packing boxes, fishing gear. I spotted my two green cases and had dragged them to the floor when someone called my name.

"Bailey? Bailey Green?"

I whirled around. To my astonishment, the voice belonged to Francine's friend Quinn Bahama. Quinn's a free-lance reporter for the *Citizen,* and she makes no secret of her goal to work up to a staff writer position. We aren't close friends, just acquaintances who admire each other's work. Two years ago when I visited Key West, Francine had introduced me to Quinn and given her a copy of my CD, hoping for a bit of publicity for me and my would-be career. That was a few weeks before Mother became ill. It surprised me that Quinn still remembered me.

All the locals know Quinn. She also waits tables at the Two Friends Patio, hoping to meet a celebrity who'll grant her an interview. Lots of service people work two jobs in their effort to pay their bills here in Paradise. Quinn also haunts the airport hoping to see some well-known people who'll give her a few minutes of their time. Like most performers, I never run from a chance for publicity, and Quinn's a good writer. Readers can depend on her for accuracy in the whos, whats, whens, and wheres of her articles.

Tonight, Quinn wore a red satin caftan and matching spike-heeled sandals. The humidity made her curly hair look like a golden chrysanthemum, and her smile reached clear to her blue eyes. Looking at Quinn made most people want to smile back. And I smiled.

"Hello, Quinn."

"Been away for awhile?"

Quinn eyed my green parka and my two matching bags. Successful performers tell me the best kind of advertising is word-of-mouth, so I surround myself in green in what I hope is a subtle attempt to promote my name and my CD titled *Greentree Blues.*

"Been home in Iowa for quite a while. I'm surprised you remember me." I slipped off my fleece-lined parka, tossed it over my arm, and felt like a butterfly emerging from

15

a cocoon. "It's winter-coat cold up north."

"Business or pleasure trip?"

"I've spent the last two years taking care of my mother. She recently passed away after a long bout with cancer."

"Oh, I'm so sorry."

Quinn did look sorry and I tried to lighten the moment. "It's really good to be back in Key West. Francine Shipton offered me a job and promised to meet me, but so far I haven't seen her."

"What kind of job?"

"Secretary. Gofer. She has some kind of a new help-the-underdog project in mind. I won't know in-depth details until I talk with her. But whatever. I needed a new scene."

Quinn raised an eyebrow, then asked, "Could I give you a lift somewhere?"

"That's kind of you, but no thanks. Something important must have delayed Francine. I'm sure she'll show in a few minutes."

"Would you use those minutes to give me an interview?" Quinn began rolling one of my bags toward a bench beside the wall.

I hesitated, elated that Quinn remembered my budding career yet torn by my need to meet Francine. If I got ahead as a singer, I needed time and publicity. Francine would arrive soon, and I hoped the job she had in mind for me would allow me time for sing-

16

ing and composing. With luck, publicity would come later.

"Well, okay, Quinn. Maybe we'll have time for a quickie. And I'll make a deal with you." I tapped the camera I always wear around my neck. "Trade you a brief interview for a pic." I followed her, wheeling my second bag.

"Why would you want my picture?" Quinn asked.

"I snap shots of eye-catching people and places. Sometimes I draw on my photos to help me create lyrics for a new song. I'm still interested in writing a lot of my own stuff."

Quinn, smiled, posed, and I clicked a shot. "What would you like to talk about?"

"Your Iowa nightclub gigs and your song-writing, of course." Quinn pulled a small notepad and a ballpoint from a caftan pocket. We sat down beside each other on the bench. "Got any new titles to introduce to the public? Or maybe to a record company?"

"No. But I'm working on a few ideas." No point in advertising that I'd had a writer's block during at lot of the time I'd spent caring for my mother.

"It's hard to make a demo and get it before the public," Quinn said. "I really

17

liked *Greentree Blues*."

I didn't tell her I was a long way from recording a second CD, perhaps even from getting a nightclub gig as a singer. When I hesitated to reply, she spoke.

"Couldn't you have hired a part-time housekeeper to care for your mother while you worked a bit?"

"In my mind, that was never an option." I didn't elaborate. I had missed singing, but family came first. Mom had needed me. "I wrote a few lyrics after Mom had retired for the night. Once I get settled at Eden Palms, I may have time to compose and sing again."

"Well, I suppose taking care of your mother took most of your time."

"Yes, it did." I began to worry about where this interview might lead. Clearly, Quinn wanted information about my compositions and I had nothing new to offer. It saddened me to talk about my mother's death. I didn't dare talk about my brother, Chet, who'd left Iowa and been assigned a new identity through the Federal Witness Protection Program.

"Can you tell me about any songs you're planning to write?"

I glanced at the doorway, hoping to see Francine. "Sorry Quinn, but I can't. If I talk about a song before I write it, it weakens my desire to write." I hesitated, afraid that Quinn might give up on me as a news source and leave. "But here's an idea. Maybe we could talk about my life in a way that would be meaningful to other musicians as well as to other mothers and daughters."

"Sure," Quinn agreed. "What do you have in mind?"

"Hold it a minute, okay? I need to check to see if Francine's outside." I walked to the doorway, stepped onto the sidewalk, and scanned the small parking lot. Double drat! Still no Francine. I returned to Quinn, and for the next twenty minutes or so I told her about my growing-up years and my relationship with my mother. Would anyone be interested, I wondered.

But when I finished my tale, Quinn flashed a thumbs up.

"That's a touching story, Bailey." She glanced at her watch then stood. "Tell you what. The *Citizen*'s short a staff writer this week — flu. If I get this story written and to the editor tonight, you may be able to read it in tomorrow's paper. The publicity will be my welcome-home gift to you."

"Wonderful, Quinn. I'll be looking for your article."

Quinn made brief notes on her notepad,

then smiled. "Francine's certainly taking her time getting here. Sure I can't give you a ride? No problem. Everything's close by here in Paradise."

"Thanks, Quinn, but as sure as I accept your generosity, Francine will arrive and be unable to find me. I'll phone her again. Great talking to you. I'll look forward to reading your article."

Quinn blew me a kiss then left the terminal.

I keyed Francine's number on my cell phone. Busy. Another plane landed and taxis appeared like homing pigeons. As I buried my cell phone in my purse, my fingers touched the strange note Francine had sent me in Iowa. I pulled it from its envelope, flattened it on my knee, and began rereading it while I enjoyed another peanut butter cup. She *had* promised to meet me, hadn't she?

Dear Bailey,

I can hardly wait for your return to Key West, and I'll meet your 7:30 plane and drive you to Eden Palms. Strange things are afoot here, occurrences I don't understand, and I'm frightened. I've received threats, and mysterious events have taken place here in my home. With your creative

20

bent, maybe you'll be good at following clues. Maybe you can help explain some of these unusual occurrences. Maybe you can explain why I'm finding snakes in the solarium. I know you'll be tired from traveling when you arrive, but I want you to attend an important 8:30 meeting here at Eden Palms. Tomorrow after you've settled into the cottage, we'll talk about the job I have in mind for you. Bless your heart for coming to my aid.

Warmly, Francine

I shoved the note back into my purse then stepped outside to scan the parking lot one more time. No Francine. Why hadn't she sent Zack to meet me if she couldn't make it herself? But maybe her son had a date. Maybe he wasn't at home. I wished I hadn't reread the note. In spite of the warm evening, goose bumps prickled my arms. I felt a hidden threat behind every palm tree on the premises. Even the trade wind carried a scent of danger.

One more try with the cell phone told me its battery had died. I pulled change from my pocket and tried the pay phone nearby. Again, the busy signal. I decided to wait no longer. But when I headed toward a pink taxi parked at the curbing, the trinket vendor I'd avoided earlier blocked my path. I swerved to the right, he stepped in front of me. I darted left, he darted too. I couldn't get around him.

2

"Let me help you, ma'am."

When the vendor reached for one of my bags, I recoiled from the sight of his grimy hand.

"You can hardly manage two cases by yourself." Ignoring my body language, he click-clacked my bag across the tiled floor and outside the door before he turned, thrusting his trinket tray in front of me again. "How about a small gift for a friend?"

I felt trapped by this unshaven man, barefoot and shirtless and carrying a strong scent of garlic. He wore a faux diamond in his right earlobe and nothing else but tattered shorts and one shark's tooth dangling from a black thong knotted at the back of his neck. My ire rose as he continued to give me the hard sell for his trinkets.

"Rings, lady? Pendants? Scarves?"

I glanced over my shoulder and then looked all around me. Where was airport

23

security? Why wasn't an attendant here to help with my bags? I glanced toward the yellow cab parked at the door. No point in trying to signal that driver for help. He leaned against his cab's fender, absorbed in yakking with another driver.

Before I could protest, Garlic Breath walked farther outside the terminal door and wheeled my suitcase toward a pink taxi. I followed him, pulling my other bag. When he stopped at the taxi door, I felt trapped into buying a trinket. Although unasked, he had provided a service I needed. I never could have pulled both bags unassisted.

The elderly taxi driver, wearing a pink shirt that matched his cab, eyed my suitcases. "Ride, ma'am?"

"Yes, please." While he stowed my bags, the vendor stood between me and the taxi, waiting — waiting.

"How about a conch shell?" He picked up a mollusk and held it toward me as if I couldn't see it on his tray. "Or maybe a scarf? A bracelet?"

"Is this man bothering you?" The cabbie stepped closer to me.

"No," I lied. "Please give me a sec to buy a small gift."

The vendor smirked at the cabbie when I chose a blue cotton square bearing the words "CONCH REPUBLIC."

"Special today," the vendor said, with a look that bordered on a leer. "Two for the price of one."

"Maybe the lady doesn't want another scarf." The cabby's eyes flashed fire. Before he could say or do anything that might start a confrontation, I grabbed two scarves, thrust a ten-dollar bill at the vendor, and headed for the taxi door.

"Where to, ma'am?" the driver asked.

He helped me into the back seat then slammed the door so quickly it caught the corner of one scarf. When I opened the door to free it, the cotton square had a grease stain on a corner. I rubbed at the stain then felt the oily residue on my fingers. So what! Folding both scarves, grease stain to the inside, I jammed them into my purse and wiped my fingers on a tissue. Never in this world would I find a use for those scarves.

"Where to, ma'am?" the driver asked again.

The vendor still stood at the open taxi window. I leaned forward and whispered the address, trying to shake the creepy feeling the guy might try to follow me.

"That's off Eaton Street, isn't it?" the driver asked, without repeating the address.

"Yes. The narrow lane opens onto a cul-de-sac, and there's parking once you pull off Eaton."

The driver slapped his forehead with the heel of his hand. "Drat! Are you in a hurry, lady?"

"I'd like to get there as soon as possible, please. There's a problem?"

"A few minutes ago, I came from the other side of the island, ma'am. Lots of traffic backed up over there tonight blocking some of the streets. Maybe something spectacular happened at the sunset celebration."

"It's long after sunset," I pointed out. "Must be nearly nine o'clock."

"But sometimes the crowd lingers, watching the artists work or listening to the fortune-tellers charm their prey. Maybe the tight-rope walker tumbled off his rope."

We turned right at the airport exit, easing onto South Roosevelt Boulevard. I peered through the rear window to make sure the vendor wasn't following us. I breathed easier when I saw him offering his trinkets to a grandmotherly type with a child in tow.

Keeping within the speed limit, the cabbie drove alongside Smathers beach. The salty breeze brushed my cheeks, and I enjoyed watching the moon and starshine silver the sea. Nobody in their right mind risked swimming in the shark-infested waters at this time of night, but a couple sat on a bench in one of the Tiki shelters, arms entwined while they shared a kiss.

We drove on toward Higgs Beach then turned onto White Street heading toward Old Town and Eaton Street. A pole light glinted on the badge of a white-shirted motorcycle cop when he approached us before we crossed Fleming Street.

"Please detour a few blocks around this area," he said. "You might try taking a right here, go around a block and then head for Duval and Front Street before you approach Eaton again."

"What's going on?" the cabbie asked.

"Can't say for sure," the cop said. "But it's hard to get onto Eaton Street right now. We've orders to ask drivers to vary their route."

We made a couple of right turns and then did the Duval crawl to Front Street. The clock at Saint Paul's chimed nine times, but a few people from the sunset crowd still lingered near the dock.

"Ma'am, I'm not sure I can get you where you want to go. Could you call someone to pick you up here? Sometimes folks who live on a congested street can get through when others can't."

"Do you have a phone?" I asked. "Mine's dead."

He lifted his cell from the seat beside him and I gave him Francine's number.

"Got a busy signal, ma'am."

"This delay's making me crazy. Isn't there some way you can get through?"

"I can drive you around until Eaton opens up, or we can wait here near the dock. I gotta keep my meter running even if we're parked. Company rules."

"Yeah, right." I tried not to imagine the fare I'd be stuck with.

The cabbie finally found a parking slot on Simonton Street. "Fare's not as much when the motor's just idling," he assured me.

Hating to waste this waiting time, I pulled the unwanted scarves from my purse and thrust one toward him. "What do you know about the Conch Republic? Is it a historic thing?"

"Don't seem historic to an old Conch like me," he said. "The story goes back twenty-five years or so, but to a chick like you . . ." He hesitated. "You interested in history?"

"Sure. I'm a blues singer and songwriter. Bailey Green." I hoped he might recognize my name.

"Suppose I should have heard of you, but I don't do much listening except for the noon news. What kind of songs you write?"

Hope died. "I sing mostly blues and some jazz. *Greentree Blues.* That's the title of my CD. You can find it at stores here in Key West. A replicating facility keeps a stock of them on hand, and my friend, Francine Shipton, sees that local stores have a ready supply."

The cabbie didn't reply. So much for word-of-mouth advertising tonight. "Tell me about the Conch Republic. I might be able to use the info in some lyrics sometime."

He chuckled. "Well . . . that might work if you're looking for humor. Back in 1982 — before you were born, right?"

I didn't supply my age or tell him I'd been born in '82. He waited a moment then continued his story.

"In 1982, the United States Border Patrol set up a blockade on Highway One north of the Keys. It stopped everyone, including Keys citizens, from driving to or from the mainland. We were stuck here like barnacles on a boat hull — stuck here on 'the rock.' Forever? Nobody knew the answer.

"Can't recall the why of the blockade right now. Do remember it made us Conchs trapped in the islands feel like noncitizens of the US of A. Our mayor flew to Miami and raised one whopper of a fuss. News reporters and TV cameras caught him in action. He stamped his feet. He waved his arms. He shouted that the Florida Keys were seceding from the Union. Then and there."

"He had the authority to do that with no citizens' vote or anything?"

"Said he did. We Conchs were foaming-at-the-mouth mad. We never questioned his say-so."

"You mean he actually made the Keys an independent nation?"

"You got it. At least that's what he said." The cabbie chuckled. "He began our rebellion by breaking a loaf of Cuban bread over the head of an onlooker wearing a U.S. Navy uniform."

"I've never read about a war between the Florida Keys and the United States. You've got to be kidding me."

"No. I'm talking for real. The mayor's rebellion raised him from mayor of Key West to prime minister of a new nation. He named it the Conch Republic. Leastways that's the story he told us Conchs — and the newspapers and the TV people."

"So what happened next?"

"Cops hauled our new prime minister to a bigwig at the navy base there in Miami.

And get this. He surrendered to Union Forces. That's the pure truth. That's what he did. Surrendered. Next thing, he demanded a billion dollars in foreign aid. Said it was for rebuilding our nation in the Keys."

"That sounds all too familiar." I laughed in spite of the fact that I wanted his story to end, wanted to be able to get through to Eden Palms and Francine.

"Well, he didn't get no foreign aid from the US of A, but in time the blockade came down. Hah! Memories of those days linger to the present. In fact, a while back, an official of that old Conch Republic raised the Conch Republic flag on a piling of the Old Seven Mile Bridge. Created a real flap in the *Citizen*."

"What was that all about?" I hated to ask, reluctant to hear more of his information drop.

"Florida has a wet foot–dry foot law as concerns Cubans trying to claim US of A citizenship. If refugees hit dry land, they can stay. If they're picked up at sea, they're returned home."

"Wonder who thought that up? Sounds crazy."

"A few refugees landed on an old bridge piling. Their feet were dry, but Florida officials sent them home, saying that section of the unused bridge was at sea."

"A debatable point, I'd say."

"Right. Conch Republic officials ruled that because the bridge piling was a part of the sea instead of a part of the US of A, they would claim it as a sovereign territory of the Conch Republic."

"Did they get by with that?"

The cabbie shrugged. "No. Not legally. But we Key Westers are both Conchs and Americans and we're proud to be both."

Before I could speak, he shifted gears and pulled into traffic once more.

"I see cars moving up ahead. I'll try again to get through to Eaton Street."

We had to wait at a few intersections, but we made it to the cul-de-sac that housed several turn-of-the-century estates. I gasped. I had no trouble spotting Eden Palms. Tonight the Victorian structure stood cordoned off by a blaze of light and crime scene tape. It looked like a glowing beacon in the dark of night.

The wrongness of the scene shocked me, left me numb, breathless. An unexplained death at Eden Palms? I knew why cops strung yellow tape. Francine? Zack? Housekeeper? Grounds man? Not Francine. My friend. My mentor. Not Francine. My mind recoiled from that thought.

"Looks like bad news." The cabbie turned off his headlights as if he hoped no one would notice us. "Sure you want to get out here? I can try to back up and drop you somewhere else. Hotel, maybe?"

"I haven't many choices. Please pull up to the path leading to that cottage set back from the street."

Once he clicked the headlights on and parked, we both alighted from the taxi. He opened the trunk and set my bags on the ground. "Want me to pull your cases to the cottage?"

Before I could answer, Zack strode across the lawn toward us, spoke for me, and reached for his billfold. "I'll take charge of the lady's bags and the fare."

Thank God. At least Zack was alive, vertical, ambulatory. Thank heaven he was the kind of guy who was first to help out in any emergency. I started to ask about Francine, but an inner caution stopped me.

"Thank you, Zack." Handsome. Rangy. Silver hair that belied his youth. Tonight his face looked ashen, as if he might have suffered a blow to the stomach. Strangely, he gave no smile. No greeting. He was wearing his usual khaki slacks and handprint shirt, but his broad shoulders sagged. A chill feathered along the back of my neck when I thought of Francine's note — of the crime scene tape. I shied away from the thought that Francine might be dead. I corked my questions and waited.

3

While Zack set my bags on the sidewalk, paid the driver, and walked alongside the cab for a ways, directing him to the easiest exit from the cul-de-sac, I stood in front of the cottage trying to get my bearings. Policemen moved like fire ants, running everywhere, congregating on the steps, on the sidewalks, on both the upper and lower verandas of Eden Palms. The mansion looked as if someone inside had snapped on every light. Francine?

Again, I thought of the note in my purse, and it, along with the crime scene tape, warned me again that something terrible had happened. But maybe not to Francine. Maybe someone else had been in the mansion. Surely Zack would have told me immediately if his mother had died. I couldn't bear the thought of more tragedy in my life. By focusing on the living scene around me, I tried to blot out thoughts of death.

This area of Old Town boasted mansions built back in the 1800s when only a scattering of hardy souls lived on Key West and when land was both plentiful and cheap. In today's real estate market, any of the four homes on this cul-de-sac would bring a million or two each. Or more. Property here seldom went on the market unless the owner died without heirs.

Tonight, near neighbors and a few onlookers gathered in uneasy knots in the street or on the manicured lawns that surrounded the Shipton mansion and swimming pool. I recognized most of them from having met them when Mom and I had spent a week with Francine several years ago. I looked across the street to where Dr. Gravely, wearing his usual navy blue walking shorts, white silk shirt, and gold-trimmed yachting cap stood talking to realtor Courtney Lusk outside his home. Above the slender columns supporting the upper wrap-around gallery of his Colonial/Victorian mansion, dim lights glowed from two arched turrets. The mansion housed his living quarters along with the private clinic he operated for wealthy patients, who preferred his surgical expertise to that of the surgeons at the local hospital.

In the smidgeon of time that I observed

them, Courtney left Gravely standing alone as she strolled toward her home. The breeze caught her wrap-around sarong, revealing shapely legs, trim ankles, and the Prada sandals she made her trademark. Gossips said she inherited her property from her grandfather. I thought Courtney's sultry appearance failed to fit in with the coral rock structure and its Spanish-colonial pillars. She climbed a few steps to her veranda and went inside. My gaze lingered on her home until I saw her appear on the mansion's second-floor balcony, almost hidden beneath royal palms.

Then a tall man wearing a black tank top, blue jeans, and flip-flops caught my attention. He skulked into the croton bushes at the side of Courtney's home, and if she saw him from her balcony, she never let on. The man had a familiar look about him, but in my brief sighting I couldn't identify him as anyone I knew or as one of the area's residents.

No lights glared from Courtney's or Dr. Gravely's homes. And at the Tisdale residence, only a small glow shone from the dormer windows that were tucked like eyebrows under the overhanging roof. In front of this home, low lights reflected in the dark water of a decorative pond. I remembered a computer-controlled ecosystem where a few white, lemon yellow, and metallic orange-colored koi enjoyed a pampered life.

I didn't see Tucker Tisdale anywhere, but I cringed at my mental image. He carried a cloying smell about him and spoke in a falsetto voice. In addition to washed-out blue eyes and hair the color of boiled parsnips, the man tried to hide a skin problem by wearing wrist-length shirts and long pants. His rough epidermis peeled continually, as if he were recovering from severe sunburn. He reminded me of a molting alligator — only I doubt that alligators molt.

The Tisdales owned an upscale funeral home and crematorium off Duval Street. Tonight, the thought of death and funerals made me shudder. His association with the dearly departed along with his personal appearance made him a neighbor I'd rather avoid — one I *did* avoid whenever I could.

I jumped, startled, when Zack returned and touched my elbow, urging me toward the cottage where Mom and I had stayed on our previous visit. Without speaking, we each pulled a suitcase along the flagstone lane to the doorstep, and Zack reached inside the front screen to unlock the teakwood door and snap on a light. Once inside, he closed the screen, but left the door open to air out the cottage. I tossed my parka onto the rattan couch and turned, dreading what he might say.

"Mother's dead."

His stark words shocked me. I should have empathized with him. I should have embraced him and offered sympathy, but his eyes were glazed. His voice sounded distant, flat, emotionless, and his terse words pounded on my eardrums like stones. For a moment I felt dizzy, and I dropped onto the couch. Fighting for equilibrium, I buried my face in my hands. Moments passed before I could lift my head.

"I'm so sorry, Zack. So terribly sorry." I managed to rise and offer him a belated embrace. In the few moments he held me close, I smelled the familiar lime scent of his aftershave and I fought a temptation to kiss him. We were not lovers, only family friends who had dated now and then. A few years ago, before I met him, his father died and he'd given up his art studies at the university to take over the family business. I admired his selflessness.

"Mother's dead." He repeated the words *sotto voce* and I still had trouble believing them, refused to believe them. He said no more, but terrible tension separated us. I fought reality. I forced myself to think about anything but Francine. My mind flashed to happier times as we both stood there mute.

My CD release in Key West. Francine and Mom had been close school-girl friends and she'd visited us in Iowa many times, but I'd never met Zack. In the store where Francine had arranged for me to do a signing, I'd accidentally upset a stack of albums. Zack relieved my embarrassment by picking them up and putting them in order. Then he bought Greentree Blues.

"Shall I sign it for you?" I asked.

"Autograph it to Courtney, please."

"Ah, you have a lady friend."

He smiled and winked. "I live in possibility."

My ruse for learning his name failed. But the man was a reader, and perhaps a music lover. He'd quoted my favorite line from Emily Dickinson. So he had a girlfriend. His silver hair, his blue eyes, his sexy smile attracted me, but no man for me right now. My budding music career required my full attention. I forgot about my mother's belief that people seldom met by accident. Later, I wondered what fate had brought Zack and me together. For surely our meeting had been predestined.

"Mother's dead."

When he repeated the words for the third

time I snapped back to the present. I wanted to run, but I forced myself to stand firm and face whatever came next.

"Tell me what happened, Zack? How . . . When?" My voice faltered and my stomach churned.

He pulled me to him, looking into my eyes and drawing me close before he stood back and met my gaze.

"Zack, what happened to Francine? Can you tell me about it?" My questions flowed in a gushing torrent. "Did she suffer? Had she been ill? Why are the police here? When did it happen? I understand now why nobody met my plane."

Zack shook his head and sighed, overwhelmed by so many rapid-fire questions. "Bailey, believe me. I didn't meet your plane because I didn't know you were arriving tonight. Had I been aware, I or someone else would have been at the airport to welcome you, to drive you here."

His words stunned me. Why hadn't he known of my arrival? Why hadn't Francine told him? Why would she have kept my arrival a secret? Maybe he was trying to tell me I was no longer welcome.

I stepped back from him. "I don't understand any of this scene, Zack. Not any of it. Recently, your mother . . ." I hesitated, unwilling to mention Francine's note or reveal its contents even to her son.

Maybe I didn't know Zack as well as I thought I did. What if he had caused the happenings that had made Francine feel threatened? A frisson of fear chilled me.

"Zack, if I'm no longer welcome here, if you want me to leave, I'll certainly go — now! Immediately!" I grabbed my parka as if I might depart that very moment. My words held more bravado than I felt. Without Francine I had no job, and I'd be hard put to find another place to stay tonight with the island already overcrowded with tourists demanding lodging.

"Of course you're welcome here. Never doubt that. Never."

"Then give me a clue as to why Francine kept my arrival a secret."

"I don't know — have no idea. But since she invited you, I'm sure she intended to meet your plane. Her fall —"

"Where? An accident? How did it happen?"

Zack started to say more but stopped when someone knocked. He opened the screen door to a short and stocky man whose pudgy face reminded me of the Pillsbury Doughboy. Red hair. Gray suit. Shirt and tie. He stood as if balancing a crown on his head, or perhaps a chip on his shoulder, and I knew from his stance and his clothing that we faced a dignitary. Few locals dressed so formally.

"Detective Cassidy," Zack said, "please meet Bailey Green. Bailey's arrived this evening from Iowa."

"Pleased to meet you, ma'am."

Detective Cassidy's flinty eyes matched his suit and I sensed his level gaze memorizing my appearance.

"Will you come inside?" Zack stood back, making room for Detective Cassidy to enter.

"No, thank you. I want you to join me at your home for a few minutes. Miss Green will remain here, please."

"Of course," I agreed. Detective Cassidy spoke in a soft, no-nonsense monotone that put me on guard even more than his probing gaze.

Before leaving, Zack walked through the kitchen to the back door, opened it, then snapped the lock on the screen and turned to tell me goodbye. Air wafted inside, relieving the stuffiness that had collected in the cottage. I watched Zack follow Detective Cassidy from the cottage and turn toward Eden Palms before I locked the front screen door behind them.

4

I dropped again onto the couch, and rubbed my eyes with the heels of my hands. Francine was dead. I waited for the tears to come. I'd lost a true friend, a dear friend, a mentor who'd bonded with me, who'd understood my need to test my wings as both a singer and a songwriter. Surely that's why she'd offered me a job.

Not only had I lost Francine, I'd also lost more of my mother. Years ago, when Francine became dependent on a dialysis machine, Mom donated one of her kidneys to her, saving her life. That part of my mother had died with Francine. I felt a hollowness, heavy, cold, and I thought about my interview with Quinn. Anything felt better than thinking about Eden Palms and Mother and Francine — and Zack. I willed my thoughts away from the present.

"Quinn, did you always get along with your mother?"

Quinn scowled before she smiled. "Mom and I have our problems, but tell all, Bailey. Sometimes it empowers people to know celebrities have problems similar to their own."

"Celebrities? You flatter me! We both know I'm no celebrity."

"I won't take notes. Just tell me things that are important to you concerning you and your mother."

She tucked her notebook and ballpoint away. "Ben's on a shrimp run — my husband. He'll be gone a few days, so I have plenty of time right now."

"And apparently, so do I." I offered her a peanut butter cup and unwrapped another one for myself.

"I grew up dirt poor. Dad played dropout when I turned five and my brother, Chet, four. Mom worked at a laundry, scratching to make ends meet. All through Mom's elementary and high school years, she and Francine had been best friends. Then Francine attended an Ivy League university, married well, and moved to Florida."

Quinn grinned. "Money. My favorite thing."

I didn't tell Quinn about the kidney transplant or about Francine's deep need to repay Mom's kindness. No point in making such private matters public.

"Francine's kept track of us all these years.

She knew I was singing on weekends and doing nightclub gigs in Des Moines. She knew I'd clerked in a music store since high school days and had saved my money for an electronic keyboard and a computer with music-writing software."

"Very special goals, considering so many people live from moment to moment dodging bills from maxed-out credit cards."

"Mom felt so proud of my singing, but she worried about me driving to Des Moines and home late at night to do the club gigs."

I didn't tell Quinn of my own inner fear — fear that I wouldn't make it as a performer or a songwriter.

"Mom had made many sacrifices for me during my growing-up years, and I appreciated them. But I'd chaffed at the live-at-home restrictions that were necessary if I saved any money. Mom wanted me to continue living at home. So I did and I made the best of it, paying Mom each month for room and board."

"Good for you." Quinn nodded. "And you sold your demo."

"Right. And my club gigs in Des Moines went well until cancer entered our lives. I set composing and performing aside and, against Mom's protests, I stayed home full-time to care for her in her final illness. We lived on her savings that she had wanted to pass on

to Chet and me at her death. Tenseness marred our relationship until she told me she wanted to leave her body to science."

"You mean to some research hospital or university?" Quinn asked.

"Right. She felt that the study of her organs might help scientists find a cancer cure, felt that others might benefit from the knowledge her body might provide. So I Googled for organ donor information. I e-mailed organizations. Mom and I talked to the bigwigs in charge. The friction between us ended after we both willed our bodies to the University of Iowa's body donor program."

"Any regrets?" Quinn asked.

"I felt wary at first. I couldn't imagine my heart pumping someone else's blood or my kidneys helping some stranger pee. But those feelings passed. I'm pleased to be able to give others a chance for a better life. At the end, Mom and I bonded. She died peacefully."

After a time, I forced myself to sit up, forced myself to think about the here and now. What would happen next? The two people I loved and needed most lay dead. I had no job. I had no place to live. I felt abandoned and afraid. Zack hadn't called Francine's death a murder. Who would want to murder Francine Shipton?

Knowing I needed to unpack sometime, I

47

decided it might as well be now. Zack hadn't mentioned returning to the cottage tonight. Detective Cassidy hadn't wanted my presence at the Shipton mansion. In fact, he'd ordered me to stay here. For a few moments, at least, everyone had left me on my own. My nervousness grew and I closed and locked both outside doors.

The cottage looked the same as I remembered it from my previous visit. Green fiber mats decorated the parquet floors, and jewel-toned cushions covered the rattan couch and chairs. White walls helped give it a typical Florida Keys ambience. Zack had done charcoal caricatures of his acquaintances, and they hung in bamboo frames on the living room wall. The likeness of his mother showed a grand dame wearing a tiara, dressed in a flowing caftan, and sitting on a throne. She held a gold-knobbed scepter in her right hand.

The charcoal likeness gave a gentle spoof at Francine's reign as president of the Key West Women's Club. Only outsiders laughed at this group. Insiders knew the women were devoted to Key West and worked hard to ensure and promote its welfare. They had proved their support many times by their projects to protect and enhance the island. When they wanted something to happen, it happened — amidst fanfare, hoopla, and good times.

Having brushed against a sketch near the doorway, I stopped to straighten it. Tucker Tisdale and his wife, Sarah. Zack had presented them ensconced on the porch swing where they sat in the early evening, enjoying the trade wind and chatting with neighbors who passed by. Francine had said she could set her watch by their appearance on the porch, knowing they had finished their TV dinners and that *Wheel of Fortune* had ended.

I rolled my largest suitcase into the bedroom, pulled a sturdy pine rack from the closet, and heaved the suitcase onto it. My electronic keyboard had arrived ahead of me, and I guessed Francine had placed it in the corner, but tonight I ignored it. Francine's death left me with no heart for thinking about music or about unpacking, but I unzipped the lid and opened my suitcase. Maybe the wrinkles would fall from my shirts and shorts by morning and I wouldn't have to iron. Iron is a four-letter dirty word here in Paradise. Key West is wash-and-wear country.

I'd learned to protect my clothes by encasing shoes in shower caps before packing them, so now I removed the plastic before placing the shoes on the closet floor. I stopped. Enough. I couldn't continue this task tonight. Let it wait until morning. Then I heard a noise at the back door. Was it a scratch? Or a true knock? My thoughts hit red alert. Maybe I'd imagined the sound. I held my breath and listened. No. I heard a second scratching.

I snapped off the light, although the window shade had been drawn to the sill and nobody could have peered inside. Feeling my path to the doorway, I reached around the jamb to click off the living room light before I crept through the kitchen toward the back door. The scratching sounded again, and my teeth began to chatter.

"Come on, Bailey, what's the buzz? Open up."

The hissing voice preceded a light knock.

"Who's there?" I whispered, although I wondered why I should be frightened with so many policemen prowling the area. To surprise the intruder, I flipped on the outside light. A dark-haired man stood propping a bike on its kickstand.

"Bailey, let me in." The man turned and whispered his order again — the young man in jeans and tank top I'd seen near Courtney's house. Now, I recognized my brother.

50

"Chet!" I shouted.

"Shhh!" he cautioned and stepped inside. "No more Chet Green stuff. My new name's Mitch Mitchell. That's the handle the feds gave me, the name people down here call me. The government's given me a new identity and helped me find a place to live. Hey! They've even given me some start-up money."

"Oh, Chet." I hugged him and gave him a kiss. "You don't know how glad I am to see you."

"Don't let *anyone* hear you call me Chet. Total secrecy, Sis. That's the price tag on my existence. I'm Mitch Mitchell. Forget that and you'll blow my cover."

"Come in and sit down. Ch— Mitch." I made sure all doors were closed and all shades drawn before I turned on the living room lamp. "The black hair's okay, but the eyebrow ring. Was *that* really necessary?"

"I thought it might strengthen my disguise. In Iowa, Chet Green wasn't a body piercing type."

"You must have lost twenty pounds."

"A guy tends to drop weight when he stops eating. I did the hair-dye job myself. You can hardly tell it, can you?"

"Hardly," I lied.

"And the tattoo on my arm — a guy on

51

Stock Island did that. My tribute to Iowa. Tattoos or the lack of them are a thing cops down here notice, and Chet Green didn't have any in Iowa."

I eyed the cornstalk tattoo and shook my head. "Realistic. But what are you doing here?"

Until tonight I hadn't a clue as to Chet's whereabouts. He'd disappeared from my life. A death-bed promise to Mom made me responsible for his well-being. I'd given Mom enough problems during my lifetime, and I felt looking out for Chet would help relieve my guilt.

I'd been the kid who set the whole town searching when I accidentally locked myself in the library over Labor Day weekend, the kid who flunked math tests involving numbers of more than two digits, the kid who study hall teachers caught reading modern novels instead of Shakespeare. All things considered, I thought it only fair that I atone for my former waywardness and my present music-career stubbornness. I'd wanted to make Mom's last days peaceful, so I'd promised to look after Chet — who had no desire to be looked after.

I repeated my question. "What are you doing here, Chet?"

"You should know the answer to that one.

I'm keeping a low profile. Only two of the druggies I testified against back home are in prison. Others are still out there somewhere cooking meth. They'll be gunning for me when I return to testify against them, but I'll go back when the police say the time's right. Until then, Key West's my new home."

"Why Key West? Out of the whole world, why here? Why a place you'd never seen before?"

"I liked your description of the island, the great mix of people. Tolerant people. You made it sound like no matter what lifestyle a guy chooses, he can play it cool, hide out here, and never be noticed." Chet blushed and looked at the floor. "And I chose Key West because I heard you were coming here. You're the only family I have left, but we have to make sure nobody knows we're related."

"I missed you at Mom's funeral." His mention of family ties fueled my sarcasm.

"Gee, Sis, I didn't dare show up for that, much as I loved Mom. I hated missing that last goodbye, hated leaving you to handle all the grief and sadness alone, all the details of closing the apartment."

"Oh, sure."

"That's pure truth. If I'd shown my face at the church or the cemetery, Bubba Bronson's gang would have shot me on sight. Believe that. They'd have tossed my carcass to rot in some hog manure lagoon. That's where police found Ron Halstead's remains — when they finally found them."

I shuddered. "I understand, Ch— Mitch. We'll survive this. Somehow. Do you need money?"

"No. I have a small stipend from the feds and I have a job."

"Where are you working?"

"At Two Friends Patio. I'm a dishwasher. The boss says I can work up to waiter if I show for work on time, reveal some talent for getting along with people."

"Sounds good, Mitch." I said his new name without stuttering. "Where are you living — somewhere nearby?"

"Yeah. I'm shacking up at a one-room apartment on Caroline Street — sometimes. Sometimes not. Courtney Lusk, your friendly realtor across the street, handles the rental. Some cool babe. She even gave me part-time work at her place — caring for the lawn, whacking coconuts and dead fronds from the palms. But mostly I hang out here and there with friends."

Some kid I'd promised to look out for! "I want to see your apartment. If you don't have adequate housing in a safe area . . ."

"You can come see it. Maybe. Maybe sometime. Don't want to give anyone reason to associate the two of us."

"I suppose that's the safe way, but . . ."

"You'll see me around now and then. When I'm not washing dishes, I do odd jobs. I made it a point to work for Francine and Courtney in your neighborhood. I may begin to mow lawns for Dr. Gravely and Mr. Tisdale, too. I've talked to them. They're going to let me know soon."

I wanted to ask Mitch if and what he knew about Francine's death, but someone knocked and Zack called out.

"Bailey, you still awake? Bailey?"

5

"Just a minute." I shoved Mitch out the
back door, hoping nobody would see his
exit. I wondered about his apartment,
wondered when I'd see him again. Once he
left, I ran through the living room, grabbed
a deep breath, and opened the door. Zack
stood waiting on the doorstep, but he didn't
mention my delay in appearing.

"The police want to talk to you and all
the near neighbors at Eden Palms. Detective Cassidy will notify us in about ten
minutes. You'll come along, won't you?
They're removing the crime scene tape
now."

I motioned Zack inside. "But —"

"Don't worry. Cassidy says this'll be an
informal meeting."

"Yeah, right. I watch *Law and Order.* The
words 'informal questioning' are a ploy.
They hope the culprit will be so nervous
he'll drop his guard, say something incrimi-

nating, and make their investigation easier."

"If you'd rather skip their questions tonight, Cassidy said you could come to police headquarters tomorrow. Your choice. Why not go tonight? Get it behind you."

"Was Francine . . . was she *murdered?*" The word snagged in my throat.

"The police haven't said for sure. They're calling their work tonight a death investigation. But since they strung tape, I'm guessing they suspect foul play."

"I'll go as requested, of course. Why don't you sit and relax here while we wait to be called?" Where was Mitch? I hoped he'd managed to leave the area unnoticed.

Zack glanced at his watch before he stepped farther into the living room. Through the open doorway we watched the activities at the mansion. One cop tugged the crime scene tape off the palms, the hibiscus, the crotons that surrounded the house, then another cop arrived to help. They stuffed the tape into a plastic bag.

"Guess they can't reuse the stuff." We left the doorway and sat together on the couch. "At least that's what Cassidy said. It's too wrinkled and stretched. They burn it later to keep it out of the hands of dumpster divers."

I nodded. "Kids love to use it instead of

toilet tissue when they decorate a home of their choice."

I sensed Zack thinking a discussion of crime scene tape would prevent our discussing Francine. But questions tortured me, and so far he was the only person who might have answers.

"Zack, you said Francine fell. Exactly what happened? Where did she fall?"

"She fell from the second-floor foyer down the curving staircase to the front hall entryway. Twenty-three steps. Twenty-three! The M.E.'s doing an autopsy, but he said from all appearances, she died from a broken neck. He'll have a full report ready — maybe tomorrow."

Why did I sense Zack withholding information? Surely I deserved to know what had happened. In a reflex motion, I rubbed my neck. When I noticed Zack watching, I dropped my hand to my side. "A broken neck. How awful. How terrible."

"The M.E. thinks Mother died instantly — if that's a comfort to anybody."

No comment. I remembered my mother's lengthy bout with cancer and how she'd suffered for months. But who could say a quick goodbye was less painful than a slow farewell? Not I. Certainly, not I. I didn't ask Zack's opinion.

"Evidently, the police don't believe Francine fell by accident," I said. "But what do you think? I mean, she'd climbed up and down those curving steps several times a day for years. She was aware of places where the treads narrowed — knew them well, but anyone can make a misstep."

"I'm hoping the police call her fall an accident, nothing more sinister. But maybe something or somebody rushed her. She'd been preparing for a meeting tonight. I know she had her cleaning lady here yesterday, but today, maybe some last-minute detail caused Mother to hurry. Her fall certainly could have been an accident. That would be an easy answer, maybe too easy."

Again, I sensed Zack withholding information. Was he privy to some esoteric secret he was withholding from me? I thought of Francine's note, but I refused to share it. Clearly, Zack and I felt wary of each other.

"Zack . . . do you believe Francine might have taken her own life?"

Zack stood and paced. "Think about that, Bailey. No. I don't believe she had an accident. And no, I don't think she committed suicide. Would you consider killing yourself by throwing yourself down a flight of stairs?"

He gave me no chance to answer.

59

"No, of course you wouldn't. Never in this world. Nor would I. Nor would Mother. She was too gung-ho on life, too caught up in the day-by-day excitement of Key West to want to exit at age sixty."

He'd given his take on the accident and suicide questions. Now my voice dropped to a whisper as I faced the only alternative. "Murder? You think someone entered the mansion and murdered your mother?"

Zack's steady gaze bored into mine. "The police haven't said murder, but that's my thinking. You're the only one I've told, Bailey. Please don't let my words go any farther until we know what happened."

"Of course." I sighed in relief, felt as if someone had hacked through the anchor line constricting my lungs. Had Zack been involved in Francine's fall, he'd promote the accident theory, wouldn't he? Or the suicide theory. A killer wouldn't suggest the possibility of murder. He wouldn't express an opinion that would be tantamount to asking for an in-depth police investigation. Would he?

It bothered me that I worried about Zack's role in this death scene. He'd never given me reason to be afraid of him, and I wasn't afraid of him now. Or was I? No. I argued with myself. No. It was only normal that I worried about him. Nobody wanted to see a friend involved in a police investigation.

Zack meant no more to me than any other good friend. Francine had told me about his teenage engagement and his devastation when his bride-to-be got cold feet and fled the church, leaving him at the altar to face several hundred guests. It hadn't surprised me that Zack kept women at a distance. But he'd been a good friend to me, and I tried to erase thoughts of his involvement in Francine's death from my mind. The police hadn't said murder — yet.

"Why would anyone murder your mother, Zack? I can't imagine her having a mortal enemy. Oh, we all may have people who dislike us, but few of us have enemies who want us dead."

Zack hesitated so long that I thought he might ignore my question. When he did clear his throat to reply, I dreaded his answer.

"Incidents have taken place in Key West that you're unaware of — political things, civic matters that surfaced since your previous visit."

"What sort of things? I tried to keep up with Key's news. I read the *Citizen* on the Internet, but I'll admit I missed many days.

Caring for Mom took most of my time. What headlines did I miss?"

"There's been a lot of flack lately about the plight of the homeless in the city."

"That's new? According to articles I've read, the homeless pose mega problems in cities throughout the nation as well as in Key West."

"Key West is home to more vagrants during the winter than at other times. They drift here seeking sunshine and warmth. They find it. They settle in and stay."

I shrugged. "Good thinking. If I were homeless, I might do the same thing."

"A recent estimate said almost two thousand vagrants live in the Keys between here and Florida City, and that eight hundred of them live in Key West."

For a moment I forgot why we were discussing the homeless. I glanced again at the cop tugging on the crime scene tape. "What does the plight of the homeless have to do with Francine's death? I see no connection."

"There is one. I feel sure of it, but you'll have to hear me out if you want the whole story as I see it."

"I want the whole story. Tell all."

"A while back the cops rounded up some vagrants on Mallory Dock at the time a cruise ship began unloading passengers. Cops prodded the vagrants into a squad car, took them to jail, tried to arrest them and toss them into a cell. But the judge came to their rescue, calling such an arrest illegal."

"I suppose the city fathers thought a lawyer on the prowl might talk some jailed vagrant into suing the city."

"Right. And the guy might win his case along with megabucks of city money. According to present law, the jailing of vagrants is illegal unless the city provides a safe shelter where they can spend the night. The judge said everyone has an inalienable right to a good and safe night's rest."

"And Key West can't guarantee that?"

"Right. It can't."

"What about the churches? What about social services? Don't they provide the homeless with bed and meals?"

"Some do, but not enough of them. So the city decided to fix the problem by building an official safe shelter on Stock Island. The project's under way — a huge tent with enough beds for those seeking nighttime safety. Plenty of security guards."

"So what's the problem? If the cops nab a vagrant, he'll have a choice — the safe tent or the jail."

"Turns out the Stock Island tent's too

small." Zack sighed. "That's where Mother entered the picture. She's always had compassion for the homeless. But she also felt that seeing panhandlers on our streets was a turnoff to the tourists whose dollars keep our cash registers tinkling. And, are you ready for this?"

Again, Zack didn't give me time to answer.

"Mother's solution to help involved turning Eden Palms into a safe house, an annex for the homeless when the Stock Island shelter overflowed."

It took me several moments to digest that news. Francine giving up her home? Unbelievable! And what about the rental cottage? It rattled me to think about living only a snail's throw from the uncouth and the unwashed.

"I can't imagine Francine giving up Eden Palms."

"Neither could I or any of our neighbors. Neither could anyone living in Old Town. People blasted negative letters to the *Citizen.* Residents demanded extra city council meetings where they could protest at length and air their personal views. Everyone thinks a homeless shelter's a great idea as long as it isn't in *their* back yard."

I wondered why Francine hadn't mentioned this turmoil in her letters. But then, she probably hated to add her problems and Key West's problems to the ones I faced in Iowa. Then I remembered the note in my purse. Did her helping-the-indigent-plan that she'd hired me to help her with involve turning Eden Palms into a homeless shelter? I could hardly believe it!

"Francine wanted to remodel Eden Palms into a safe house for the homeless?"

"She not only wanted to, but she had the bucks to do it. I argued, but although the mansion's my home, too, she wouldn't listen. She forged ahead, discussing blueprints with building contractors, architects, plumbers, electricians. Of course, in their gulosity, those businessmen were eager to line their pockets with Shipton money."

"I can see she might have made enemies."

Zack nodded. "Right. Whatever Mother wants, Mother gets — one way or another. You know that. She enticed you here against her long-time friend's wishes — your mother's. She ignores those who disagree with her. She uses protestors' toes as stepping-stones to her goals. I'm sure she saw her idea as a noble cause, her contribution to humanity."

"From what I hear, some of the homeless hate the idea of living in a shelter. They prefer their wild-blue-yonder zip code."

"Here comes Detective Cassidy now. Please don't mention anything we've discussed unless you're asked direct questions, okay?"

"Okay," I agreed, but before Detective Cassidy reached the cottage, he veered in another direction and left us waiting again.

"I don't understand how Francine could believe that her disrupting this neighborhood would help anyone."

"It wouldn't." Zack shook his head. "You're right. Many vagrants don't want help. It'd mean no more alcohol. No more drugs. Some of 'em are on the lam. Fleeing from the cops? Maybe. Or perhaps from their families. They may be tired of paying child support or alimony. They can think of worse things than being homeless in Paradise."

"So you're thinking someone in the area may have murdered Francine to put an end to her homeless shelter project?"

"It's a possibility. In fact it's the only motive I can think of. A safe house here would make neighbors feel endangered. It'd lower their property values — and don't think the people living on this cul-de-sac would stand still for that."

"What'll happen to Eden Palms now that Francine is . . . gone? Had she already signed papers donating the property to Key West?"

"No, but she had her lawyer working on it. As things stand now, I'll inherit the property. I'm her only son and heir."

"Oh." I tried to cut off the fears tugging at my mind. How well did I know Zack Shipton? Sometimes he startled me, reminding me of the aloe cream I used for sunburn — smooth but with a sudden burning coolness.

"Oh." I couldn't manage more than the one syllable.

"Yes, oh, indeed. If the police cry murder, I'm sure I'll be number one on their suspect list. I've been vocal in my disapproval of Mother's plans. And anyone who inherits a fortune from a murder victim is bound to face scrutiny."

"Here comes Cassidy again." I nodded in his direction, glad now to have his company — his protection. After we left the cottage, I turned to lock the door.

6

One by one, cars headed to the mouth of the cul-de-sac and turned onto Eaton Street. I recognized the medical examiner who had given me information for some dark and down song lyrics. I also recognized a police photographer who had given me tips on taking pictures. Those men probably didn't remember me, but I remembered them and all the help they offered.

Someone moved through Eden Palms, snapping off the lights. First the third floor blacked out. Then the second floor. Even without crime scene tape marking a disaster area, the Shipton mansion loomed cold and formidable. When I climbed the coral-rock steps I realized it had been Francine's personality and charm that had given the mansion warmth.

White pillared columns on the veranda supported a second-floor balcony where a pine railing enclosed its perimeter. Francine told me the railing's spindles had been hand-carved in the 1800s. Sailors whiled away hours at sea by carving decorations for their future homes. I didn't try to look up at the small third-floor roof and its widow's walk. The head-back position would make me dizzy, and that, coupled with my inner fears, could make me fall.

Once inside the mansion, I vowed to avoid looking at the staircase, but I failed. The curving steps magnetized my gaze. I tried not to imagine Francine's body crumpled in the foyer, and I jumped, startled, when Zack touched my elbow and nodded toward the solarium. The sunroom with its bay windows facing the south still held the day's warmth along with the fragrance of damp earth and jasmine. Water from an ornamental fountain almost hidden beneath an elephant ear plant dripped like a monotonous threnody.

"Take seats, please," Detective Cassidy ordered. "I believe I've enough chairs for everyone. If not, we'll bring in more."

True. He or some ancillary officer had arranged a semicircle of Francine's bridge-table chairs in front of the plethora of tropical plants she tended daily. Huge terra cotta ollas held an assortment of ivies, miniature hibiscus, aloes — even small trees. I couldn't come close to naming all the varieties. Francine had been a walking green thumb. How could she have thought of removing lush foliage from this sanctuary and replacing it with beds for the often-raucous homeless?

"Ladies and gentlemen," Detective Cassidy began, "please make yourselves comfortable. This's an informal meeting, and I intend to talk to each of you. It will take time."

"Do we need a lawyer?" Courtney blurted the question and yanked her yellow sweater more closely around her shoulders.

Her throaty voice and pragmatic question startled me. I scrutinized the group, wondering if anyone else might question the detectives. Dr. Gravely? Zack? How had Tucker Tisdale and his wife escaped this gathering?

"Ms. Lusk, if you'd feel more comfortable with a lawyer at your side, feel free to summon one. The telephone's at your disposal. Let me make it clear that nobody's under arrest. The cause of Francine Shipton's death is yet to be established. This's an informal questioning to help me ascertain what went down here tonight."

"Then we're all under suspicion?" Dr. Gravely rubbed his cheek where a nervous tic pulled at the flesh under his right eye. "Correct?"

"Of course not," Detective Cassidy said.

"I feel that everyone here's under close scrutiny," Courtney said. "I don't like this one bit."

"There's a telephone on the kitchen wall, ma'am," the detective said. "You're free to make a call or calls, or you're free to leave."

At that point a strange man entered the solarium from the kitchen hallway, paused, and then stood near the doorway behind Detective Cassidy. I wondered who he was. Did he plan to grab anyone who tried to escape?

Cassidy turned toward the stranger. "Please let me introduce Detective Joe Burgundy. Detective Burgundy and I are partners, and we'll be working together on this case."

I liked Detective Burgundy on sight. He stood tall and when he smiled a greeting, his smile lit his whole face. Although he stood at attention for Cassidy's intro, he relaxed when he entered the solarium, moving as if his bones were strung on elastic. I wondered if he'd worked a murder case before. In his casual suit and crew-neck shirt, he looked like a poster boy for Banana Republic. I wished I could snap his picture for future reference. But then, I guessed I'd be seeing him often enough if a police investigation developed.

"Are all the neighbors here?" Cassidy directed his question to Zack.

"Tucker and Sarah Tisdale are absent," Zack answered. "He's at his funeral home, and his wife's off-island — up North Carolina way visiting her sister."

"Detective Burgundy, please drive to Tisdale's place of business and ask him to accompany you here?"

"Yes, sir." Detective Burgundy turned and left.

Detective Cassidy paced before the semicircle of chairs, eyeing each occupant with his probing gaze.

"Are you sure we aren't under arrest?" Courtney squirmed, an action foreign to her usual mannerisms.

"No, Miss Lusk. I answered your question earlier. Nobody here's under arrest. As I told you, this will be an informal meeting, important but informal."

"How important?" Courtney demanded.

How did she have the nerve to question the detective in charge!

"The meeting's important both to you and to me. This's the start of our mysterious death investigation, and I need everyone's help."

I wondered what right Cassidy had to hold

us here, but I didn't blurt my question. Blurting was Courtney's style, not mine. I hoped she would ask, but she didn't.

"If the medical examiner gives me information that someone murdered Francine Shipton, I'll need facts quickly. If the police have no strong lead on a suspect within twenty-four hours, the investigation can drag on for days, weeks, or months. It could end up as a cold case, unsolved but still open many years from now. I don't want that to happen. I don't intend that to happen. Someone in this room may be able to offer clues as to what transpired in this home today."

"You believe Mrs. Shipton's death was murder?" Now Dr. Gravely spoke up. "I think that's what you're trying to tell us."

"I have an open mind," Cassidy said. "You people were Francine Shipton's neighbors and friends. You are the people with whom I'll start the investigation as to the cause of her death."

"What time did she die?" Courtney asked. "I've been showing property and making sales calls all day. If I need an alibi, I have one."

"If there turns out to be a need for alibis, I'll be checking on those later," Cassidy said. "And I won't release the time of death until I get that information from the medical examiner — probably later tonight or early tomorrow."

The telephone rang and nobody spoke.

"It's your home, Zack. Answer the phone, please, but be aware that we're recording all conversations."

Was that legal? I wondered. But I guessed it was or the police wouldn't be doing it. I cocked my head, trying to overhear Zack's telephone conversation. Impossible. He kept his voice whisper low. When he returned to the room, his expression revealed nothing.

"The call's for you, sir."

"Thank you." Detective Cassidy nodded and I wondered if his face would crack if he risked a smile. He walked to the kitchen. He didn't stroll. He didn't hurry. He moved like a man used to having others wait for him. When he returned to the solarium his words did little to relieve our curiosity.

"Detective Burgundy's returning to join us." He looked at Zack. "We'll need two more chairs, please."

Zack brought in more chairs, placing them next to Courtney's, and a few minutes later all heads turned when Detective Burgundy entered the solarium urging Tucker Tisdale and Mitch ahead of him.

My heart pounded. Where had Detective

Burgundy found Mitch? What had my brother been doing since he left my cottage? Where had he been?

"Gentlemen," Detective Cassidy eyed Mitch and Tucker Tisdale as if they had broken some law and were up for reprimand. "Please be seated." He nodded toward the empty chairs. "I'm sure Detective Burgundy told you why we're here and why you've been asked to join us."

Tisdale and Mitch both nodded. Tisdale pulled his shirtsleeves low onto his wrists. Mitch looked straight ahead.

"Young man," Detective Cassidy said, peering at Mitch, "since you don't live in this neighborhood, I'll begin my questions with you and then you'll be free to leave."

Be careful, Mitch. Be careful. My mind shouted the warning, yet I knew Mitch had experience in handling himself around police investigators. But this situation was different. This time Mitch might be on the other side of the law. If Detective Cassidy delved too deeply into Mitch's past he might discover Chet Green from Iowa. I thought of no way I could help my brother now. I could only hope the Federal Witness Protection Program would keep him safe.

"I'm going to ask each of you to answer my questions. I'll be taking notes for future reference." Cassidy looked directly at Mitch. "Young man, your name please."

"Mitch Mitchell."

"Your address, please."

Mitch supplied the address of his Caroline Street apartment.

"What brought you to this neighborhood tonight?"

"Curiosity, sir. I work for, worked for, Mrs. Shipton and Ms. Lusk. Mowed their lawns. Sometimes I helped Mrs. Shipton with heavy lifting. Now and then she asked me to change the position of the plants in this room. Tonight, when I heard sirens and saw emergency vehicles heading this way, curiosity got to me. I followed them on my bike."

"What was your reaction when you learned Mrs. Shipton was dead?" Cassidy avoided mentioning or suggesting that Francine had been murdered.

"The news shocked me. Surprised me." Mitch looked at the floor and his face flushed. "And to be frank, I felt sorry to know I'd lost a good customer."

"Do you know the rest of the people in this room?"

"Yes, sir. At least I know who they are — their names and where they live."

"Miss Green only arrived here tonight.

You're acquainted with her, too?"

I held my breath, but Mitch looked directly at me as he answered.

"I know Bailey Green by hearing Mrs. Shipton mention her. She felt excited at having hired a famous person to work for her and live in the guest cottage."

"Famous?" Cassidy asked.

"At least sort of famous," Mitch said. "She's a singer and a little bit famous. I mean, she's cut a record that's for sale in Key West. At least that's what Mrs. Shipton told me."

"When did you last work for Mrs. Shipton?"

"This morning, sir."

"What duties did you perform?"

"I mowed the grass, weeded around the hibiscus bushes and plucked off the withered blossoms. She wanted everything to look neat for the evening meeting she planned."

"Was that all you did?"

Mitch hesitated, and again I held my breath, afraid of what he might say next.

"No that wasn't all. Mrs. Shipton told me she'd seen a snake in the solarium this morning. She asked me to come inside, look for it, and get rid of it if I found it."

"Did you find it?"

"Yes, sir. It lay almost hidden under the leaves of that elephant ear plant." Mitch pointed, and we all looked at the plant and the ornamental fountain beside it as if the snake might still be there. "The creature must have slithered inside unnoticed when the door opened. That sort of thing happens sometimes. It's no reflection on Mrs. Shipton's housekeeping. None at all. This's a good room for snakes, sir. I mean . . ." Mitch hesitated. "I mean the warm dampness inside the room, the sunshine filtering through outdoor plantings and flickering through the windows . . . The room offers the sort of protected environment snakes enjoy."

"What kind of a snake was it?"

"A blacksnake, sir. About four feet long. Big but harmless. I'm not surprised that seeing a snake in her solarium startled Mrs. Shipton."

"How do you happen to know so much about snakes?"

"I've read about them. I like all sorts of critters, and I wish more people realized snakes are their friends."

"Do you see snakes around here frequently?"

Mitch shrugged. "Only now and then. I sometimes see them around that koi pond up the street. I don't bother them."

"What did you do with the snake you found in this solarium?"

"I asked Mrs. Shipton for an old towel. I wrapped the snake in the towel, and then I put it in my bicycle basket and took it to the brushy area around the old salt ponds near the airport. I turned it loose there where it wouldn't hurt anyone and where nobody would hurt it."

I breathed easier when Cassidy abandoned the subject of snakes, and I thought Mitch had handled the questions well. As a kid he had loved snakes and frogs and newts — any creature that lived in the outdoors. Both Mom and I had shrieked and cringed when we found a toad or a handful of grasshoppers in his pants pockets on wash day.

"When was the last time you saw Mrs. Shipton alive?"

"This morning, sir, when I removed the snake from the solarium and took it away."

"Detective Burgundy says he saw you loitering behind the cottage next door. What reason did you have for being there?"

"When I arrived here earlier in the evening, I parked my bicycle there because it's the spot Mrs. Shipton suggested I use during my working hours. Tonight it seemed like a safe place. There are seldom many cars in this cul-de-sac, but tonight there were lots of vehicles moving about. I didn't want my bike to be in the way, and I didn't want some car to smash it."

"Thank you for your time, Mitch Mitchell," Cassidy said. "We may have more questions for you later in the week. You're free to go now, but don't leave Key West without my permission. Is that clear?"

"Yes, sir."

Mitch rose and left the room. My heart and my fears went with him. Earlier, I'd seen him skulking around Courtney's home, and Detective Burgundy had seen him behind my cottage. What had Mitch been up to tonight? Plunking oneself in the middle of a police investigation didn't match my definition of keeping a low profile.

I shuddered. Surely I wasn't suspecting my own brother of Francine's death.

7

All eyes followed Mitch from the solarium and watched through the window while Detective Burgundy motioned him into a patrol car, stowed his bicycle in the trunk, and drove away. The group snapped to attention when Detective Cassidy cleared his throat.

"Mr. Shipton, since you're the owner of this property, I'll resume my questioning with you. Your relation to the deceased, please?"

"Francine Shipton was my mother."

"Your occupation, Mr. Shipton?"

"I'm president of Shipton Boatyard and Salvage Company."

Cassidy's ballpoint refused to write. He discarded it and pulled another from his pocket. After testing it, he jotted Zack's reply in his notebook as if he hadn't already known the answers before he asked.

"Where's your place of business located,

Mr. Shipton?"

"The main location's on Stock Island where I maintain a business office and an active construction operation. I also moor salvage boats at my Stock Island dock so I'll be ready to answer distress calls from boaters in trouble. Salvaging's a necessary service in the Keys."

"Yes," Detective Cassidy said. "Our department has called on you for help from time to time. You have offices other than the Stock Island location, right?"

"Yes. I have a boatyard on Marathon, and I'm expanding, building a third one on Key Largo."

"Do you visit your places of business on a daily basis?"

"I try to, but not always. It's a long drive to Key Largo. I go there only when necessary. I've hired a manager on Largo who's capable of overseeing the new construction."

"Where did you work today?"

"I stopped briefly at Stock Island this morning before spending the afternoon at my Marathon office."

"About fifty miles from here?"

"Right."

"I understand that your mother had scheduled a meeting of friends, near neighbors, and not-so-near neighbors at Eden Palms tonight. An eight-thirty gathering, I believe."

"Right."

"Did you plan to attend that meeting?"

"Yes. The meeting concerned ideas for remodeling and reconstruction here at my home. I wanted to be present."

"What time did you leave your Marathon office?"

"About five o'clock."

"Did you drive directly to Key West?"

"No. Business matters interfered. I stopped at Toppinos on Rockland Key to discuss renting a crane. May have spent an hour there. Got home a little after seven. You and your people were here when I arrived. But you know that."

I wondered if this was Zack's alibi for his whereabouts at the time Francine died. I hoped he had an unshakable alibi — for my own sake as well as for his. I'd never sleep well knowing a killer might be living next door. I felt trapped. I guessed Detective Cassidy planned to give us all the same order he gave Mitch — don't leave Key West without his permission.

"When did you last see your mother alive, Mr. Shipton?"

"Rather late last night. I live here on the

first floor. Mother lived in a second-floor suite. Those were her wishes."

"She didn't mind using the stairs?"

"No. I never heard her complain about climbing up or down the steps. She recently celebrated her sixtieth birthday in good health. She preferred living upstairs. She felt it gave her more privacy — especially at night. Key West has an unsavory reputation for crime in the nighttime."

If Detective Cassidy considered Zack's explanation of their living arrangement a slur directed at the police department, he ignored it.

"Getting back to my question, when did you last see your mother alive?"

"She came downstairs to tell me good-night around ten o'clock last night. We told each other our plans for today, and then she went back upstairs and to bed."

"So nothing unusual happened yesterday evening."

"Nothing that I know of."

"Did you notice anything unusual around your home or your yard this morning before you left for work?"

"Nothing, sir. Everything looked okay to me. I left for work as usual and then re-turned much later to find —"

"What was your relationship with your

mother, Mr. Shipton? Did the two of you get along well?"

"Yes. We got along fine." Zack snapped the words, exasperation creeping into his tone.

"You never had any arguments?"

"No."

Detective Cassidy gave a sardonic smile that never reached his eyes. "How lucky you were, Mr. Shipton. Few people living in close proximity can boast of such a placid relationship."

Zack's face flushed, and I thought he should have had a lawyer at hand to protect his rights. Before he could respond to Detective Cassidy's barb about mother-son relationships, a car stopped out front. Footsteps scraped on the steps, then Detective Burgundy entered the solarium.

"Please be seated," Detective Cassidy nodded toward the empty chair Mitch had vacated, barely taking his gaze from Zack. I thought he'd ask more about Zack's relationship with Francine, and his next question surprised me.

"What are your hobbies, Mr. Shipton? How do you occupy yourself in your spare time? What activities do you enjoy spending money on?"

Good question. I like to read, and I know

I learn a great deal about a story character by the hobbies that character pursues or would never dream of pursuing. I waited, eager to hear Zack's reply.

The flush of anger left by Cassidy's previous question drained from Zack's face, leaving it ashen again.

"I like to sail. I'm building a sailboat for my own personal use. I like to fish. I spend time reading — especially about the sea. Also, I'm an amateur artist. Caricatures. Sometimes Mother auctioned my sketches at benefits, using the money for some cause that interested her. A few of her favorites hang in our cottage."

"Miss Green's temporary home?"

Did I imagine it or did he emphasize the word "temporary"?

"Yes. Miss Green has arrived to take up residence on the Eden Palms estate."

In the next instant, Detective Cassidy focused directly on me. "Miss Green, how long have you lived at the Shipton cottage?"

I felt like a germ under a microscope. Since I'd arrived after Francine's death had taken place, it surprised me that Cassidy wanted to question me. Had someone hinted that I might have killed Francine? I struggled to keep my voice pleasant.

"I arrived only this evening. Francine had

offered me a job as her secretary and aide. Housing in her cottage was to be a part of my payment."

"What time did you arrive, Miss Green?"

"My plane landed around seven-thirty. Due to traffic gridlock I didn't reach the cottage until almost nine o'clock."

"Can you explain the lag time between the plane landing and your arrival on the Shipton premises?"

I could and I did, skipping the parts concerning my interview with Quinn Bahama and my encounter with the intrusive vendor. My account must have been enough to satisfy Detective Cassidy. His gaze returned to Zack.

"Had you noticed any unusual activity around your house in the few days preceding your mother's death?"

Zack sat silent a while before he answered. "I can think of nothing unusual that happened here lately. Nothing."

Again, Cassidy looked at me. "Miss Green, since you have arrived to live on Shipton property, I'll continue my questions with you. What was your relationship to Francine Shipton?"

I answered his questions as completely, but as briefly, as possible, unwilling to reveal too much — or too little. The only information I withheld that might pertain to the investigation concerned Francine's note in my purse. It was a no-ask, no-tell situation. If he asked about our correspondence in the future, I'd have to reveal the note. But not now. As I'd expected, Detective Cassidy ordered me to get his permission before leaving Key West.

I had no choice but to remain. The cottage was now my residence unless Zack asked me to leave. Perhaps he could find part-time work for me in the Shipton business. I had no home to return to in Iowa, and even if I could find another rental in Key West, I couldn't afford to leave the Shipton cottage unless I found a full-time day job and worked on writing lyrics at night.

I hoped to avoid that. I wanted to give songwriting and performing my best shot, and I couldn't do that and worry about the responsibilities a full-time day job would bring. It unnerved me to realize an unknown murderer might be at large in Key West, but I saw nothing I could do about that. I promised myself to be strong and unafraid. Well, at least I'd admit no fear to anyone.

I listened to Detective Cassidy call on Courtney next. Now and then I caught myself squelching a yawn, but I zoned in on

Courtney's alibi. On my previous Key West visit, she'd never ranked as my favorite person, but I had no concrete reasons for my feelings. It's hard for me to warm up to a person who dotes on wearing Prada and who never has a bad hair day.

"Miss Lusk, where were you this afternoon and early evening?"

"I was showing houses to a family new to the city who expressed interest in making Key West their permanent home."

"Who were these people?"

"The Gordon Jamell family from Jackson, Michigan."

"They occupied your whole afternoon?"

"Yes. After I left them, I stopped at Pier House for a sandwich. After that, I met friends who were visiting the island and staying at Pier House. The Haynes. We attended the sunset celebration before they caught a plane for Miami."

"They will corroborate your statement?"

"I feel sure they would if they were available. They planned to fly to Miami tonight, stay there until morning, and then fly abroad."

"Do you know where they were planning to stay in Miami?"

"No."

"Where were their plans going to take

them once they left this country?"

"They mentioned renting a car and touring England."

Courtney's words sounded evasive to me — too many unexplained time slots. I had to blink fast to keep from going to sleep, but I jerked to attention when Cassidy began questioning Dr. Gravely. Was I the only person present who hadn't known Gravely had been the one who found Francine's body?

"Tell us more about this," Detective Cassidy asked.

"I'd been attending a luncheon at Kelly's Caribbean. A group of us were planning a special Conch Republic celebration dinner for friends who'd missed the regular celebration last year. After we finalized our plans, I drove home and then walked to Eden Palms — purely a courtesy call. I wanted to ask Francine if I could do anything to help with last-minute details for her evening meeting. And since my hibiscus plants are in full bloom, I offered to bring her a bouquet."

"And what did you find?"

"I found her sprawled on the floor at the foot of the staircase. I called 911."

"You knew she was dead?"

Gravely hesitated only a moment. "I'm a doctor, sir. I knew."

Zack's face grew crimson and for a moment he glared at Gravely, but he said nothing.

Detective Cassidy dismissed Dr. Gravely. Why so quickly, I wondered. I had lots of questions. It was a Sherlock Holmes moment. Had the door been unlocked? Were there signs of a struggle? Had her clothing been disarranged?

With a nod, Cassidy focused his attention toward Tucker Tisdale. I looked away from Tisdale's scaly skin, the parsnip-colored hair. His falsetto made him sound like a prepubescent boy, and he had little information for Cassidy. He'd been working at his funeral home, and he felt sure his staff would vouch for that. Cassidy didn't inquire as to the nature of that work. Thank goodness.

Detective Cassidy let his gaze sweep the solarium, stopping briefly on each person present. In the silence we heard water dripping from the fountain, the squeak of Courtney's chair when she leaned forward, preparing to rise.

"Thank you for your attention," Cassidy said. "You may go now. If you have reason to leave the island, please clear your departure with me first. Thank you."

For a few seconds nobody moved, then in

a nanosecond the solarium scene broke apart like a jigsaw puzzle someone had kicked by accident. I headed for my cottage, glad I'd locked the door before leaving it.

8

Few streetlights illumined this cul-de-sac, but at least I'd remembered to leave the porch light on. The night had grown chilly. Why hadn't I thought to slip on a sweater! Why indeed! Tonight had been no time for remembering mundane things like sweaters.

A mourning dove, probably disturbed by my footsteps, twittered a plaintive cooing from the sea grape tree near my front door. The eerie sound sent goose bumps prickling along my arms. I forced firmness into my steps, determined to appear strong to anyone who might be watching, and at the same time I wondered *who* might be watching. Zack? Courtney? Cassidy?

Stop borrowing trouble, you dope. Nobody's watching!

I wondered if my brother might be somewhere near. Detective Burgundy had escorted Mitch away in a patrol car, but nothing could prevent him from riding his bicycle back. I wanted to talk with him, but I doubted he would return here tonight. Did he have a telephone at his apartment? Maybe he carried a cell phone. If only we'd had a few more minutes together before Zack interrupted us.

My key scraped into the keyhole and the lock clicked open. I closed the door in slow motion, fighting my inclination to bang it shut. After pushing the lock button in the center of the doorknob, I thrust the deadbolt in place. But even as I took those precautions I wondered who else carried a key to this cottage. Francine had kept one in case someone locked himself out. Where was that key now? And wouldn't Zack have a master key to every door on the property? I considered calling a locksmith tomorrow and adding my personal lock to the cottage. But could a renter do that to property owned by someone else?

I turned on inside lights before I snapped off the porch light. In the bedroom I ignored my keyboard, the suitcase on the luggage rack, and the second case standing unopened beside it. Reaching into my bag, I pulled out a sleep shirt and headed for the bathtub, looking forward to a warm soak with lots of bubbles. In minutes my muscles relaxed, and the steam and the gardenia fragrance of the bath oil almost lulled me to sleep in the tub. I pushed fear from my mind. How could anyone be afraid in Paradise?

A brisk knock on my front door answered my question. I didn't shout "coming." Maybe I could ignore the knock. Grabbing a bath sheet from the towel rack, I wrapped myself in it and tiptoed to the door. One peek through the peephole revealed Zack on my doorstep carrying a tray of sandwiches and mugs of hot chocolate with floating marshmallows.

"Zack!" I called through the closed door. "One a minute, please. Be right with you." Hurrying to the bathroom, I slipped on my sleep shirt; then rushing to the bedroom, I pulled a robe from my suitcase, rammed my arms into the sleeves, knotted the sash.

When I reached the living room again, I released the lock, the deadbolt, and opened the door to Zack, who stood looking embarrassed.

"Sorry to bother you, Bailey, but I thought we both needed some refreshment after that session with Cassidy." Zack stood back as if he might change his mind about coming inside.

"How thoughtful, Zack. I can smell hot chocolate and barbecue sauce from here, and the Cuban sandwiches look great. Pulled pork — my favorite. Come on in."

When I opened the door wider, I saw Courtney standing at her upstairs window watching. Zack's gaze followed mine. I fought a temptation to wave, to let her know we'd caught her watching, but before I lifted my hand, a drapery fell in place. Courtney and Zack go out together now and then, and that's fine with me. But in the past when Zack and I had gone out, I don't think it was fine with Courtney. I think she'd enjoy retiring from real estate and devoting full time to being Mrs. Zack Shipton.

Zack stepped inside and I closed the door, glad Courtney had seen Zack enter. I didn't care about making her jealous, but I wanted Zack's whereabouts and mine recorded in someone's mind. I led the way to the snack bar, and we sat on barstools to enjoy Zack's treat.

"Zack, what's your take on Cassidy's question session? You think he believes someone shoved Francine down the steps?"

"It's hard to know what a detective thinks or believes. Cassidy's probably unsure himself — thus all the questions. I hope you weren't bent out of shape by his prying and prodding. You've had a hard day of travel — and then all that."

I took a bite of sandwich and followed it with a sip of hot chocolate. "Wonderful treat, Zack. Wonderful. But I have lots of questions. I'm new here. I've met the neighbors, but I don't know them well. Or the yard man."

"Well, the yard man's new, but I've known the neighbors for years. I'd trust them with my last dollar."

"But maybe not with your mother?"

"Bailey! I trust everyone present in that solarium tonight. Even the yardman. What motive would Mitch Mitchell have for pushing Mother down the stairs? He doesn't own property around here. At least I don't think he does. Why would he have cared if Mother established a homeless shelter?"

"You're right. He'd have no motive. But what about the others? Tell me about Dr. Gravely. Everyone seems to like him and give him lots of respect."

Zack hesitated. "Known Winton Gravely all my life. I think it strange that nobody told me he was the one who found Mother's body. That irritates me. But I trust him implicitly. We grew up together. Went to Key West high school together. We both love the outdoors and we fish together now and then."

"Only now and then?"

97

"He likes trolling on the open sea, and I like fly-fishing in the back country."

I smiled. "Fishing is fishing, isn't it?"

Zack chewed his sandwich thoughtfully. "Fishermen who go in for trolling like being on the water more than they like fishing. They pull alongside a bait boat and buy whatever bait the skipper's selling. Then off they race at high speed, gung-ho to find a promising spot, bait their lures, and begin dragging them behind their boats. They're eager to reel in any fish that happens to snag their hook."

"And backcountry fishermen? They're more discriminating, more particular?"

"Lots more." Zack grinned. "Sometimes I use a spinning rod, but more often I prefer a fly rod. I spend lots of time tying my own flies. There's an art to fly tying, you know."

"I'm sure there must be, but it sounds tedious."

"I like to work with a magnifying glass, a vise, with feathers and artificial insects. It took me a long time to learn to tie the eclectic knots a discriminating fly fisherman needs. But I'm a detail man. I find attention to details worthwhile. I like to stand on a poling platform or maybe on the bow and search the clear water until I see the fish I want to catch."

"You can be that particular?"

"Sure. No point in hooking up with some trash fish I'll have to release — maybe lose my lure and snarl my line. Would you like to go fishing sometime?"

"Maybe."

"Maybe you'd rather go sailing. When I finish work on my sailboat, I'll take you for a sail."

"That sounds nice. When will you finish it?"

"It's almost done. Just a few details left."

Did I really want to be at sea and alone in a boat with Zack? I hoped Courtney would remember she saw him come in here tonight. And I hoped Zack would remember that Courtney had seen him enter the cottage. I enjoyed a half-melted marshmallow then changed the subject back to fishing.

"When you spot a fish you'd like to catch, do you usually catch it?"

Zack laughed. "Not always, but if I miss, I try again. I'm willing to take my chances. Sometimes I go out with Winton on his speedboat and sometimes he goes out with me in my backcountry skiff. We humor each other. We brag a lot about our catches, give each other put-downs, but no hard feelings. It's all a part of our friendship."

"So you trust Gravely. What about Tucker

Tisdale?"

"Tucker's an okay guy. I don't envy him being in the funeral business, but to each his own. He inherited the business from his dad same way I inherited mine. No sense walking away from a good thing. Tucker's okay in my book. He sometimes soaks people big bucks for his services, but on the other hand I've seen him provide free funerals for the families of indigent people. Tucker's both community minded and generous."

"Guess that leaves Courtney, doesn't it?"

"Courtney and I've been friends for years. We date now and then, but there's nothing serious between us. We both understand that."

I took another bite of my sandwich and looked away, feeling that what Zack understood and what Courtney understood might be two different things.

"You might say Courtney's the new kid on the block. Her husband, Sidney Lusk, died in a car crash about five years ago. She inherited her home from her grandfather, and she and Sidney lived there until his death."

"Zack, since you seem to trust these neighbors, yet you think Francine's death wasn't accidental, what *do* you believe happened? Police don't do death investigations unless they suspect something suspicious about the death."

"I don't know who's responsible or what happened. I've come here tonight to bring refreshments, and I've also come to ask for your help."

A foreboding of danger put me at guard. "What sort of help? What do you think I can offer, Zack? Of course, I'll do whatever I can."

"I've already mentioned that as the person who inherits Mother's fortune, I'll be the number-one suspect."

"I'd hoped you'd have an airtight alibi."

"I do have an airtight alibi — more extensive than the one I gave Cassidy tonight. If the police call Mother's death a homicide, I'll reveal all in the hope they'll keep my words out of the media. Once made public, my alibi could jinx an important business deal — reveal too much information to a competitor."

"So what can I do?" Clearly, Zack wasn't going to reveal his alibi to me. At least not now.

"Help me solve this mystery, Bailey. If the police call Mother's death a homicide, then I want you to help me find the culprit before the police have to reveal my alibi. As I remember it, you're a mystery reader, right? So am I. We both know how to follow clues."

I set my mug of hot chocolate aside and stared at Zack. "You know for sure that someone murdered Francine, don't you? And I think Detective Cassidy knows that, too. Why are you holding back this information from everyone? The safest thing for me to do might be to catch the next flight out of here."

"I can understand your feelings, Bailey. But you're involved whether you want to be or not. Mother's death may be called an accident or it may be called murder, but either way, you're involved. You've had correspondence with Mother. She mentioned writing to you now and then. Sooner or later the police will call you in for in-depth questioning."

"I suppose you're right. And I did hear from Francine frequently." I hated to see Zack looking so sad and reflective, and I wished I could lift his spirits.

"Please agree to help me solve this mystery, Bailey."

"Let me think about it. Please let me think about it. Will you give me until tomorrow?"

"Of course. Mother was always there for me and I'm hoping you will be, too. And I'm going to ask another favor. Will you come to the mansion early tomorrow morning? I want you to play hostess. When you were here before, Mother introduced you to her friends as her substitute daughter. In fact, people might think it strange if you weren't on hand to greet callers since you're on the island."

"Who are you expecting?"

"People who arrive to express their condolences, of course. There'll be friends calling as well as business associates. And under the circumstances, there'll be reporters. It wouldn't hurt your performing career to have the locals as well as the tourists see your name and maybe a few shots of you in the *Citizen.*"

"Okay, Zack. I'll come over for you and for Francine, not for the publicity."

"And I'll have breakfast ready. I do cook, you know."

"No. I didn't know."

"And I also know you haven't had time to shop for groceries."

"I'll be there, Zack. You can count on it."

Zack stood, stepping away from the snack bar and reaching for the tray.

"Leave the dishes. I'll wash them and bring them with me when I come in the morning."

Zack stacked the mugs and plates on the

tray. "I'm not the kind who prepares food then leaves the cleanup to others. I'll see you in the morning."

We walked to the door, and I opened it for him. "Thanks for the snack. I needed it." I looked toward Courtney's home, but I saw no drapery move. Since she had seen Zack arrive, I wished she'd also see him leave.

Once alone again, I snapped off the lights and stretched out in my bed to think and to start making the decisions I knew I must face. In my heart I knew Francine had been murdered. The probable why of it seemed to make sense, but I couldn't begin to guess the who of it. I could barely believe a killer lurked hidden somewhere here in Paradise — perhaps in this cul-de-sac.

I had to trust someone. Mitch. I'd promised Mom to take care of Mitch. I could trust my brother, but how could I make contact — especially make emergency contact when I might need his help? I'd have to be careful not to reveal our relationship.

At least for the present, I needed to trust Zack. I couldn't go on living in this cottage without trusting him. He anticipated my coming to his home tomorrow morning, so at least I was safe for tonight. Wasn't I?

9

Sometime after midnight I drifted to sleep. I could sense myself tossing and squirming, first feeling too chilly and pulling a blanket around my shoulders, then feeling too warm and shoving it off again. Without turning on any light, I rose from bed, raised the window shade and opened the window. The full moon was doing its thing, and the night looked almost as light as day. When I spotted a bright green iguana perched on a hibiscus branch outside my window, I stood watching it for several moments as I cooled off. Iguanas! Fascinating. I had forgotten how much they look like miniature dragons. This creature sat dining on a pink blossom until it suddenly came alert and stared at something in my back yard.

I looked where the iguana looked. A man carrying a paper sack was approaching the cottage. It took me a moment to recognize Chet. Grabbing my robe, I hurried to the kitchen door before he had a chance to knock or call out to me.

"Chet! What are you doing here at this hour?" I opened the door so he could slip inside.

"It's *not* Chet. It's *Mitch,* remember?"

"I'm trying, Mitch. Old habits die hard. And — it's difficult to remember new stuff when it's past midnight and I'm half asleep." I closed the door quickly. "What if someone's watching?" I hurried to the bedroom to close the window I'd just opened and lower the shade. Thank goodness Courtney didn't have a view of my back door.

"Who do you think will be watching at this time of night?"

"One never knows. Detective Cassidy may have targeted this whole area for surveillance. If the M.E. calls Francine's death a murder, Zack Shipton thinks he'll be the prime suspect. Plainclothes detectives in unmarked cars could be parked nearby watching Eden Palms as we speak."

"So I've taken a mega-chance coming here in hope of a shower?"

"What's wrong with showering at your apartment? No water? Bad plumbing? Behind with your bills?"

"None of the above, Sis. So far, I've never lived in that apartment. Sure, it's rented in my new name and I've pocketed the key. But I'm steering clear of the place until I feel sure no druggie has followed me here from Iowa."

"So where are you living?" I held my breath, unwilling to hear the answer I felt sure he'd offer.

"On the street."

The words submerged in the silence like sharks preparing to attack while I tried to think of an appropriate reply.

"No way can you persuade me to use the apartment, Sis. No way. Be a pal and share your shower. Just this once, okay?"

"Don't you stop by the place to pick up your mail? You could bathe then."

"What mail? Nobody's writing to me."

"Someone might."

"If they do, I'll stop for it at the post office. I've rented a box."

Mitch's mail was unimportant when compared to matters closer at hand — or at nose. "How long's it been since you had a shower?"

"Don't ask."

"Okay, rescind the query. Why don't you use the restroom shower at Smathers? Beach restrooms aren't the greatest, but if . . ."

"Don't talk to me about Smathers! I don't

even sleep in the sand around there. Lots of guys do, though, but have you ever grabbed a whiff of that restroom?"

I didn't bother to answer. Instead, I turned on a night light, stomped to the linen cupboard, and pulled out a towel and wash-cloth.

"Here. Be my guest. But don't make this a habit."

"Thanks, Sis. I knew I could count on you."

"This time. This *one* time. After tonight, use the shower in your apartment. You have Federal Witness Protection. The government's at hand to help."

"Government help." Mitch laughed. "What an oxymoron!"

He disappeared into the shower, and I lay on my bed again, feeling wide awake in spite of my exhaustion. Mitch splashed a bit before he began to sing.

Iowa, Iowa, my home. Iowa, the tall corn state.

"Enough, Mitch! Enough! Someone might hear."

He stopped singing. In a few minutes the water stopped flowing, and presently he appeared dressed in fresh jeans and tank top. He patted the sack under his arm. "Got my dirty duds in here. I don't suppose . . ."

"Right. Please don't suppose I'm into the laundry business. Use the facilities at your apartment." Mitch had a soulful way of looking at people that made them want to help him. He'd had Mom and me wrapped around his finger for years. I relented — as he'd known I would. "Okay, leave your bag. I'll do your stuff when I run a load."

"You're a pal, Sis." Mitch planted a kiss on my cheek and headed toward the door.

"Wait just one little minute." I grabbed his arm. "Where are you spending your nights? And who are you spending them with? You could get in big trouble if —"

"You wouldn't know the place or the people. They're just friends I've made since I arrived here in Paradise."

"What sort of friends?"

"The sort that like sleeping under the stars. You oughta try it sometime, Bailey. Give me a little notice, and I'd be more than glad to share some prime space with you any night you want to stop by."

"You're more than generous. But don't hold your breath while you're waiting for me to show."

"You'd be surprised at the sense of freedom you'd get from feeling the sea breeze cooling your face, from feeling the good earth mold to your warm and weary body, from feeling —"

"Mitch, be real! Most of our family vacations turned into camping trips because you liked to sleep in a tent. I've had enough of that scene. I can't believe you really enjoy sleeping out now — with the homeless derelicts of society."

"I don't always sleep out. If it rains, Wizard shares his tent with me. Princess offers me tent space, too, but I never accept. Doesn't seem right. She's a heavyweight. I'd crowd her. But it's good of her to offer, right?"

"Wizard? Princess?"

"Don't suppose those are their real names, their legal names," Mitch admitted. "I'm still digging for that info. I'd like to see them reunited with their families."

"Doesn't it occur to you that they may not want to reunite with their families? You can't take homeless people in. You can't baby them, treat them like you used to treat stray cats and dogs."

"Don't know why not," Mitch said. "Sometimes I buy special treats — burgers and fries and donuts to share. They follow me then, just like the tabbies and mongrels used to. My new friends like to have someone take care of them. I got nothing else to do right now."

"Maybe their families kicked them out. Maybe they're drug abusers."

"They're just people down on their luck. Now and then I pay their doctor bills or take them to a dentist. They need family."

"Maybe they prefer a bottle to a family. Mitch, it's dangerous to hang out with these people. You read about that guy on Big Pine? He murdered his mother, his cousin, and his wife before he hanged himself. Who knows how many others he murdered! You never know what strangers might do."

"For the most part they're kind folks. You treat them good, they'll treat you good."

"Well," I corrected. "You treat them well."

"That's what I said — what I meant. I don't have a problem with any of them — at least not so far. But I empathize with them and I want to help."

"Where'd you sleep last night?"

Mitch hesitated, pretending he couldn't remember. Then he cocked his head and replied. "Last night I camped with Wizard on the Bridle Path. It's an unused path on South Roosevelt where the old timers say people used to pleasure ride their horses. Hasn't been used for that in years."

"When you end up in jail, don't call me for bail money."

"Won't end up in jail. Police can't arrest

us 'cause the city hasn't provided us a safe place to sleep. Wizard says sleeping on the Bridle Path isn't as safe as it used to be. Here lately some tourists have realized that they, too, can camp there without being arrested. Now *that's* a scary thing. Nothing worse than a deadbeat tourist."

"To each his own."

"I'd rather sleep on the ground next to Wizard than next to some cheapskate from Wisconsin."

"To each his own."

"Cut me a little slack, Bailey. Before your mind hardens against Wizard and Princess, let me introduce you to them. They're my present projects and I'd like you to meet them."

"Present projects?"

"Right. I know I can't help all of the homeless that hit on Key West. But, I might be able to help one or two of them to a better life united with their families. Will you let me introduce you to Wizard and Princess?"

"I suppose so. But we'll have to stage the meeting in some secret place. We don't have any reason to contact each other, and if people see us together they might ask questions I'd rather avoid."

"That's true. I don't want anyone to know

you're my sis."

"Mitch, what were you doing today? I mean do you have an alibi for late afternoon?"

"You don't suspect me of murdering Mrs. Shipton, do you?"

"Of course not, but I want to know where you were and what you were doing. Think about it. Get that question and your reply set in your mind. And don't change your response. Sooner or later the cops are going to call you in and demand an in-depth answer."

Mitch paused to think. "Hmmm . . . I worked at the mansion in the morning and in the afternoon and early evening, I worked at Two Friends Patio."

"Anyone who'll vouch for that?"

"Sure. The manager was in and out but, Quinn Bahama made sandwiches in the kitchen all the time I washed dishes. She'd vouch for me."

"I hope that won't be necessary, Mitch, but keep it in mind. I'm glad you have a good alibi."

Mitch left the cottage as quietly as he had entered, and I returned to bed. It seemed as if only two minutes had passed before the telephone rang.

In my grogginess, I knocked the phone

from my nightstand, and the receiver hit the rattan mat before it skidded onto the parquet floor. I rolled onto my stomach and groped for it, but even before I could pick it up, I heard Zack shouting.

"Bailey? Bailey? Are you all right? What was that crash?"

"Good morning, Zack," my voice croaked through early-morning hoarseness.

"Are you okay?" he asked.

"I'm fine. Guess I didn't hear my alarm. Sorry about that."

"That's okay and understandable. You had quite a day yesterday. Are you still planning to come over this morning?"

"Yes. Yes, of course." I spoke with more enthusiasm than I felt, and I managed to focus my gaze on my watch. A little after seven. "Are people arriving this early?"

"None so far, but why don't you come over as soon as you're dressed and have breakfast? I know you haven't had time for grocery shopping. Since I didn't know of your arrival plans . . ." His voice trailed off, and I wondered if we both were thinking of Francine's special blueberry coffee cake — a treat she had often shared with friends and neighbors and guests.

"Thanks, Zack. Except for your snack last night, I can't even remember the last time I ate anything more substantial than airline pretzels."

"Come on then." He sighed. "I can give you a great choice of cold cereals and some O.J. Don't feel like cooking today."

"Any cereal's okay. See you." I hung up, then replaced the phone on the nightstand. Cold cereal and orange juice sounded good, but the thought of sharing breakfast with Zack unnerved me. I wondered how I'd get through the morning — and the next few days.

My stomach growled in anticipation of food, and I got up and began dressing. What to wear. Now I wished I'd unpacked last night. After slipping into a pair of skimmers, I turned to face the morning.

I straightened the bed before I began a quick unpacking, and from the mound of clothing I picked up my favorite green shift and shook out the wrinkles. To iron or not to iron. That is the question — a very small question today. I have outfits that offer comfort, and this was one of them. I pulled the shift over my head and then ran a comb through my tangled hair before I pulled it into a ponytail. My keyboard called to me, but I ignored it and left the room.

My camera still lay on the living room couch where I'd dropped it last night. I picked it up by its strap and held it for a moment before tucking it out of sight in my closet. It was terribly out of date, but I'd kept it because it had been a present from Mom years ago, and it still worked well. I had no desire for one of the new digitals.

On impulse, moments before I left the cottage, I paused and opened the refrigerator for the first time since I'd returned. Francine had stocked the shelves with breakfast necessities — milk, orange juice, eggs, and cereal. Bread? Bread in the refrig? Of course. Francine's solution to Florida's ongoing ant problem centered on storing all food in the refrig.

My inclination to call Zack and regret his breakfast invitation died quickly. So did the idea of inviting him here to share Francine's bounty.

Some of the mansion's coldness dissipated when Zack met me at his door, towering over me and smiling while he led the way to Francine's state-of-the-art kitchen. He wore his casual khaki pants and hand-print shirt that I mentally called his uniform of the day — every day. He could modify the pants into shorts with the flick of a couple zippers. But he never did. At least I'd never seen him in the walking-shorts version. This morning dark circles ringed his eyes and a red chin scrape told me he had nicked himself shaving.

"Get a good rest?" I asked.

"Yes, indeed. I thought maybe I couldn't sleep, but exhaustion kicked in. And you?"

"I slept fitfully, but I liked hearing wind swishing palm fronds instead of snowflakes."

Zack motioned me to a chair at the glass-topped table near the bay window in his breakfast alcove. Although Shipton ancestors had built Eden Palms over a hundred years ago, Francine had remodeled the kitchen. Zack moved quickly and easily between the refrigerator and the sink, which was set in a stainless steel island at room center. In moments we sat enjoying corn-flakes, juice, and toast.

"What are your plans for the day?" Zack asked.

"That depends on your plans for me. I'll help however I can. Francine had lots of friends who'll want to assist, to express their sympathy. If you need to be away to make funeral arrangements, I'll stay and greet callers. Or, if you want to choose one of Francine's friends as hostess, I'll keep in the background."

"Don't know how I could choose one friend without hurting the feelings of a dozen others. Your presence will save me from that angst."

"Have you considered funeral arrangements?"

"I've talked briefly with Tucker Tisdale about private services. Under the circumstances we think that's the way to go. It'll involve a lot of phone calls and a discreet announcement in the *Citizen*."

"Maybe I can do the telephoning."

"Great, but Tucker can't schedule anything definite yet. The police haven't released Mother's body."

"Wonder when they'll do that?"

"I don't know, but look." Zack nodded toward the window. "I see Cassidy and Burgundy pulling up right now. Maybe they'll have some answers."

I studied the detectives as they got out of their unmarked Ford. Cassidy stomped up the sidewalk, his stomach leading his bulk toward the front door. Gray suit. Gray hair. All his gray could mask the Florida sunshine. Burgundy followed him, towering above him. His loose-jointed gait and the spring in his step drew my gaze away from Cassidy. Had they planned it that way? Maybe they did a good cop–bad cop routine, using their looks to enhance their act. If they had big news for Zack, I hoped they'd present it quickly and leave. But it never happened that way.

10

"Good morning, gentlemen."

I heard footsteps in the foyer as Zack greeted the detectives and invited them into the solarium. Intent on eavesdropping, I jumped, startled, when Zack appeared at the kitchen doorway.

"I told them you were helping me today, Bailey, and they want you to hear what they have to say."

Bad news? Good news? I didn't try to guess. But I could think of nothing good about a suspicious death. It surprised me that they wanted to share information with me. I left my cornflakes and juice and followed Zack to the solarium. After we exchanged greetings and sat rather uneasily in Francine's easy chairs, Cassidy dove straight to the point of their visit.

"We have the medical examiner's report. He estimates the victim died between three and four yesterday afternoon, and we're investigating Mrs. Shipton's death as a homicide. We're informing you first and withholding that news from the public — at least for the time being. I wish we could spare you the headlines sure to come, but we've no control over the media."

Someone pushed Francine down those stairs. The thought etched itself into my brain.

"Someone shoved Mother to her death." Zack's voice shook when he verbalized my thoughts.

"Yes," Cassidy said. "We believe that's what happened. But we're only releasing the information that she died from injuries sustained in a fall."

"Why?" Zack asked. "Why delay the truth? There's bound to be speculation and gossip."

"We want to get a feel for public reaction to the news. We have certain people under surveillance. Whoever caused your mother's fall must be guilt-ridden and insecure right now — perhaps in a ready-to-cut-and-run mode. Out of nervousness and fear, the culprit may do something to incriminate himself — or herself."

"A woman?" I blurted.

"Quite possible. Murder's an equal-opportunity employer, and it takes little muscle to push an elderly lady down some stairs."

"And after that?" Zack asked. "After you've issued your bit of misleading information, then what?"

"Mr. Shipton, we're here now to release the whole truth of your mother's death to you and Miss Green. To you two, only."

I imagined an anchor line tightening around my stomach. Detective Burgundy watched both Zack and me, but Cassidy looked straight at Zack, who met his gaze without flinching.

"Your mother's fall broke her neck. She died immediately. Following that fatal fall, the perpetrator coiled a dead blacksnake around her neck and wedged the snake's head into her mouth and throat. That was the way the murderer wanted someone to discover her body. But she died of a broken neck, not of suffocation, as the killer may have wanted the police to believe."

Zack jumped up and color drained from his face. Clearly, he was hearing these horrid details for the first time. My stomach rose into my throat, and I looked toward the door hoping for escape.

"If you're feeling ill, Miss Green, you may be excused." Detective Cassidy glared at me and leaned forward as if to rise. Something about his demeanor, his arrogance in thinking I'd crumple at his news, made me swallow my gorge and remain seated. He sank back into his chair and nodded to his partner.

Burgundy reached into his attaché case and withdrew photos that he fanned across the coffee table. I closed my eyes, but not in time to avoid seeing Francine and the snake.

I heard Zack stride forward, brush the photos to the floor. After I forced my eyes open, he stomped the pictures, kicking them toward Cassidy. Then he picked up two of the photos, tore them in half, and flung them at Burgundy's feet. Blood had rushed to his face, and I thought he might be having a heart attack, or a stroke. He stood with his arms at his sides, both fists doubled, his eyes flashing fire.

"Why wasn't I told these details sooner?" Zack demanded. "Why am I the last to know? I'll . . . I'll . . . Winton found her body. My so-called *friend,* Winton Gravely. He knew of this horror last night while you were questioning us. Gravely knew even before that — when he found Mother's body. Why didn't he tell me!"

"Please calm yourself, Mr. Shipton," Cassidy said. "We can explain our actions and Gravely's. Once you hear our reasoning, I think you'll agree we did the right thing. Please remember, our job is to find the murderer, not to comfort the survivors."

"I'll have your head for my breakfast!" Zack shouted. "I'll, I'll . . ."

"Please hear us out, Mr. Shipton." Detective Burgundy rose and stood beside Zack. "Handling the information in the way we did may help us as we investigate this case. Before last night's questioning, we ordered Gravely to say nothing about the snake. We wanted to note everyone's reactions to our questions as well as to the answers given by those present. Many times we count on initial reactions to reveal important clues."

"How could such secrecy have helped? I'm calling my lawyer." Zack turned and started to leave.

"You're welcome to call anyone you care to," Cassidy said. "But do hear us out first. Please listen to our comments. Then, if you have questions we'll do our best to answer them."

Zack sat again. "All right." He glared at each detective in turn. "Why was Winton allowed to know information that you denied to me? And why is Bailey being put through this unpleasantness? You know she was en route to Key West when the murder took place."

"Would you rather have broken this news to Miss Green yourself?" Cassidy demanded.

Zack shook his head and stared at the floor. "Of course not. Nobody likes breaking this kind of news to anyone. But that doesn't excuse you from allowing Winton Gravely —"

"We swore Gravely to secrecy until we announced the details of your mother's death to the media. He remains under oath to keep silent. Now we're demanding the same thing of you and Miss Green. Secrecy. Police frequently withhold facts from the public. Often it's that one withheld detail that causes the perpetrator to stumble, to reveal his guilt. We feel it possible that someone in this room last night knows exactly what happened to your mother."

"Who?" Zack demanded. "Tell me right now. Which person, who of my friends and neighbors do you suspect. Who?"

"We're revealing no more details yet and we want both you and Miss Green to keep the information we've revealed to you this morning a secret."

"There'll be a thorough investigation?"

"Of course. We've been working to unravel this mystery since yesterday when we received Winton Gravely's nine-one-one call around six-thirty — about half an hour before you arrived home."

"And you think someone who was in this room last night is guilty? I can't believe that one of our neighbors —"

"You're jumping to conclusions, Mr. Shipton. We said that's a possibility. A total stranger may have murdered your mother. Police deal with such homicides frequently, but according to statistics, murders are most often committed either by some member of the victim's family or by a close associate."

"What about the yardman?" Zack demanded. "We know nothing about him except that he showed up one day asking for work."

I wanted to scream at Zack, to tell him to hush up about the yardman. But I corked my thoughts and forced myself to listen.

"Tell us about the yardman. He was a stranger to your mother?"

"That's right. She'd known him only a few weeks — a month at the most. Mitch, Mitch . . . what's his last name?"

Burgundy pulled a notebook from his jacket pocket and supplied the name. "Mitch Mitchell. Might be a phony name. Or maybe the Mitch part may be a nickname."

"According to Mother, Mitchell worked

hard and had no trouble following her instructions concerning her lawn, her trees and plants. The neighbors joked about Mother's nitpicking when it came to attention to her yard. When she hired someone she approved of, they'd vie to hire that person too. I've watched a succession of yardmen come and go."

"You never did the hiring and firing?"

"No." Zack banged his fist against his chair arm. "Mother did her own hiring and firing. Mitchell admitted being inside this very room. He admitted to finding a blacksnake here. He admitted liking snakes to the point that he'd go out of his way to protect one. I want to talk to Mitch Mitchell up close and personal."

Warning signals flashed in my head. I had to warn Mitch.

"Of course the yardman will get close scrutiny. Mitch Mitchell. His name's on our list of suspects."

"Have you dusted the house for fingerprints?" Zack asked.

"Yes. We did that before you arrived home from work yesterday, but we're releasing no information on the results just yet."

Detective Burgundy tucked what remained of the torn photos back into his attaché case. "We thank both of you for your cooperation."

"We expect you to remain silent about the details of this investigation," Cassidy reminded us — again. "We'll inform you before we release the whole story to the media."

"Thanks," Zack said. "I'll appreciate that. I'll expect that."

We watched the detectives get into their car and leave before we returned to our breakfast. Although I didn't feel like eating, Zack began making fresh toast.

"Now what?" I don't know what I expected Zack to say. I'd agreed to stay and greet callers. I regretted that promise. I needed to get in touch with Mitch, to put him on guard against whatever the police might have in store for him.

"I'd like to lock the doors and disappear," Zack admitted. "I'm sorry you've been sucked into this horror."

"I appreciate your feelings, Zack. But I'm glad you don't have to face this scene alone."

"Did you notice anything strange about the conclusions the detectives were reaching?"

I thought for a moment. "I don't believe they said anything about reaching conclusions. I feel as if the investigation stands wide open and they're waiting to find the perpetrator or to have him reveal himself."

"That's the feeling they left me with, too. They may give the impression they suspect Mitchell, but I didn't hear them letting me off the hook. No way. Anyone else's motive for murdering Mother might hinge on protecting the neighborhood from an influx of homeless people. I'm the only one with a dual motive."

"Protecting the neighborhood and claiming your inheritance."

"Right. There's no way I've been dropped from their suspect list. I'm in the number-one spot."

I hated to admit that Zack was right, and I felt more wary of him than before, although I could think of no reason why he'd want to harm me. I brushed my feelings to a far corner of my mind, and for a moment I forgot about them when I glanced out the window and saw Courtney crossing her lawn and heading directly toward Eden Palms.

11

Courtney made it a point to let the neighbors know she jogged five miles every morning rain or shine. Of course, in Florida it was mostly shine. This morning she wore a yellow tank top that struggled to cover her bustline and spandex short-shorts slung low enough to reveal her pierced navel. Suddenly, my silk shift had all the charm of a garage-sale special. Courtney was the only jogger I knew who could look glamorous while wearing sweaty hair pulled back with an elastic band. Walking toward Eden Palms, she looked as if she'd reluctantly stepped from a lemon-and-spritzer world into a scene of mourning. I pulled my stomach in and stood straighter.

Zack and I both walked to the front door to meet her. I stepped back while he held the door open wide, allowing her to make a dramatic entry with the gold and silver gift bag she dangled from two fingers. How, I wondered, did she manage to smell like Chinese orchids?

"Oh, Zack!" she hugged him with her free arm. "My deepest sympathy to you in the loss of your dear mother. My very deepest sympathy."

"Thank you, Courtney. I appreciate your empathy and concern. Do come inside and join us."

At the word "us," Courtney peered over Zack's shoulder, seeing me for the first time. She managed to change her initial reaction of dismay to one of pleasant surprise.

"Bailey! How nice to see you here . . . too. I didn't know you were such an early bird."

I forced a smile, fumbling in my mind for a suitable response and finding none. Courtney causes me to think of suitable responses a day after I need them. Before I could speak she continued.

"I've brought you sustenance, Zack." She turned her body so that it all but blocked me from the scene while she thrust her gift bag toward Zack as if offering the crown jewels. Her fingers touched his and lingered while she took exaggerated care to make sure he had a firm grip on the bag's handles.

"Zack, I realize this's a time of great stress for you, and I want you to take care of yourself. You've probably no appetite at all, but you must eat. I insist on it."

I tried not to gag. One minute she played the part of a temptress, the next minute, the part of a wide-eyed ingénue waiting for a pat on the head — or the butt.

When Zack opened the mouth of the bag and peered inside, the enticing aroma of onions, peppers, and Cuban salsa wafted to us.

"Ahh," he sighed and inhaled deeply.

"Yes, an aroma to die for, and I'm here to see that you eat right now before mourners begin arriving and fragmenting your day."

"How very thoughtful of you, Courtney."

"I had a late, late supper at Naked Lunch last night. The chef made this special serving at my request. I warmed the juicy meat to perfection in the microwave only minutes ago and it's ready for you to enjoy. I know you're a hardy type who likes roast beef for breakfast."

"How thoughtful of you, Courtney." Zack led the way to the kitchen. Courtney followed him. I followed her. Since Naked Lunch is a clothing-optional bar and restaurant on Duval, I wondered which option Courtney had chosen yesterday evening. When we reached the breakfast alcove, Courtney sniffed and raised an eyebrow when she saw the soggy cornflakes and toast we'd abandoned.

"Away with all this." With an air of determination, she flushed our uneaten breakfast into the disposal then began setting the table afresh. Clearly, she'd done this before. She had no problem finding dishes and placemats. But why should she? She and Francine had eaten here frequently. I wondered why my mind rejected the idea that she and Zack might have breakfasted here, too. Who Zack shared breakfast with was no concern of mine.

Courtney began by setting out two place mats. "Can I persuade you to join us, Bailey?"

"Of course she will," Zack answered for me. "It's going to be a long day for all of us."

"That's true. I just thought that since Bailey wasn't on Key West at the time of Francine's passing, she might want to opt out of the police investigation, if there is to be one, and fly right back home to Iowa."

"No," I said. "I hadn't thought of leaving — especially not before the funeral services. Francine meant a great deal to me and to my family."

"Well, of course," Courtney agreed, "but I haven't seen your colorful car around and I assumed you might already have gone."

I couldn't miss her sarcastic tone on the word "colorful." To celebrate on the day *Greentree Blues* hit the Key West stores, Francine had flown our family to the Keys and presented me with the car — an emerald green Lincoln that she'd outfitted with a vanity plate bearing the word BAILEY. It broke my heart to have to leave it in Key West, but Mom became ill and we had to fly home quickly. Francine had wanted to ship the car to Iowa, but we decided to leave it here for a short time, thinking Mom would recover soon and we could return for it. But the short time grew into a long time — a time very long and sad. We'd seldom mentioned the car.

"I took the Lincoln to our mechanic for a checkup," Zack said. "Mother and I both drove it now and then to keep the battery up, to keep the mechanisms operating. You know how it is in the Keys when it comes to motors — use them or lose them. Since the car had been idle more than it had been used, I felt it needed a professional look-see."

"Thank you, Zack," I said. "There've been so many things going on, so much to think about, I haven't had time to peek into the carport — yet. I appreciate your taking care of it for me."

"What were the detectives doing poking around here this morning?" Courtney asked.

Her sudden change of subject startled me. How dare she ask such a personal question! But Zack deflected it with adept courtesy at the same time he brought out a third place mat, a third plate with napkins and silverware.

"Oh, they were just being thorough," he said. "They thought of questions they hadn't touched on last night."

"I thought they covered things in depth yesterday," Courtney said. "They certainly went out of their way to try to make me look guilty of murder. I couldn't believe their insinuations."

"I don't think they intended to make you or anyone else look guilty," Zack said. "Detective Cassidy insisted again this morning that last night's question-and-answer session was informal — only necessary to his peace of mind. He wanted to be sure, as sure as he could at that point, of what had gone down here at the house. Try not to take it personally, Courtney."

Courtney divided the roast beef and its fragrant sauce and juices into three portions, making sure Zack received the largest. Her gift bag also contained rolls and tiny pats of butter in ceramic containers. She warmed the rolls in the microwave, giving Zack one and splitting the other between the two of us — with reluctance, I thought.

We ate in silence for a few moments before Courtney began a forced conversation. "I'm sorry the chef didn't have your favorite chutney glaze, Zack."

"This bland Cuban flavoring hits the spot this morning," Zack said. "I didn't realize how hungry I was. Guess I forgot about eating dinner last night."

Had he forgotten the sandwiches and hot chocolate we had shared, I wondered. The meal dragged on and on. I had to admit the beef was so tender I barely had to chew it, and the mixture of Cuban flavors left me wanting more. Zack answered a phone call concerning his business on Key Largo, and after he returned to his chair, we soon finished our meal. Courtney made a show of clearing the table and loading the dishwasher.

"Thank you so much for your thoughtfulness," Zack said when at last Courtney headed toward the front doorway.

"You're entirely welcome, Zack. If there's anything else I can help you with be sure to let me know. As a realtor, I can juggle my schedule to suit the occasion." Then she turned to me. "And Bailey, when *do* you plan to head north? You can count on me for a ride to the airport if Zack's at his office."

"My plans are tentative, Courtney, and although I have no present plans for returning to Iowa, I appreciate your offer."

Courtney was less than subtle in her effort to urge me on my way north, and I felt sure Zack noticed. A painful thought crossed my mind. Had Zack said something to her about anticipating my departure? But when would he have had time to talk with her privately? With Francine gone, I felt my situation at Eden Palms had changed. I wondered if Courtney already saw herself ensconced here as Zack's wife. I wondered about the closeness of their relationship. With Zack's wealth, good looks, and business success, many women in Key West might consider him the catch of the day. I tried to ignore his charms. I reminded myself again that I had no place in my life for a man right now and maybe never would have.

"If you've vetoed a return to Iowa," Courtney said, breaking into my thoughts, "then perhaps you'll be seeking other living arrangements here in Key West."

"Spoken like a true realtor, Courtney,"

Zack laughed. "Bailey's welcome to continue living in our cottage for as long as she cares to."

Courtney smiled at Zack then winked at me as if we shared a secret. "Give me a call if you decide to make a change."

Deep in thought, I stared after Courtney's departing figure until Zack cleared his throat.

"Bailey, sometimes Courtney overplays her hand. Please try to take anything she says with a grain of fault — her fault."

"Maybe she's right in her insinuations. Maybe I should pack and go." I met Zack's gaze, trying to read answers there. My staying might make an awkward situation for him.

"I'm not rushing you off, Bailey. Francine offered you the cottage, and although her plans for you haven't worked out, I'm sure I can find temporary employment for you in one of my offices for as long as you want it. From my point of view, it's better to have the cottage occupied than vacant."

"We don't have to decide on my plans right now. But if you think my continuing to live here might cause gossip . . ."

"Forget that, Bailey. Key West's a live-and-let-live island."

How well Zack knew that. I smiled, thinking about his almost-wedding and Francine's words. *"Zack returned the wedding gifts, repaid his fiancée's family the wedding expenses, although those duties were the girl's obligation. During a post-fiasco dinner, Zack stood and gave a toast.*

'To me — the guy who's spent his last dime on a non-wedding.'

For a while everyone nicknamed him Dime. Although his fiancée had hurt him deeply and although gossips gossiped, Zack put up with the name until everyone forgot it. Live and let live, that's Key West."

I'd been standing in the doorway peering at Courtney's departing figure. Now I turned, and followed Zack into the solarium. Francine had coaxed a gardenia plant into early bloom, and its fragrance greeted us, heady, cloying, reminding me of funeral flowers.

"Zack, I don't want to go back to Iowa, although it's a great place. I remember one summer when Chet and I were hiking. We'd been following a creek that babbled through a cornfield. When we came to a railroad trestle spanning the creek, we used wild sumac branches for handholds and climbed the bridge."

"Courting danger?"

"Yes, but luckily, no train rumbled within

sight or sound. I turned to look back, and I've never seen such beauty, not even in the Keys. The sun shone between a fluff of cotton candy clouds onto a sea of green cornstalks undulating in the breeze. A hawk soared toward a willow tree, and three red-winged blackbirds perched on swaying cattails at the brook's edge. I drank in the scene until I felt the railroad ties vibrating. Chet shouted a warning. We escaped from the bridge minutes before a freight train blasted its whistle."

"A memory like that might tempt you to return to Iowa — beautiful land. Isn't that what the Indians called it?"

"Yes, but I'll never go back. I also remember blizzards, sub-zero temperatures, and streets that remained ice-packed for weeks. One winter we were without power for six days. Friends took us in until we found a hotel room — a room of sorts. After the ordeal, people asked us if we paid the hourly rate or the night rate."

Zack smiled. "Guess I've never experienced true cold."

"In spite of the frosty winters, Iowans were warm and friendly. It's memories of my dad deserting us, of Mom struggling to support us, of her battle with cancer — those memories hurt."

We saw a delivery boy approaching, peering over the top of a miniature hibiscus plant full of salmon-colored blossoms. Zack turned to answer his knock, and my thoughts masked Zack's conversation with the boy.

In the distance, I heard the clatter of a Conch Train carrying tourists to see the interesting and historic spots on the island. The train's a boon to the tourism that keeps the island alive. Most locals seldom rode it more than once. Nor did they rush to the sunset celebration on Mallory Dock unless visitors had arrived and needed to be entertained for an evening.

"Beautiful, Zack," I said when he returned to the solarium with the hibiscus. "Where would you like to put it?"

"On the coffee table?"

"Fine." I slid a conch shell to one side, making room for the plant while Zack opened the card tucked into the leaves.

"Why don't I make a list of the friends who've sent remembrances?" I asked. "It'll help when you write the courtesy notes later."

"Good idea, Bailey. Thank you. My mind's not in gear yet this morning. Guess we were discussing your leaving or staying."

I sorted through my thoughts. I felt guilty

at arriving too late to help Francine. I might have prevented her death. She'd asked me to help her find the cause of the strange happenings here.

Surely Francine hadn't expected me to play detective, but she had asked for help and I'd failed her. I had to stay here. I had to help bring her murderer to justice if I could. I couldn't walk away from that obligation, nor did I want to. I thought about my brother, too. I couldn't desert Chet, either. I loved him, and I'd promised Mom . . .

"What are you thinking, Bailey?" Zack broke into my thoughts, and I managed a smile.

"Thinking about Key West." I couldn't tell him all I'd been thinking. I certainly couldn't mention my brother — Mitch, not Chet. I had to remember that.

"People either love Key West or they hate it." Zack adjusted the hibiscus plant on the table.

"I've listened to lots of people, Zack. It's a thing songwriters do. They listen. Many locals view all the tourists down here, especially the ones on Mallory at sunset, as an unwanted mass of humanity."

"You see it otherwise?"

"Definitely. At sunset, I see a rich tapestry

of strangers. Sometimes I feel that I've known them all before in some faraway land."

"A land of your imagination, but I hope that'll persuade you to stay here. By the way, the plant's from Winton Gravely. I'll find a notepad if you're serious about keeping track of the gifts."

"Sure thing."

Zack disappeared, then reappeared carrying a yellow notepad. "I have an ulterior motive for wanting you to stay here, Bailey."

His low tone made me wary, put me on guard. "What could that be?"

"I know I'm facing an in-depth police investigation. According to law, any suspect's supposed to be considered innocent until proven guilty. But, instead, sometimes a suspect has to take the lead in proving himself innocent. I think you can help me with that."

"How?" My mind backed off another step from Zack.

"We talked about the how of it last night — briefly. Again, I'm asking you to work with me, covertly of course, in finding the person who murdered Mother. Your experiences have put you around clues, motives, suspects. I hope you'll help me now."

"All right. I'll try." I hoped my quick

143

response masked my reluctance. "But I can tell you right now, I don't know where to start."

I couldn't tell him that he loomed as a key suspect in my thinking. The neighbors all had tentative alibis as to their whereabouts during the estimated time the murder might have taken place. Zack had accounted for his time, too, in a general way. But if the others were all occupied elsewhere, how easy it would have been for him to have returned home unseen and . . .

I could barely stand to think of Francine, the snake, the staircase. Could I bear to go on living next door to a man who might be a murderer? Might I be his next victim?

12

A steady stream of visitors came to the mansion bringing food and flowers. In spite of his consternation over the death-scene photographs and Detective Cassidy's visit, Zack managed to be gracious to the callers. I carried cakes, pies, and salads to the kitchen, hoping the refrigerator would hold the must-keep-chilled dishes. After each visitor left, Zack and I worked together, recording each person's name, address, and a brief description of the gift.

"Oh." Zack rose and looked out the window. "Here come the servicemen returning your car."

I jumped up. A dream car. It glistened in the sunshine like a green magnet pulling me toward it.

"Go ahead." Zack nodded toward the door. "I know you've missed it. Take it out for a spin."

"I do need to pick up a few groceries from

Fausto's. But I won't be gone long." We hurried outside, and while Zack chatted with the servicemen, I slid beneath the wheel, waved to them, and eased into the Tuesday morning traffic on Eaton Street. Three mopeders cut in front of me, and I braked to avoid a mishap. I didn't honk. They rode on, unmindful of their danger — or mine. Even after two years, the interior of the Lincoln still held the new-car smell. I inhaled deeply, admiring the cream-colored leather seats and reaching overhead to open the sun roof and allow a sea breeze to cool me.

Doing a slow Duval crawl, I inched along, enjoying a quick glimpse of Fast Buck Freddie's, Margaritaville, Sloppy Joe's. I took a longing look at The Sandbar where Francine had managed to have me invited as a guest soloist on my previous visit to celebrate the release of *Greentree Blues.* I hoped the owner might hire me for some gigs now that I would be living in Key West. A few people gawked at my car, and a male voice shouted, "There goes Bailey." For a moment I had forgotten my name was on my license plate. Could I consider that word-of-mouth advertising?

I spent only a few minutes in the grocery store. A bag of M&Ms. Some peanut butter cups. A half gallon of milk. The fragrance of freshly baked donuts tempted me, but I thought of the food arriving at Eden Palms. Zack would share.

Back at the cottage, I parked at the door while I carried my purchases inside, and moments later, I eased my car into the carport that sat out of sight behind the mansion. I smiled when I entered the kitchen. Zack sat nibbling on a chocolate chip cookie. Sometimes food does help minimize one's troubles — at least momentarily.

At mid-afternoon, during a lull in the flow of visitors, I wandered into Zack's art studio. North light flowed into the spacious room and I eyed the easel draped with a white cloth sitting near the door. I smelled the faint but pungent scent of oil paints and turpentine when I peeked under the cloth at the likeness of a white boat with kelly-green sails.

"Beautiful, Zack," I said when he followed me into the studio. "Do you manage to find a regular time for your art?"

He smiled. "Not every day, but I live in possibility. Someday I'll finish the painting — and the boat."

I heard the wistfulness in his voice, and I empathized with him when I thought of my own work-in-progress on a new blues composition. I'd hoped to have plenty of writing time. I owned software that allowed me to compose at my computer, and my electronic keyboard would coax me to work every day. Yet few new ideas for lyrics or fresh rhythmic patterns had flowed to me in recent months. I told myself that was understandable, considering my mother's recent death — and now Francine's.

"My face aches from smiling." Zack held a sheet of notepaper on a clipboard toward me. "I'm taping this note onto the door, thanking visitors for coming and promising to get in touch later."

"If you'd like, I'll stay here and greet people."

"No. You've already done more than your share and I appreciate it. People will understand our need for a respite. Go on to the cottage and grab some rest. I need to take care of details at the funeral home, and I promised Ben Bahama some help. He's been waiting since yesterday."

"Quinn's husband?"

"Yeah. Know him?"

"No. But Quinn mentioned him when we were talking at the airport last night. Said he'd gone shrimping."

"Guess those were his plans, but he won't be going out today. His boat's at the bottom of the bay near Land End's Village."

"Accident?"

"No. The boat's old — a floating disaster. Or, as of last night, a sunken disaster. I promised to help salvage it, and he really needs it today. He's having a rough time financially and *The Seawitch*'s under water almost as much as it's floating. If I get over there and winch it up this afternoon, he may be able to dry it out, do some makeshift repairs, and take his crew out tomorrow night."

"Can't you send some of your workers to do the job?"

Zack shook his head. "I do it personally — as a favor. Ben keeps me supplied with fresh shrimp. Besides, my employees face deadlines on other projects."

"What about a late lunch before you go?" I asked. "I saw a chicken casserole that looked delicious."

"Not hungry. But you help yourself. Take it to the cottage if you'd feel more comfortable eating there."

"Think I'll do that." I went to the kitchen and picked up the casserole, feeling it warm my hand even though it'd been in the refrigerator a few minutes. Before I left, I turned to Zack. "Give me a call if there's anything more I can do here."

"Thanks. Will do."

When I left the mansion, a cloud blocked the sun and a mist began to fall. I hurried to the cottage. Strange to have rain in January, but it matched my mood. Once inside, I enjoyed a helping of the casserole along with a piece of toast covered with Francine's special guava jelly. Everything I saw or did reminded me of Francine. Busy as she always was with her bridge groups and civic activities, she always took time to pick the summer-ripe guavas from the tree beside the carport and spend hours turning them into jelly.

The casserole hadn't tasted as good as I hoped it might, but I finished the serving on my plate. *Clean your plate if you expect dessert.* My mother's voice did an instant replay in my mind. Why, I wondered, did my mind focus so sharply on the dead?

I'd gone to my bedroom to unpack when the phone rang.

"Hello," I'd expected to hear Zack's voice requesting some bit of help, but instead I heard Chet — er, Mitch. Even in my mind I had to learn to think of him as Mitch.

"Hi, Sis. What's the buzz? Can we get together for a while this afternoon? I've tried to call you several times this morning. You been away?"

I explained my morning to him. "What do

you have in mind?"

"You promised you'd let me introduce you to a couple of my friends, remember?"

"Your homeless friends?"

"Those are the ones. How about it? They're good people. All they need's a little help from someone who cares about them. This afternoon would be a good meeting time for them and a good time for me, too. Nothing much going on in my life today."

I wanted to tell him about the blacksnake, the special horror concerning Francine's death, the pictures, but Detective Cassidy had demanded secrecy.

"Well, there's plenty going on in my life right now. I haven't even had enough free time to unpack."

"I saw you doing Duval in your car. Remember hearing someone yell at you? Well, that was me."

"Thanks a lot — Mitch."

"Seems to me, if you have time to joy ride, you should have time to meet my friends."

"I wasn't joy riding. Well, not exactly. I loved seeing my car again, so I made buying a few groceries a reason for taking it out for a drive."

"So take it out again. I'll introduce you to Wizard and Princess. We can give them a spin around Old Town. They probably haven't ridden in a Lincoln anytime recently. How about if I bike over to your place, and we can drive to the bridle path? They live near there."

"No way. Think, Mitch. Think. We can't risk being seen together. What would Zack and his neighbors think of my sudden friendship with their yardman? Or with a part-time dishwasher at a local eatery? What would the police think?"

"You ashamed of me?"

"Of course not." I hesitated, wishing I could warn him about the police investigation, wishing I could tell him how he might have compromised himself with his tale of the blacksnake. "Of course I'm not ashamed of you. Honest work makes anyone respectable in my thinking. It's you I'm concerned about. What if someone guesses we're related? Guesses your identity? Your life could be on the line."

"Yeah. You're right. Sometimes I forget I'm a new person. Thanks for the reminder. We'd better avoid togetherness. Especially togetherness in your car. Those wheels grab plenty of attention. So why don't you park at Smathers and hoof it, cliché intended, to the bridle path. I'll meet you there. You're a strong walker, and the path's close to the beach. Once we meet, it'll be easy for you to disappear with me into the thicket."

I eyed my tumbled clothes in the suitcase and sighed. "Okay, Mitch. Give me half an hour, okay?"

"Okay. See you then."

In that half hour I managed to unpack only one suitcase — the one that held the glamorous gown I had worn when I performed at The Sandbar. I felt the cool smoothness of the jewel-toned satin. I could hardly wait to wear it again. I sighed, tucking the empty case into the back of my closet before I hoisted the other bag onto the luggage rack — the sturdy bag that held my laptop. Enough. I slung my camera around my neck, glad that it was an old friend I'd owned since high school days, a camera I could depend on. Maybe someday I'd invest in a new digital variety, but not yet. I headed for the Lincoln and the beach, glad for the diversion even if it involved meeting my brother's indigent friends.

Sunbathers crowded the sand this afternoon, but I found a parking place and fed quarters into the meter. A mixture of enticing aromas wafted from the many vendors' trailers parked bumper to bumper next to the sidewalk that separated beach from boulevard — hotdogs, pizza, barbecued pork.

Dreading this secret meeting with Mitch's newfound friends, I stalled now and then, stopping to drink in the scene at hand. In the distance the gray silhouette of a cargo ship inched across the horizon. High overhead a blue and gold hot-air balloon trailed a streamer advertising tonight's harbor sail, promising dinner as well as a sunset. Below the balloon, a plane towing a parasailer grabbed my attention. I stood gawking, but I heard the warning shouts.

"Outta the way, lady! Duck!" A blue volleyball whizzed by, barely missing my head.

"Sorry, lady." A sunburned boy wearing nothing but a red Speedo retrieved the ball. Amid catcalls and whistles, he rejoined his pals waiting ankle deep in sand on the volleyball court.

I walked faster, narrowly missing a collision with a guy flying a giant turtle-shaped kite. Then I jumped aside in time to avoid a head-on with two skateboarders intent on eating huge puffs of pink cotton candy. Horns honked when I jaywalked across the highway toward mounds of dirty beach sand that had been bulldozed from the street following hurricanes Georges and then Wilma.

A few yards farther on I walked under palms that shaded the old bridle path. I found it hard to imagine anything as sedate as a horseback rider enjoying this trail. Such activity must have taken place in another day, another age. Right now, I wished Mitch had been more specific about our meeting place, but I needn't have worried. In a few moments he stepped from the thicket beside the path.

"Thought you were going to stand me up," he said. "Been waiting a while. But come on. Follow me."

"Where to?"

Mitch was alone, but I glanced over my shoulder now and then while I followed him a few yards into a small clearing hidden from the street. We stopped when we reached a tattered blue tent blocking our path.

"Okay, people." Mitch lifted the tent flap and leaned into the opening. "She's here. Come on out. Meet my friend."

Thank goodness he'd kept our relationship a secret! The woman appeared first, then the man.

"Princess. Wizard. I want you to meet my good friend, Bailey Green. And Bailey, I want you to meet my friends."

I muttered my hellos while Mitch spouted bits and pieces of information like a tour guide. *Very comfortable here. Got police okay to pitch the tent. Got friends all around us.*

While he rattled on, I couldn't take my gaze from Princess. In her sixties? Maybe. That was a wild estimate. She was built like a pyramid on stilts, and she could have been forty or seventy or anywhere in between. She wore a fraying straw hat. Her orange, pot-scrubber hair and her scarlet lipstick clashed with the blobs of pink rouge dabbed on her raddled cheeks.

"Like my new outfit?" She twirled before me like an obese child showing off for Grandma. "Mitch lent me the money, and I bought the whole outfit including the hat for only three dollars on Flagler at the Salvation Army store."

Her twirling released the sick-sweet fragrance of perfume. I fought a desire to step back. Her white peek-a-boo blouse and black satin skirt, along with the red and white polka dot cummerbund spanning her wide middle formed a one-of-a-kind outfit. Pink ballerina slippers were losing a half-hearted struggle to contain her feet.

"What a colorful outfit, Princess! I'm sure you'll enjoy wearing it a long time."

"Your brother is very generous." Princess grinned at Mitch until he blushed. I wondered what real name might be on her birth certificate, if she had one. But everyone has a birth certificate somewhere, right?

"Where's your home, Princess?" I looked away from the tent. "I mean where does your family live?"

"Don't remember. Maybe don't have no more family."

"Wizard hails from New Jersey," Mitch frowned at me, trying to change the subject and put Princess at ease. I gave the balding scarecrow of a man my full attention, determined to ask no more embarrassing questions. Wizard looked a lot like the vendor I'd encountered at the airport. I backed off a step. Could it be the same guy?

"Pleased to meet you. Wizard."

"Likewise, I'm sure." His voice was a guttural rumble.

Wizard wore no shirt under his bib overalls. He'd rammed bare feet into hiking boots whose toes had been cut out for comfort — or maybe for ventilation. Wizard's appearance made me think of the plethora of food at Eden Palms. I wondered when he'd last eaten a good meal. Did he patronize the soup kitchens? An odor emanating from him made me guess that beer might be his main form of sustenance. I looked at the tent from which these two had emerged. Did they live together?

"Mitch, where do you live — I mean where do you sleep?"

"We all sleep on pallets under the stars, Bailey. The tent's only for emergencies such as rain or sudden cold or mean tourists who might tell us to move on."

The three of them sat on the ground and I joined them, hoping this get-together would soon end and that nobody would see me.

"I want to help these people, Bailey. They're down on their luck right at the moment. Wizard used to be a telephone line repairman, but he walked when the company discriminated against him — promoted others when he should have been promoted. And Princess has had a lot of troubles, too." Mitch stopped to grab a breath. "She was an ace housekeeper, but her employer fired her when some of the family jewelry turned up missing. No fault of Princess's. None at all. The woman's kid probably swiped the stuff and sold it for drug money. I'd like to help both these people get their lives back on track, help them reunite with their families. There're many reasons for family estrangements, but with a little effort, a little understanding, these people could be happy living with their loved ones again."

Mitch rattled on as people sometimes do when they know they're presenting a weak case. When I looked at Mitch, my mind flashed back to the kid who used to bring in stray cats and dogs. Now he'd graduated to stray people.

"And what do Princess and Wizard think of your plan?" I tried to keep sarcasm from my voice. What did I know! I could be wrong. Maybe these two did want to reunite with family.

"I'm happy right here," Wizard said. "Nobody around prodding me to find a job or stop dirking or —"

Princess broke in. "Mitch wants to help us, and we appreciate him and we like him a lot, but we don't really need no help." She paused, looking down at her clothes. "Well, I did need help in getting this new outfit. But Mitch didn't try to boss me around. He let me choose every piece of it myself."

"I'm helping them out when I can," Mitch said. "I give them a little money for food, a little help with doctor's bills, some cash for medicine. All they need is someone to lend them a helping hand."

It appalled me to know these two were scamming my brother with their hard-luck stories. I stood. There was little hope of changing Mitch — or Wizard and Princess. I opened my purse. I felt guilty leaving these people without giving them something, some token of my visit. But what? Unlike

159

Mitch, I refused to dole out money I felt sure they'd spend in the nearest bar. Instead, I poked into my purse and pulled out the two scarves I'd purchased under duress at the airport. I extended a smile and a scarf to each of them. If Wizard had been the man who had sold them to me, he didn't let on.

"I've enjoyed meeting you both, and perhaps you'll enjoy wearing these mementos of Key West."

Princess's eyes lit up and she smiled her thanks as she folded the blue scarf into an oblong and tucked it into her polka-dot cummerbund. Again she twirled, expecting my admiration.

Wizard folded his scarf into a triangle and tied the ends of it at the back of his neck, letting it hang like a bib. I'd forgotten about the grease stain and now it embarrassed me to see it front and center, but Wizard didn't seem to notice.

"Thank you, ma'am. This'll make a useful sweat rag once the temp begins to heat up."

I reached for the camera slung around my neck. "May I take your pictures?"

Princess posed, smiling and tilting her head like a movie star. "People are always wanting to take my picture," she said. "This's my Britney Spears pose."

I snapped the shot and turned toward

Wizard. He didn't smile, but he looked straight into the camera as I took his picture.

"Thank you both very much. It's been a pleasure meeting you." Then feeling like a Scrooge, I gave in, reached into my purse again, and pulled out a fiver for each of them. Mitch walked me back to the bridle path, and I felt Wizard and Princess watching me as I left. I trusted Mitch, but Wizard and Princess could be dangerous. I hoped they didn't know where I lived.

13

"What did you think of them?" Mitch asked when we were out of earshot of his friends. "They're interesting people, Bailey. Once I got to know them, I learned all sorts of interesting things about their pasts. I can understand why they prefer to live on the street."

"They're taking you for a ride, Mitch. Thousands of people hunting jobs, and Wizard walks out on one! And Princess! Maybe she stole her employer's jewelry and maybe she didn't. Are you sure any jewelry existed to be stolen? Maybe she imagined the whole thing."

"Cut 'em some slack, Sis. You just don't understand them. You don't understand how harshly the world can treat some people."

"Right. I don't. But I do understand that your new friends could be dangerous. Sure, they've given you hard-luck stories, but you've no proof they're true."

Mitch scowled. "You think that by ignoring their situation it'll go away? Be real."

"I think you'd be better off donating your chump change to the organized agencies trying to help people like Wizard and Princess. Let the professionals do their thing."

"We have differing opinions, as usual."

"Right. As usual."

"Thanks for showing up to meet them." Mitch turned and headed toward the hidden tent. "I won't walk you to your car."

"Thanks." I didn't storm off in a huff. Huffs had never worked for me when dealing with my brother. My promise to Mom to look after him made me realize I had to keep a line of communication open even though we were living on different planets.

The morning sessions with the detectives, with Courtney, with Zack, to say nothing of my meeting with Mitch and his friends, all were taking their toll. I felt wiped out. Once I reached my car, I didn't want to go home, so I inched through the bumper-to-bumper traffic on Duval Street to the dock. Parking lot almost deserted. Too early for the sunset crowd. I strolled to a bench near the water. I could almost taste the salt in the sea air. No cruise ships blocked my vision, and I sat enjoying the breeze and the water until I felt refreshed enough to drive home and face whatever might await me there.

Once I turned into the cul-de-sac, I wished I'd stayed at Mallory. Detective Burgundy stepped from his unmarked car when he saw me turn toward the carport. I took my time parking, wondering what he wanted. Maybe he'd come to see Zack. One could hope.

When I returned from the carport, he walked toward me in his loose-limbed way. Puppet on a string. That's what he reminded me of, a tall, good-looking puppet. Forget that. A cop was a cop was a cop.

"Good afternoon, Bailey. I called ahead a few times, but when you didn't answer I decided to drop by and wait. Do you have some free minutes?"

"Yes, of course." I paused at his car, drawing a deep breath. "How can I help you?"

Burgundy glanced at his watch. "Detective Cassidy and I want you to come to headquarters for a formal interview. Would you be willing to do that now?"

I wanted to ask if I had a choice. But no. I knew I didn't. His smile and friendly attitude belied his true intention. If I refused to go, they could deliver a summons that would force me either to appear or to risk breaking the law.

"Why does Detective Cassidy want to question me further? I assume it's about Francine's death."

"Right. It is."

"I told you everything I know yesterday — Monday. I didn't arrive in Key West until late in the evening."

"We're aware of that. But we'd like to make more careful notes on your account of the happenings since you arrived."

"Will I need a lawyer?"

"That's your choice, of course. If you'd feel more comfortable with a lawyer at your side, you may call one when we reach headquarters. Or, I suppose you could even call one from here and have him meet you at our office. Might save some time."

I considered my options. It irritated me that Detective Burgundy assumed all lawyers were men. I did know a lawyer — a woman whom Francine had asked to offer me legal advice concerning certain aspects of writing lyrics and song titles. But why bother her now? She might not even remember me from several years ago. I knew so little about yesterday's happenings at the mansion that I felt sure I wouldn't say anything to incriminate myself.

"I'll not bother with calling a lawyer,

Detective. How long should I plan to be away?"

"I'll have you back here within the hour unless we encounter interruptions. If you need to let someone know your whereabouts, I'll wait here while you make a call."

"Thank you, but that won't be necessary."

He opened the car door for me, and I eased onto the passenger seat. We headed toward North Roosevelt and drove to police headquarters, stopping in front of the station grounds when we heard sirens begin to wail. The police and fire stations are adjacent to each other, and we waited while a fire truck exited the driveway. Then, once Burgundy entered the parking lot, I saw signs marking reserved parking slots for both Detectives Burgundy and Cassidy.

After opening the car door for me, Burgundy walked alongside me toward the station. The walls looked pink in the afternoon sunlight — an unusual color for a police station, I thought. We hurried inside the smoky-smelling entryway and took an elevator to the detectives' second-floor office.

"Please have a chair," Burgundy said, "and I'll tell Detective Cassidy you've arrived."

Two steel file cabinets, two pine desks with captain's chairs, and two folding chairs for visitors almost filled the office. A closed window overlooked the street below, and the stench of cigarette smoke hung in the air. Did I dare ask that the window be opened? No, probably not. I decided to speak only when spoken to, and I didn't have to wait long.

"Good afternoon, Miss Green. Thank you for coming in on such short notice."

"Good afternoon, sir." I wondered if Cassidy wore the same suit every day or if he had a closet full of gray lookalikes. Both officers sat at their desks and pulled out yellow legal-size pads and ballpoints. Steely-eyed and grim-faced, Cassidy fired the first question. It didn't scare me.

"Your name and address, please."

A warm-up formality. I replied although we both knew he already had my name and address well in mind. I braced myself for the next question.

"Miss Green, I understand your plane landed at Key West International last night at seven-thirty as scheduled."

"That's right."

"And you didn't reach Eden Palms until around nine o'clock due to traffic problems in the area."

"That's right."

"At that time, did you suspect that Francine Shipton might be dead?"

The question shocked me and I felt a deep uneasiness. "No, sir. I had no reason to believe that she might be dead."

"Who had planned to meet you at the airport?"

"Francine Shipton." Cassidy's gaze was monodirectional, but so was mine. I didn't intend to be the one to look away first.

"What did you think when she failed to appear?"

"I thought she must have been delayed by something beyond her control. I waited for a while expecting her to arrive at any minute, and when she didn't, I took a taxi. I hoped we wouldn't pass each other en route to our destinations."

"When you reached the mansion, what was your first impression?"

"When I saw the crime scene tape, I knew it indicated serious trouble, that police usually use it in the event of an unexplained or suspicious death."

"Who did you think might have died?"

I refused to tell Cassidy about my note from Francine. He hadn't asked about my correspondence with her, and I wouldn't tell unless asked. I hesitated too long, and Cassidy repeated his question.

"Miss Green, who did you think might have died?"

"Since Zack came toward my taxi to greet me and since only he and Francine lived in the mansion, I had to admit the possibility of Francine's death."

"Had she given you any indication that she might have been in danger."

'Yes, sir. She did. She wrote a note urging me to hurry back to Key West."

"Did she say why?"

"She said strange things had been happening at the mansion and that she had received threatening notes. She mentioned finding snakes in the solarium and that she felt frightened."

"She give any names of the person or persons she felt might be frightening her?"

"No names. None at all."

"Do you know of any enemies she might have had?"

"No. None. I'm rather new to the island, and I don't know all of her acquaintances. But I'd never heard her mention having an enemy."

"In the few times that you've visited the cottage and the mansion, have you ever encountered a blacksnake?"

"Encountered one? You mean inside the cottage?"

"Inside or outside. Either one. Have you seen blacksnakes in the area?"

"Only once, sir."

"And when was that?"

"One morning about two years ago, I saw a blacksnake slither across the street and disappear into the grass in Courtney Lusk's yard."

"You're good at identifying blacksnakes?"

"What do you mean — good at? I'm no herpetologist, if that's what you mean. But in Iowa, during my childhood, my younger brother introduced me to a variety of midwestern snakes. All I can really tell you about the snake I saw that day is that it was black."

"Did it scare you?"

"No."

"You're unafraid of snakes?"

"My brother taught me to be unafraid of them, and they don't terrify me. However, I'd always rather see a snake before it sees me."

"What would you do if you saw a snake today near Eden Palms?"

"I'd give it its space and walk in the other direction."

"You'd make no effort to kill it?"

"Never. My brother taught both Mom and me that most snakes are harmless unless you frighten or threaten them. Snakes improve the environment by ridding their habitat of pesky creatures."

Drat. I looked away first. What was with this man? Did he think I'd been shipping snakes to Key West for the express purpose of scaring Francine?

"Miss Green, do you still have the note Francine wrote you? The one in which she mentioned solarium snakes, being threatened, being afraid?"

I felt an adrenalin rush. I could say yes. Or I could say no. I didn't want the police to involve me in this case. But I did want to do anything I could to help them apprehend Francine's killer.

"Yes. I still have the note."

"May we stop by your home and pick it up as a piece of evidence?"

"No need for that, sir." I opened my purse, withdrew the note, and leaned forward to place it on his desk.

"I thank you for your cooperation, Miss Green. Detective Burgundy will drive you home now. You're free to leave Key West if you care to, but please inform someone in this office of your travel plans."

"Yes, sir. I'll remember that." What did that mean — that I could travel but they planned to keep track of my whereabouts?

Detective Burgundy escorted me to his car and we headed for my cottage.

"You handled that quite well, Miss Green. Sometimes Detective Cassidy can seem formidable."

A good description, I thought. Formidable. "That's understandable. He has a tough job. I guess he can't smile and risk giving people the impression that he isn't taking his job seriously."

When we reached the cottage, Burgundy walked me to the door and saw me safely inside. I flopped down onto my bed feeling a need to relax. I'd dropped off to sleep when the telephone rang, and I sat up, too startled for a moment to pick up the receiver. I lifted it on the third ring.

"Bailey speaking."

"It's Zack. Been trying to get you for a while, but . . ."

He hesitated, but when I didn't offer to tell him where I'd been, he continued.

"I've invited the near neighbors in for a snack, Bailey. There's an overflow of food here and I've no family to help me eat it. Anyway, everyone I've invited is a suspect in this murder case. Did you hear the announcement on the five o'clock news?"

"No. Oh, Zack! The police have announced the whole story?"

"Most of it. But nothing about the snake. That's still hush-hush."

"Thanks for the heads up."

"We need to get together — all of us. We need to discuss our various situations before the police haul us in individually for formal questioning. Will you come over? Courtney's already here helping me organize an informal buffet."

"Sure, Zack. I'll be over as soon as I freshen up." For some reason I didn't want to tell him I'd already been in for questioning. Nor was I eager for another meeting with Miss Perfection in Prada.

14

After a quick shower, I searched my closet for something to wear. It irritated me to think I might let Courtney influence my decision. She'd be dressed to — I avoided the word "kill" — to attract attention — especially from Zack. So what. I refused to enter a costume competition. She might need a man to make her life meaningful, but not I. Yet, if she planned to use Francine's death to point out a hole in Zack's life and perhaps to entice him into marriage, that might concern me — a lot. Her first act as the new Mrs. Shipton might be to demand that I find another place to live.

Don't go there! I shoved that concern to the back of my mind. If necessary, I could find another apartment. Maybe. I slipped into a green tee, white capris, and Kino thongs before I ran a comb through my hair. After adding a gloss of coral-toned lipstick, I felt nervous and wary but determined to face whatever lay ahead. I locked the cottage and dropped the key into my purse. On second thought, I retrieved it and tucked it into a pocket of my capris.

Tucker Tisdale's cream-colored Cadillac sat at the curb in front of Eden Palms. The other guests must have walked. Maybe Tucker felt he might need to make a quick exit. Funeral directors could be summoned on the spur of the moment. And so could doctors. I didn't see Dr. Gravely's Lexus, but I squinted as the sun flashed against the silver of Courtney's BMW in her carport.

Zack met me at his door.

"Come in, Bailey, and have a chair." He eased me toward the living room. Dr. Gravely and Tucker Tisdale sat at opposite ends of a leather sofa, and Zack had pulled armchairs into a semicircle for the rest of us. "We've decided to meet in here and enjoy a few snacks. Nobody felt in the mood for a formal meal. I doubt if anyone has much of an appetite."

"You hear the news?" Dr. Gravely shot the question at me, almost interrupting Zack's welcome. "Homicide." His piercing gaze probed my eyes.

I nodded, careful to keep the source of my news to myself. "Tragic," I muttered. "Unthinkable." The others murmured in agreement.

My feet sank into plush carpeting as I faced Gravely and Tisdale. I didn't see Mitch, and that didn't surprise me. Although he'd been present last night, he wasn't one of the near neighbors. I hoped he wouldn't be involved in a homicide investigation.

"Hello, Bailey," Courtney called from the kitchen doorway, where she stood holding a pitcher of iced tea. "Glad you could join us."

I murmured a greeting to Courtney and to the others and tried to ignore Courtney's outfit. But nobody could ignore Courtney for long, especially not this evening when she undulated between kitchen and dining room, carrying snack trays and glasses. Her lemon-colored sarong flowed from her slim neck to her ankles. The long auburn hair she usually wore in a sophisticated French braid or an upsweep now fell around her shoulders and onto her back. Eleanor Roosevelt once said another person couldn't undermine your poise unless you allowed it. I wasn't about to allow it.

"I've arranged snacks in the dining room," Courtney called to everyone, very much at home as Zack's hostess. "Do come along and help yourselves. We can talk later."

Zack arranged a TV table beside my chair, and then the others let me lead the way into the dining room. Portraits of Shipton ancestors peered at us from ornate gold frames. In the center of the teakwood dining table, Courtney had floated a yellow hibiscus in a Waterford bowl. Around it she'd arranged salvers of crackers along with shallow bowls of plantain chips and, in close proximity, crystal bowls of crab dip, guacamole, and smoked oysters. Only Courtney would dare use Francine's palm-print paper plates and napkins on the same table with Waterford and make the combination seem a perfect choice.

"Shrimp scampi. Calamari. Grouper fingers." Courtney roll-called other delicacies, but I had no appetite. I took a small helping of curried chicken to be polite.

Courtney's bright chatter about the menu didn't call up huge appetites from anyone. When we sat again in the living room, we picked at our food. I couldn't think about eating while sitting so near the spot where Francine had died. Zack tried to make casual conversation.

"Bailey, I saw a dozen copies of your CD this afternoon. Front window at Island Book Store. The owner had surrounded it with books on music and composers. Stuck

177

my head in the doorway long enough to tell him he'd made a great window display. Francine must have made arrangements for it."

Zack avoided mentioning the title, *Greentree Blues*.

"You've listened to the recording?" Dr. Gravely asked.

"Certainly," Zack replied. "Mother owned one of the first CDs available after its release. It's there on the coffee table if anyone wants to borrow it. You had a chance to hear it, Tucker?"

Everyone glanced at the coffee table and the CD with my picture alongside a likeness of a graceful palm tree bending in the breeze.

"Don't have much time for listening." Tucker smiled apologetically and tugged at his shirt sleeves. "But my wife said she listened to it the same day it came out. Said it was her kind of song."

"Thank you," I murmured. "That's good to hear."

"What about you, Courtney?" Gravely said. "I know you're a music lover. You listened to *Greentree Blues*?"

Courtney nodded a yes. "Francine gave me one of the first copies available. I still listen to it now and then."

So. Francine had asked Zack to buy my CD for *her* to give to Courtney. It bothered me that it made a difference to me. As we continued to pick at our food, the conversation grew more fragmented.

"Lovely decorations in this room." Tucker Tisdale broke an uncomfortable silence. "Francine loved to patronize struggling artists. And she had an eye for choosing the best. I like that early Wyland above the piano." With his fork, Tucker pointed to the oil depicting a manta ray swimming above sea fans, angel fish, and coral. "Francine guessed Wyland would be famous one day."

"I like the seascapes," Courtney said. "And the tall ships. Nothing's more graceful than a sailboat tilting under a breeze."

"I'm redecorating the walls of my waiting room at the clinic with historical memorabilia," Gravely said.

"From what era?" Zack asked. "I thought you concentrated on photos of exotic fish and fishing boats."

"Lately I've become interested in the 1980s. I've been framing flags and old newspaper articles about the Conch Republic and Key West's colorful mayor."

"Mayor Wardlow." Zack smiled. "I was in my teens, but I remember him."

"My patients like my new décor. Guess a

little humor helps lift their mood."

"I'd like to see your photographs, Dr. Gravely. I'm always seeking ideas, for subject matter other songwriters may have overlooked. I hadn't heard of the Conch Republic until yesterday when a cabbie told me about it. Would it be possible for me to see your waiting room some time?"

Gravely hesitated a moment before replying, and I worried that I had intruded into the privacy of his clinic, but he smiled. "Of course, Bailey. I'll give you a call one of these days."

Suddenly, I regretted having asked the favor. All our stilted chit-chat this late afternoon had made me forget for the moment that Winton Gravely was a murder suspect along with the rest of us. I had no intention of visiting his clinic anytime soon.

"Bailey?" Zack nodded toward the piano. "How about singing us a short number? A little music might lighten our mood."

"Right!" Dr. Gravely rose, opened the cover on the keyboard, and pulled the bench out for me.

I sat down at the elegant grand reluctantly. It hardly seemed the time and place for singing and playing blues, but I began with an arpeggio to warm up my fingers.

"One of the main challenges a songwriter

faces in addition to clever lyrics is creating a left hand piano rhythm that anchors the bass line while it gives the vocalist freedom to create a melody line with enough importance to make the composition hang together."

I shared only a few lines of an original I had begun and then abandoned — *Dreams at Midnight.* When I hesitated for a moment, Courtney applauded lightly and spoke.

"Thanks so much, Bailey. I know your next CD's sure to be a hit. Now, thanks to your generosity, we can say we were first to hear a preview of it right here at Eden Palms."

I took Courtney's cue, stopped playing, and slid from the piano bench.

"More! More!" Gravely cried.

"Another time," I said. "Another place."

"Thank you, Bailey." Zack made a point of helping me back to my chair. "We all want to hear more, but let's get to the point of this meeting. There's no avoiding it. We're all suspects in this murder case and we need to discuss how we can best defend ourselves once the police start bearing down on us."

"We may be suspects," Gravely said, "but there are certainly other people who might also be under investigation. Just because we're near neighbors, doesn't rule others from police scrutiny."

"Any Key West resident who abhors seeing this neighborhood blighted with a home for derelicts could have felt he or she had reason to put an end to such a possibility." Tisdale looked at us, seeking agreement.

"The police might find a homeless person guilty," Courtney said. "Some of those street sleepers are mentally deranged. Nobody knows what to expect from them. Maybe one of them hated the thought of a new shelter where he might be forced to live under rules prohibiting drugs — and alcohol is one of their favorite drugs."

"Or perhaps some building contractor had a fit of jealousy," Tucker said. "Someone might have hated seeing lucrative contracts go to a competitor." He nodded as if he'd struck on a great idea.

"And what about that yardman?" Winton asked. "There's a guy who's been inside this house looking for . . . a snake. He certainly deserves an investigation into his background. How did he decide on *this* neighborhood when he went job hunting? We need answers from that guy."

Zack cleared his throat. "I think we should keep the information we have to ourselves — information the police gathered from us last night. People besides the police will be asking us questions. The less we say, the better. That's the point I want to get across tonight."

"I agree," Courtney said. "No comment. Isn't that the line people toss to reporters when they want to avoid answering questions?"

"Right." Gravely slapped a fist into his palm. "No comment."

"I can't imagine anyone low enough to do away with a human life in such a dastardly manner." Tucker rose, shoving his TV tray to one side. "Clearly, police will call it a hate crime."

Dastardly. I'd heard that word before and I'd read it in print, but this was the first time I recalled hearing anyone say it aloud. *Dastardly.* Very descriptive.

Dr. Gravely stood and followed Tucker to the door. "Thank you for the hospitality, Zack. You, too, Courtney. Good of you to help out. Wish it could have been under more pleasant circumstances."

Courtney's gaze followed the men until Zack ushered them out the door. When he returned to the living room, she began gathering the snack plates. "Give me a minute, Zack, and I'll have everything cleared away."

Zack stepped between her and the nearest

TV table. "No, no, Courtney. You've been a life saver, but you've done enough for today. Bailey and I'll finish setting things to rights again."

I didn't know if I felt glad or sorry. I didn't mind the setting-things-to-rights statement, but being alone in the mansion with Zack made me feel more uneasy than it had early this morning. Zack didn't wait for my agreement. He began urging Courtney toward the door in a way that would have made her refusal to leave an embarrassment for all of us.

After Courtney left, Zack stood in the doorway watching Tucker drive away, watching Winton Gravely's brisk step as he hurried toward his house, stopping briefly to view the Tisdale's Koi pond. He watched Courtney head across the street until she turned to look over her shoulder. Then he closed the door, pretending not to have been watching.

"I'll cover the snacks and set them in the refrig," I said, hoping to be on my way to the cottage as quickly as possible.

"Thanks. I appreciate your help." Zack grabbed the paper plates and napkins and stuffed them into the kitchen wastebasket. When we were through, I broke the awkward silence.

"I must go, now, Zack. It's been an exhausting day for both of us."

"Tomorrow will be another of the same kind, and with police interrogation thrown in for good measure."

"They called me in this afternoon."

"Damn! How could they! Don't tell me they did mug shots and fingerprints! If they put you through that scene, I'll . . ."

"No. Nothing like that. They wanted to know my thoughts, my thinking about Francine, about her life, and about any hints of danger she may have shared with me."

"And what did you tell them?"

"I had little to offer."

I didn't tell Zack about the note. For all I knew I was talking to a murderer, standing in a killer's home alone and unprotected. I moved toward the door, but Zack moved faster, blocking my way.

15

I tried to ease past him gracefully, but he stood firm. I backed away from the door and managed to smile as I met his gaze.

"Wait, Bailey. I want to talk to you."

"But we've been talking." I glanced at my watch. "I know you're as tired as I am."

"I need to talk to you alone. Let's go somewhere for dinner."

"I'm sorry, but after all those snacks, I've no appetite."

"You hardly touched your food. I watched. I noticed. I'm not hungry either, but we both need to eat."

We. We. In past times, I might have welcomed his linking us together, but now I stepped back from him, determined to hide my fright. It unnerved me to think he'd been watching me, noticing my actions.

"It's a poor time for either of us to flaunt a large appetite in public, Zack. I'll just go on home. You never know who may be speculating on our whereabouts." I wondered if Courtney might at this moment be standing at a window watching.

"You're right about attracting public interest, but we both need to eat a real meal. It's going to take strength to face tomorrow. Let's go out somewhere even if we only order a hamburger and a salad."

I smiled at that. Many of the locals here in Paradise consider it a breach of conduct to order beef in preference to seafood.

"I can tell you're weakening," Zack said. "Come on. Let's go."

He took my hand and, quashing my fears for the moment, I followed him to the carport and let him help me into his convertible. But before he backed out and headed toward the street, I spoke up.

"Zack, even in Key West, people will talk if they see us together tonight. Your mother's death will be uppermost in everyone's mind. We'll be inviting gossip that might implicate us later." When Zack looked down at me, I read hurt in his expression.

"Bailey, are you afraid of me? Surely you don't think I killed my mother — do you?"

"No. I'll never believe that. Never." In spite of trying to hide my fear, my tone must have belied my words.

"I can tell you have doubts." Zack

187

pounded the steering wheel with his fists and breathed deeply. Then he relaxed and sighed. "All things considered, I guess I can't blame you for your feelings. But surely you've known me long enough to know I'm not capable of harming anyone — especially not my mother."

"I believe you." Maybe if I said that often enough I really would believe it. I wondered if Courtney had seen us leave the house. Was she standing behind a drapery watching and counting the minutes we'd been sitting in the carport out of her sight?

"Okay. I'll try to understand your doubts, but I have a favor to ask."

"What?" I tried not to hold my breath.

"I'm asking again. I want you to work with me, want us to work together to find Mother's killer. I know the police are investigating, but we may be able to look into details they have no access to."

"Like what?"

"Like facts involving the other suspects' alibis. I know people on this rock that I can talk to privately in a way the police can't. I have markers I can call in. And there's no way Cassidy or Burgundy can match your woman's intuition. We'll work well together as a team."

"I don't know about woman's intuition,

Zack. Not really."

"How about it, Bailey? Will you help me find Mother's killer? We can use special ways to investigate — ways the police may overlook. I need you."

How could I refuse! Down deep, I didn't want to. I liked Zack. Our friendship had been pleasant and platonic. Surely if Zack were guilty, he wouldn't be spearheading a personal investigation. I wanted to believe in his innocence. I wanted to work with him for his sake. I wanted to work with him for Mitch's sake. How I wished Mitch had never mentioned snakes.

"What are you thinking, Bailey?"

"I'm thinking that I agree with you. Perhaps we can do more toward finding the culprit than the police can. What are your plans? What should we do first?"

"Go out to dinner. You're probably right about not being seen together in Key West, so let's drive up the Keys to a smaller island."

"Agreed." To my surprise I felt hungry. "Do you know of some out-of-the-way restaurants farther up?"

"None of them are out-of-the-way during tourist season. Let's head out and stop at some place that grabs us. Do you need a wrap?"

"Good idea." Again, I wondered if Courtney hid watching while I ran inside the cottage and returned with a sweater.

Darkness had fallen hours ago, but a harvest moon brightened the sky — harvest moon if you're from Iowa, seafarer's moon if you're from the Keys.

"Think we'd be less conspicuous if we put the top up?" I asked.

Zack grinned, and I think it was the first time I'd seen him smile since I'd returned. "No need. You forget we're in Paradise. Convertibles are more common than seashells. A car with the top up on a night like this would be the one to attract attention."

"I'll take your word for it." I loved to watch the moonlight silver the palm trees as we left Key West and later the mangroves growing between the highway and the sea.

A genius must have designed the bridges connecting the islands. Instead of railings at eye level like the ones I remembered in Iowa, these bridges had low concrete walls. Passengers could enjoy an unrestricted view of the Gulf of Mexico on one side and the Atlantic Ocean on the other. I wondered who had decided exactly where the two bodies of water met.

"Lovely night," Zack said. "I'm glad I have business that draws me out of Key West now and then. The drive between offices refreshes me. Some of the locals seldom leave the rock or travel north of the Boca Chica bridge."

I tried to imagine we'd left our worries behind us and I enjoyed the wind in my hair, the salt scent of the sea. We'd driven only a short distance before I slipped on my sweater.

"Shark Key. Sugarloaf. Cudjoe," I said, naming the keys we passed. "Interesting place names. I wonder where they originated."

"I've heard several theories about Cudjoe. Some say it came from the joewood, a small tree that thrives in the area. But more likely the name came from Africa."

"When sea captains brought slaves here?"

Zack nodded. "In those days, Cudjoe was the common name of an African boy born on the first day of the week."

"Interesting."

"There's also the story that an early homesteader with a speech impediment had a cousin named Joe and that he often talked about his Cudjoe."

I laughed. "I like the joewood theory best."

"Now we've passed Ramrod Key, and there's a turn coming up soon that I don't want to miss. Help me watch for it. It's just before we reach Big Pine Key. There's a restaurant overlooking the bay called *Parrotdise.*"

"Have you been there before?"

"Oh, yes. Many times."

I wondered who he'd chosen as a companion on those visits, and it bothered me that I wondered. The moonlight must be getting to me.

Zack found the obscure road he'd been looking for, turned onto it, and then slowed the car. The tires crunched on gravel and I smelled dust. But after a short distance, neon signs marked an entryway and he turned again, this time onto a concrete slab.

"Whew!" he exclaimed. "Hate to coat my car with gravel dust, but the entrees here are worth the sacrifice." He parked in a visitor's slot below a coral-colored restaurant supported by tall pilings and overlooking the water. A heron called in the distance, and once we left the car, Zack took my hand to guide me up a dozen wide steps At the restaurant's entry we stepped into a dimly lit room where candles flickered in hurricane globes. A sign said "Please seat yourselves."

An assortment of long-haired men wearing jeans and tank tops perched on stools at the bar. A few sat eating boiled shrimp.

Most of them were drinking beer and watching either the comely waitress or the basketball game blaring from an overhead TV. Zack led the way past the bar and to a row of high tables set alongside open windows that offered a view of the moon-silvered bay and a small dock where two moored runabouts bobbed in the waves.

"Look, Zack." I pointed at the water where a small boat with white sails drifted with the current. "Some lucky couple's taking a moonlight sail. What a beautiful scene."

"Someday we may be able to do that — if I ever find the time to work on my sailboat."

"Sounds like fun. When do you plan to finish it?"

"Who knows! Building a boat takes a lot of time, and sometimes life interferes."

I laughed. "Sounds much like composing song lyrics." The boat drifted from our view, and I glanced around the restaurant. Pictures of exotic parrots hung on the walls and parrot paintings decorated the kitchen and restroom doors.

Thank goodness we were the only dinner customers — at least so far. Zack had selected an excellent spot. Beautiful. Secluded. We sat on spindle-legged stools at a high table. After a short time, a waitress wearing a t-shirt with the word "Parrotdise" embroidered on the neckline, jeans, and a scarlet hibiscus in her hair approached us. She brought menus and a dazzling smile — for Zack. I studied the parrot-decorated menu while I waited, wondering if she'd tell Zack she was a poor girl working her way through college.

"What may I bring you to drink?" Merry Sunshine asked, her gaze still focused on Zack.

"What would you like?" Zack asked me.

"A Coke, please."

"Make it two," Zack added. "I'm the designated driver."

Merry Sunshine's smile faded when she saw her tip dwindling. "Square grouper fillets are the special of the day." She slapped the menus in front of us and left to get our Cokes. If Zack noticed or resented her sudden change of demeanor, he didn't comment.

"Square grouper?" I asked.

Zack grinned. "It's a joke. This place's noted for its grouper entrees. A square grouper refers to a bail of marijuana locals sometimes find in the sea if a smuggler's had to jettison it to avoid shore patrol arrest."

"Oh. An insider joke."

194

"So now that you're an insider, what would you like to order?" Zack perused the menu. "Forget the hamburger and salad. Let's go for something elegant and eclectic. You might like their gazpacho and Cajun crunchies for starters. And their coconut-crusted shrimp are the best in the Keys."

"Sounds great to me." I glanced on down the menu. "And look at this dessert special. Cappuccino bread pudding with White Russian Chantilly cream. Would you split one of those with me?"

"Sure you can't eat a whole one?"

"Positive. Halfies."

"You got it."

Merry Sunshine returned. After she took our order, she brightened. I could imagine her mentally tallying the bill, calculating twenty percent. I peered out the window. Below us miniature floodlights glowed on a pool where a baby shark and a barracuda swam among tendrils of seaweed. Snappers shared space with the biggies, swimming as if unconcerned about being selected as their next meal.

While we waited for our order, we talked about everything and about nothing, avoiding the topic uppermost in our minds — Francine's death. When our appetizer arrived, the gazpacho and crunchies whetted our appetites for the entrees yet to come.

Later, the shrimp lived up to Zack's description. "It's the best I've ever tasted."

Zack laughed. "I told you so."

When I saw the dessert, I almost wished Zack had ordered one for each of us. The cappuccino flavor, the sweetness of the White Russian cream made the perfect finale for a perfect meal. Once we'd finished eating, I excused myself for a restroom visit while Zack paid the bill. When I returned, the smile on Merry Sunshine's face told me Zack's tip had been more than adequate.

We held the pine railing on our way down the steps, but before Zack headed for the car, he led me around the building for an up-close-and-personal look at the fish darting about in their pool. Leaning forward to get a better view of the elusive 'cuda, I lost my balance. Zack caught me, pulled me to safety, and then into his arms. Instead of protesting, I clung to him, enjoying his nearness.

"Bailey," he murmured into my ear. "I'm really glad to have you living in the cottage."

My brain warned me to break the embrace, but my heart ruled. My career escaped my thinking for the moment, but I stopped short of telling Zack I was glad to be in the Keys — and his cottage.

Before I could say more, he tightened his embrace and our lips met in a warm kiss. And another. Then when I looked above us, I broke from Zack's arms, and stepped away from the pool.

"Bailey! Please. I didn't mean to . . ."

My look stopped his apology. "Don't be obvious, but glance up at the dining room."

Zack glanced then took my hand and led me toward the car.

"Detective Cassidy, Zack. I'm sure that's who we saw watching us. Do you think he followed us here?"

16

When we returned to the parking lot, we counted three cars in addition to Zack's convertible. Detective Cassidy's gray Ford? No.

"That looked like Cassidy to me," I said. "Maybe he owns a second car. Maybe taxpayers raise a storm if they see Key West's finest driving a city vehicle while off duty."

"Possible and probable," Zack said. "But we only caught a glimpse of the guy in the window. It might have been someone else. We're thirty miles from Key West, and it's past the dinner hour for most people."

"You're right. Cassidy doesn't seem the type to be enjoying a late dinner at such a romantic spot."

Zack sighed. "Probably spends his evenings at home sucking on a beer and watching reruns of *Court TV*."

Zack took my hand while we approached

his car. The evening had grown chill, and he pushed a button that raised the top and then settled it in place. Good plan. I felt less exposed in the closed car, but it irritated me that Cassidy had the power to make me nervous. Zack held my hand while we drove to Eden Palms. I didn't pull away.

When we turned into the cul-de-sac, Courtney's house loomed before us, stark and dark. In case she stood beside some curtained window watching, I didn't give her the satisfaction of seeing me look in her direction. A dim light glowed from deep in the interior of Winton Gravely's home — maybe a night light for his patients. Zack stopped in front of the cottage, walked me to the porch, held his hand out for my key. I waited while he unlocked the door and entered, uninvited. I held my breath. Was I afraid of an intruder? Or of Zack? After making a thorough inspection of the interior, he stepped outside.

"Bailey, you call me if anything frightens you."

"Don't worry about me. I'm not afraid, and I'll be fine."

"I have business on Stock Island tomorrow morning, but if you'll be free in the afternoon I'd like to begin checking on some of the stories we've heard."

"Fine with me. Any ideas on where to start?"

He paused for a moment. "Maybe with Tucker Tisdale."

My mind recoiled from my mental image of Tisdale, his falsetto voice, his flaky skin. "Why him first? Any special reason?"

Zack stepped back, ready to return to his car. "No special reason except that he seems elusive. His absence Monday night when Cassidy called everyone in for questioning makes me wonder. Remember? Burgundy had to go get him, bring him to the solarium."

"I didn't think that strange at the time. The man's in the funeral business. There'd been a death of a friend and neighbor. Wouldn't it be normal for him to be at his funeral home overseeing his staff?"

"Could be, but I didn't call Tucker. I didn't ask for his services. At that time, nobody had told me his services were needed. Someone may have tried. I may have been on the road between offices. Mother's body had been removed from the house by the time I arrived home. I thought that strange. I resented it."

"So who called Tisdale? I remember Gravely saying he called nine-one-one, but

I don't think he mentioned phoning Tisdale."

"I'll check on that tomorrow. Maybe the medical examiner made the call. Since the police were dealing with a suspicious death, the M.E., under Cassidy's orders, may have called the shots. Since Tucker and his wife are long-time friends and neighbors of ours, the Tisdale Funeral Home would have been my choice. And Mother's. She prepaid her funeral arrangements years ago — wanted to spare me having to make those decisions later."

"How like her. How thoughtful." I paused before closing the door. "Have you decided on the time of the funeral?"

"No. The police haven't released her body yet. Until they do, the service will be on hold."

"The indecision makes it hard on everyone."

"Funerals are never easy. What do you think, Bailey? If you object to starting our investigation with Tisdale, we'll choose someone else."

"No. Your idea's good. I'll begin thinking about him, his words, his actions. Maybe I'll remember some little thing that might make a deeper look-see in his direction interesting."

"Okay, I'll call you as soon as I get home from Stock Island — probably shortly after noon. We can go somewhere for lunch and fine-tune our plans."

"I'll be ready, Zack. And thank you for a wonderful dinner."

"My pleasure." He brushed a kiss on my cheek then waited until I closed and locked the door before he strode to his car. I heard him turn into his driveway and park in the carport.

Once he'd left, I double-checked all door and window locks and lowered all shades to the sills before I drew the draperies. Thinking of snooping into Tucker Tisdale's activities left me too wired for sleep, so I tried to count my blessings. At least Zack hadn't suggested starting our investigation with Mitch. How easy it might have been for him to try to blame the yardman, the stranger, instead of one of his long-time neighbors and friends.

I set up my keyboard and laptop, never an easy job for me. My mind balks at dealing with cables, three-pronged electrical plugs, and power packs. And in the Keys a surge protector's a must. I think a competent serviceman or perhaps Bill Gates himself should be included as basic equipment with every laptop when it leaves the factory.

I played a few melody lines and tried to fit words to them, but nothing seemed to work so I went to bed. Even with my head on the pillow, I couldn't close my eyes. I lay staring at the ceiling and thinking of Tucker Tisdale. Had he known his koi pond attracted snakes? Had he seen snakes there? Had he dealt with so much death in his business that one more body meant little to him?

Then I thought of Tucker's wife away visiting her sister. Francine had told me Mrs. Tisdale was friendly and outgoing and that she doted on their koi pond. Zack told me he had sketched some of the colorful fish while she coaxed them to the surface with food. His sketches turned out well but I'd never seen them hanging at Eden Palms. Maybe he had given them to her.

Had Tucker chosen this time of his wife's absence to murder Francine? Perhaps he was depending on her absence to give him extra time to foolproof an alibi. Surely the need to hide an evil deed from a spouse *and* from the police would add to any culprit's angst. I'd read where the wife of the serial killer on Big Pine had suspected his blood-covered clothes were a result of more than a successful night of fishing. Why hadn't she told the police her suspicions? Why had she waited — and let him take her life, too?

Could I be playing the same kind of deadly waiting game? No. Impossible. I had no firm reason to suspect anyone of Francine's murder.

I slept fitfully, turning my pillow from side to side, waking only when a cock crowed under my window. Still drugged with sleep, I rose to open the drapery, raise the shade. Sunshine had dried the morning dew, and its rays glinted on a rooster's black and russet feathers, its red comb, while it chased a hen across the yard. I smiled.

Francine had written to Mom that when the state passed laws forbidding cock fighting, some irate bird owners released their gamecocks to roam the city. Now, years later, many tourists think roaming chickens lend quaintness to the island. Residents have mixed emotions — depending upon whose window the cocks choose to crow under.

When I answered the telephone, Zack's voice flowed across the line.

"Everything okay at the cottage? It looked quiet there when I left earlier."

"Everything's fine. I overslept."

"Can you be ready if I pick you up around two?"

"Fine. I'll be expecting you."

Zack broke the connection, and I sighed

as I poured a glass of chocolate milk and made myself a peanut butter and jelly sandwich. Flying into Key West on Monday, I'd looked forward to getting to work on a new song. That plan had gone down the tubes — at least for one more day. I needed time to rethink some options. I like to work in the early morning when I can blot the world out and live for a few hours with my melodies and their variations. And then there are titles to consider. Titles are always hard for me. I'd been unable to come up with any good ideas. But my computer sat at the ready in case free moments and ideas presented themselves.

When Zack stopped the convertible in front of the cottage, I hurried out and slid onto the passenger seat.

"The neighborhood's deserted," I said. "Except for a few chickens. No cars in the carports. Of course we can't tell for sure about Dr. Gravely's."

"I've already stopped at the funeral home," Zack said, turning toward Eaton. "I called earlier and learned Tisdale's in Miami for the day, so I stopped by his business before I called you. Thought it'd be a good time to talk to his staff."

"Learn anything?"

"Nothing important. I asked a few subtle

questions and I believe his story. All day Monday he worked in his office, doing inventory — getting ready to prepare his tax forms. He didn't leave his office on Monday until the call came notifying him of Mother's death."

"Who called him? Gravely or the police?"

"The police made the official call, but Gravely had phoned him first, not as a funeral director but as a neighbor and friend delivering unpleasant news."

"Then I guess I don't have to think about Tisdale — at least not today."

"Right."

"Thank goodness, Zack. That man gives me the creeps. Even talking about him gives me a chill. Got no logical reason for my feelings. I just don't like his looks — don't like his koi pond. Guess the only thing I do like about him is your mother's description of his wife — a nice person. Not the sort of woman you'd find watching *Wheel of Fortune* with a murderer."

"Agreed." Zack turned toward Old Town. "Now let's hear your suggestions on what to do next."

"How about driving to Mallory Square? We could stop in at the hospitality center and ask a volunteer about Courtney and her guests."

"Might work." Zack braked the car, narrowly avoided hitting a bicyclist. "Courtney and friends may have stopped there to pick up brochures."

"Right. The sooner we ask about Courtney's guests, the less time the volunteer will have had to forget them. Those women see dozens of people every day."

"But Courtney makes a memorable impression on people."

"One way or another." I corked further comments, not wanting Zack to think I might be jealous.

I'm convinced Zack has a good-parking karma. Near the Shell Warehouse he found an empty spot at a meter with time left on it — a bit of serendipity that seldom happens in Key West. He plunked in a few more coins. With each quarter good for only ten minutes, both locals and tourists consider metered parking a mega pain. But meters, when you can find one, are better than having to walk to the distant parking ramp.

Conchs. Scallops. Murex. On a previous visit to Key West, the Shell Warehouse with its rough-planked floor supporting the thousands of seashells piled in wooden bins always made me want to stop and browse. Even the musty smell of the building enticed me. But no time for browsing today.

Zack led the way along a narrow sidewalk until we reached the white-washed Hospitality House. While we paused outside, planning our line of questioning, I glanced toward the edge of the dock, where a cruise ship rocked at its mooring and where sturdy dock pilings shaped like pointed crayons discouraged pelicans from perching and leaving their calling cards.

"What a neat ship," I commented. "When I'm rich, I'm going to take a cruise."

"Hospitality House used to be the ticket office for passengers traveling to Cuba. But those days are long past. Maybe gone forever." The nearby rattle of a Conch Train and the blatant call of its driver yanked us from dreams of travel.

"We're delaying the inevitable, Bailey. Let's go on inside."

17

We stepped into the air-conditioned building where tourists stood browsing at the wall racks, choosing brochures that advertised events and places of local interest. A bouquet on a countertop near an orange juice dispenser wafted jasmine scent into the room. I approached a silver-haired volunteer behind the counter, feeling it my turn to speak up since Zack had done his bit at Tisdale's.

"May I help you, ma'am?" The volunteer wore a sea-blue smock and a badge bearing the name Lucy.

"Thank you, Lucy. I hope you can. Were you working here late Monday afternoon?"

"Yes, I was. Did you lose something?" Her gaze traveled toward a cardboard box labeled "Lost & Found."

"No. Nothing like that. I'm wondering if you happened to notice an acquaintance of ours who might have stopped here. She accompanied two friends who were visiting Key West and seeing Mallory for the first time."

Lucy laughed. "That description could fit lots of people. Can you be more specific?"

"Our friend's a local," Zack offered. "Pretty lady. Stands about five feet five inches, auburn hair probably worn in an upsweep."

Why did it irritate me that Zack could give such a detailed and accurate description?

"If she's a local, I may know her," Lucy said. "What's her name?"

"Courtney Lusk," I said. "If she stopped here, she might have had two guests with her."

"Oh, Courtney Lusk. Real estate business, right? I've known Courtney for years. But, no. I haven't seen her lately. And I'd remember. She catches one's eye, and besides that, she knows me well and would have stopped to say hello. Sorry I can't help you today."

"Thanks, Lucy," Zack said, turning and steering me toward the door.

Good. I smiled, thinking Courtney had lied to us. "Maybe Courtney has more to hide than she let on to Detective Cassidy. Why else would a person say she'd been in Hospitality House when she hadn't?"

"Did she actually say she came here,

Bailey? Or did we surmise that she might have brought her friends here since they were doing the tourist thing?"

"Oh, my. I wish I'd been able to take notes at that meeting. Do you suppose one of the detectives might have carried a tape recorder in his pocket?"

"Hard to answer that one."

"Now what?" I looked up at Zack. "There were probably a hundred vendors on Mallory on Monday. And the same ones might not be here today. Anyway, it's early for the vendors to be arriving."

"Look. There's a cruise ship in port. There'll be vendors."

"There's no way we have time to talk to each of them, but we might question a few."

We strolled along the dock, watching cruise passengers board their ship, showing their passes to the guard at the sloping gangplank. The blast of the ship's whistle startled us and we stopped gawking and walked on, pausing to question an artist sketching a seascape, a vendor selling t-shirts, a man tossing a fire baton. Yes, they had been on the dock on Monday afternoon. No, in the masses of tourists they had not noticed anyone matching Courtney's description. Time was slipping away and before long the sunset crowd would begin to drift in.

"Look." I nodded toward a sagging canvas tent directly ahead. "Someone's pitched a tent right on the concrete."

Zack laughed. "Some guy's defying the cops — setting up his living quarters in plain view of cruise passengers."

A closer look revealed a battered bicycle and the owner of the largess himself. He sat unshaven and in tattered cutoffs, dozing in a canvas chair. A cardboard sign pinned to his tent flap held a warning in dark block printing: "NO CHEATING. PICTURES $1. NO CHEATING. PAY UP."

I pulled a dollar from my purse and dropped it into the empty coffee can at his feet, then focused my camera. The man watched me through one half-open eye.

"Thank you, ma'am," he muttered as we walked away.

We strolled on past a boy playing jazz licks on a trombone with the instrument's open case inviting tips. Zack dropped him a dollar, and we strolled on. Fifty feet farther on, I stopped and touched Zack's arm.

A shirtless and barefoot man with greasy hair pulled into a ponytail sat on a canvas stool. A green iguana reclined on his bare neck and shoulders. A blacksnake, coiled around his right arm, watched us from yellow eyes. I reached for my camera and started to approach the man in spite of my inner qualms.

"Wait," Zack whispered, reaching for my hand and trying to pull me back before he gave in and followed me.

"You're very brave," I said to Reptile Man, trying to hide my apprehension. "Aren't you afraid of those creatures?"

"Nothing to be afraid of, lady. Maggie and Nero and me be long-time buddies. I treat 'em well. They treat me well."

"Where'd you find the snake?" Zack asked.

"What's it to you, buddy?" The man's demeanor suddenly became guarded, belligerent. His eyes, the color of black onyx, smoldered as he spoke.

"No offense intended," Zack said. "I merely wondered where a person would find that kind of snake around here."

With slow deliberate movements, the man pulled the iguana from his shoulders and set it under his chair. He uncoiled the snake from his arm before dropping it into a green palm-frond basket and closing the lid. Then he approached Zack with a scowl and a growl.

"You suggesting I stole Nero?"

Zack backed off. "Look fellow, I'm not

suggesting anything. Nothing at all. My friend and I are interested in all the people on the dock and in their activities. We find a man garbed in reptiles unusual to say the least."

"I'm a vocalist and songwriter." I stepped between Zack and Reptile Man, giving him my best smile. "Always looking for ideas for new compositions. Have a CD out titled *Greentree Blues*. A friend's made it available in most Duval Street gift shops and book stores. Have you heard it?"

"Don't care for blues. Country-western's my thing."

"I'm interested in people that I might draw on when I create lyrics. May I take your picture?" I reached into my purse, found a dollar bill, and waved it in his direction.

"No way, lady. No way." The man took another step toward us.

His response surprised me. A few bills protruded from a basket sitting beside his chair. Clearly, he had come to the dock to offer tourists a chance to take his picture — for a price. What was going on here? Zack's question had made the guy mad. Maybe he'd stolen the snake or the iguana or both. From where? Where in Key West would one go to steal such creatures?

"The both of you better bug off and leave me alone. Any more of your lip and I call the cops. Tell 'em you're disturbin' my peace."

We retreated, leaving Reptile Man to cope with his disturbed peace. I snuck only one quick glance over my shoulder to make sure he wasn't following us. Zack looked back, too, and gave an uneasy laugh.

"Guess we can relax. He's coiling the snake around his arm."

I glanced at my watch. "It's getting late, Zack. Maybe we'd better give it up for today."

"Suits me. Maybe we'll have some new ideas by tomorrow."

"I suppose we need to go to Kelly's and check on Dr. Gravely's story."

"That should be easy," Zack said. "His group probably had a reservation. No doubt the waiters will remember him — might even recall the names of the people in his party."

"Sometimes a tip will improve memories."

Zack drove us home, finding very little traffic on our side of the street. Cars, bicycles, mopeds, and pedestrians vied for space in the other lane, heading for the sunset celebration.

Zack stopped in front of my cottage, and

it relieved me when he didn't suggest going out for dinner. I welcomed an evening alone, planning to reread my notebook of lyrics and titles. It'd been weeks since I'd had time to do any songwriting, and I hoped a review would give me the insight I needed to push some new ideas forward.

Once I finished nuking and eating the last of the chicken casserole, I stacked my dishes in the dishwasher. I'd gone into my bedroom to my work desk when the phone rang. Almost nothing arouses my curiosity more than a ringing telephone. This time Quinn Bahama's voice greeted me, and she arrowed right to the point.

"Bailey, may I come over for a few minutes? I have an important matter to discuss with you. Did you see my article on you in the *Citizen*? I knew I'd get it in soon."

"Wonderful, Quinn. Congratulations. Chalk one up for success! I haven't had time to pick up a paper today, but I'll take a stroll to the paper box soon." I squelched a sigh, seeing my quiet evening slipping away. "I'm working tonight, Quinn. But I can give you a few minutes. What time would you like to stop by?"

"How about right now? I promise I won't stay long."

"Okay. Come ahead. I'll snap on the porch

216

light. You can park in front of the cottage."

"Thanks, Bailey. I appreciate."

I began reviewing CD titles in my note-book, thinking Quinn would arrive shortly, but wanting to get in all the reading I could. *Moonlit Bay*? Trite. I crossed it out. *Starshine Serenade*? Only a tad better. I sighed. Almost half an hour passed before Quinn knocked.

When I held the door open, she slipped inside so quickly I wondered if she was try-ing to elude someone. Before I could dwell on that thought, I glanced across the street and saw Courtney slide into Zack's convert-ible, watched them drive away. Hmmm. I squelched my curiosity.

"What's up, Quinn?" Again I glanced toward the street. "Where's your car?"

"I walked. Didn't want my car seen at your house. I kept to the shadows. Hope nobody saw me, recognized me coming here."

"Why all the secrecy?" As I closed the door behind her, I felt wary. "Tell me what brings you here surrounded by so much mystery?"

"I have a favor to ask. A big favor. It has to do with Francine Shipton's death."

18

I wanted to shove Quinn outside and lock the door. What right had she to ask for favors concerning Francine's death? But wait. Maybe she had information to offer, facts that Zack and I needed.

"Give, Quinn. Come sit down. Tell me what sort of a favor you need."

"You know I want a permanent job as staff writer for the *Citizen* — had my application in for ages."

"Right." I sat beside her on the couch. "Any luck? Have you submitted another article?"

"Yes. The editor accepted a human-interest piece on the monthly used-book sales our library sponsors. Look for it this coming Sunday. He gave me thumbs up on my writing style, and before he forgets how much he liked both articles, I want to drop a new one on his desk tomorrow — on spec, of course."

"And I can help?"

"Yes, Bailey. I *know* you can."

"How? What's your topic?"

"The inside story on Francine's death."

The words hung between us sizzling, ready to explode. My face flushed, and my hands shook in anger and surprise. When I didn't reply, she pushed harder.

"Bailey, you're an insider. You know the skinny. *Why* did Francine fall? The police say homicide, so did someone push her? Did someone startle her into hurtling herself down the stairs? The public wants to know the why, who, and how. If I had those answers, maybe even *one* of them, I could write an article that'd scoop the whole staff."

Quinn's plethora of words revealed her nervousness. I stood to make my position firm and clear. "Ms. Bahama, you're asking the impossible. I have no answers for you. None."

"I'd never reveal my source, Bailey. Never!"

"I believe you, but I have no intention of being your source." I walked toward the door, hoping she'd take the hint and follow me. She didn't.

"It'd be privileged material, Bailey, protected material. I'd go to jail before I'd talk.

I'd be like that writer who interviewed Deep Throat years ago in the Watergate investigation. You remember reading about that guy, don't you?"

"Quinn, believe me. I don't have any answers for you. None. And even if I did, I couldn't tell you."

"Couldn't or wouldn't?" She rose and approached me.

"Maybe both. I'd never betray Zack Shipton by revealing information that might skew the police investigation, nor would I risk putting myself in jeopardy, maybe setting myself up for in-depth police queries."

"Betray Zack? A slip of the tongue, Bailey? Or does that mean you think Zack knows more than he's telling about his mother's death?"

"Quinn, if you're —"

"Put yourself in jeopardy? You're afraid you're on the suspect list?"

"I didn't say that."

"I can build an article around any tidbit of information you'll tell me. I can turn any fact you'll give me into a scintillating article. I'm begging, Bailey."

"No. Forget it." I eased her toward the door.

"I thought we were friends, Bailey. I got you publicity in a paper that thousands of people read. Here's your the chance to return the favor. I'm only asking for a tiny nugget of information."

I hated Quinn's persistence in the face of my refusal. I needed to end this conversation — now. Even so, I felt afraid she might twist my words and write an article that would harm Zack or me — or maybe Mitch.

"The answer's no, Quinn. Let's forget you came here tonight. Let's forget you questioned me. But please, let's not let this disagreement spoil our friendship. Okay?"

Quinn didn't answer. She turned and almost before I could move aside, she stormed outside, banging the door behind her. I hated to see our meeting end this way, but she had asked the impossible.

I snapped off the living room light and stood in the open doorway, peering after her. Clouds hid the moon and she melted into the darkness. So much for my plan of working on song lyrics! I couldn't concentrate tonight. I took a long shower and dropped into bed. My radio tuned to soft music didn't lull me to sleep. The scene with Quinn replayed in my mind until the scene with Courtney sliding so easily into Zack's Thunderbird replaced it. I turned restlessly for a long time before I fell asleep.

The next morning an announcer wakened

me with the day's weather report. Sunshine. Winds at twenty. Small craft warnings. Only a nanosecond later I remembered Quinn's visit. I must phone Zack. He needed to know her intent, know she'd been nosing around. But that call could wait until I dressed and ate breakfast.

As soon as I'd downed a piece of toast and a glass of chocolate milk, I opened the door and checked the carport for Zack's convertible. Yes. Still there. I'd started to turn away when I saw a note taped low onto the screen. Had I missed an early-morning caller? Quinn? Zack? Had I been sleeping that soundly?

A corner tore from the folded paper when I pulled it from the screen, and I opened the note quickly, thinking Zack might have left a message to avoid wakening me. I didn't start shaking until I'd read the words.

Take care, Bailey Green, if you want to live to record another CD. Stop snooping into affairs that are none of your business.

The note wasn't signed. Death threats seldom carry signatures. I darted inside, closed and locked the door. Who? Who had written this? Who had come skulking to the cottage and taped this threat to the screen? Quinn Bahama? She'd left last night thwarted and in high dudgeon. Was this her way of getting even? Childish. Did Quinn really think she could frighten me with a note? I wouldn't admit fright, but she'd shaken me. I called Zack as soon as I'd calmed down.

"I'll be right over," Zack said. "Don't handle the note. The police may be able to lift some fingerprints."

I should have known better than to touch the note, but I never dreamed it would contain a threat. I pulled a plastic bag from a utility drawer, and using kitchen tongs, I lifted the note and laid it inside the bag. The only prints on it should be mine — and those of the person who taped it onto my screen.

Zack ducked his head as he entered the cottage, a protective habit tall people develop. The scent of lime aftershave accompanied him. He'd unzipped the bottom half from his pant legs and I wondered why he didn't wear shorts more often. He looked good in them. His casual appearance told me he didn't intend to go to his office.

"Where is it, Bailey? Let's see the note."

When I handed him the baggie, he grinned. "Good work, detective." His grin disappeared as he read the threat.

"W-who . . ."

"I think I know who." I told him about

Quinn's visit, her request for information. "She stormed out of here last night, banging the door. She must have returned later to leave the note."

"You didn't hear anything?"

"Nothing. Nothing at all."

Zack studied the note again. "Where's the piece that's missing? You tear it getting it off the door?"

"Guess I did. It'd been taped to the screen." I followed Zack who'd already headed for the door, and I stopped him seconds before he touched the paper. "Fingerprints. Remember?"

I used the kitchen tongs to remove the torn scrap, took it to the snack bar, and stuck it inside the baggie before we tried to examine it.

"It's so tiny, Zack. I don't think there's anything on it. Guess I didn't destroy any evidence after all."

"Maybe not. But look at this." Zack had turned the baggie over and used his thumbnail, pointing to a dark S-shaped line.

"A snake." I leaned closer to be sure I hadn't made a mistake.

"Yes, a snake." Zack scowled.

"So what do we do now? I'm not the Nervous Nellie type, but this scares me."

"I'll call the police."

"Wait. Let's think a minute. Quinn's nobody to be afraid of. Anyway, I don't see her that way. Maybe we both need to calm down before we call the police. Maybe we should call Quinn and talk to her about this."

"Think, Bailey. Quinn couldn't have written this note. So far the police have released no information about a snake. None."

"Then if Quinn already knew about the snake, maybe she had something to do with the murder. Or maybe she knows more than she's telling. That's hard to believe. She's the last person I'd suspect of murder."

"Forget Quinn for now. I'm thinking about that guy we saw on the dock yesterday afternoon."

"Reptile Man? He flared up because he thought you were accusing him of stealing his snake. But, Zack, he had no way of knowing our names or address. And even if he did know, why wouldn't he have left the note on your door rather than on mine?"

"I don't know how that guy fits into the picture, but he seems at home with reptiles. Maybe he supplied a snake to some unsavory character — maybe to the murderer. That's possible. He may know more about Mother's death than we think." Zack tapped the baggie with his finger. "We need to get this note to the police right now. You may be in danger."

Zack stepped to the phone and punched Cassidy's number. When he had him on the line, the one-sided conversation told me Cassidy would arrive here in living color soon.

"We couldn't bring the note in for him to examine at the police station?"

"No. He wants to check the area around the cottage and the mansion for footprints or other signs of disturbance."

I brewed a pot of coffee and set three mugs on the snack bar.

"Better make it four," Zack said. "Burgundy will come with him."

I brought out another mug and added more Oreos to a plate. We'd each had a cup of coffee and several cookies before the detectives arrived in their unmarked car, which to me had become an oppressive hallmark of their presence.

Detective Burgundy towered over Cassidy on the bar stools as they examined the note.

"Good thinking to place it in the bag." Burgundy's smile dissipated some of the tension in the room. Cassidy never changed his dour expression, acting as if underlings always presented him evidence prewrapped in see-through plastic. He spent several minutes listening to my story and studying the note from every angle before he spoke.

"I'll take a look around the cottage, Joe." Without a smile and without saying thanks for the coffee — and six Oreos — Cassidy tucked the note into his jacket pocket and nodded toward Zack's home. "You take a look around the mansion. If we find any unusual footprints, we can get some photos — maybe make a plaster cast."

Zack and I drank more coffee, devoured more cookies. I'd opened a fresh bag of peanut butter cups before Cassidy returned to the door.

"Found nothing significant," he said. "I'll take the note to headquarters and have it checked for prints. We find anything, we'll let you know."

19

"Well, there goes the morning." We watched Cassidy and Burgundy drive away. In the distance, a cruise ship sounded its noon whistle, punctuating Zack's words. "And all we know's that someone dislikes our snooping around playing detective."

"*Our* snooping? The note was on *my* door. I think Quinn Bahama wrote it. She's a writer and writers like to write. She left here in a rage because I refused to give her information, then she wrote the note, returned, and taped it to my door. She's trying to scare me. I don't think Reptile Man had anything to do with it."

"How can you be so naive? I think he's the logical suspect. The snake drawing on the note makes him number one in my mind. Remember — Quinn knew nothing of the snake. Nada. Zilch."

"That's true, Zack, but yesterday at the dock, Reptile Man vented his anger at you, not at me. If he wrote the note, why didn't he leave it on *your* door?"

"Good question. Why? I don't have the answer, but someone's threatened your life. That's never a thing to dismiss lightly. Think I'll phone Cassidy's office again and demand police protection for you." He stepped toward the telephone.

"No way." I stood, easing between him and the phone. "No way at all. I've had more than enough of police presence since I arrived. If we're going to investigate your mother's death, we can't do it with detectives snooping around."

Zack nodded and stepped away from the phone. "You're right. I really don't want the police tailing you, either. But don't let that note get to you. I've guys working for me who'll be willing to do some subtle watchdogging — especially around the cottage."

"I hate the idea of being spied on or of having the cottage under scrutiny. I'll watch my back. I'm not afraid." I spoke with ebbing bravado. The words on that note were etched into my brain. Even though I've taken some judo training, I'm not eager to put it to use.

"For now, you're safe enough with me, so let's go on with our plans for the day. Gravely said he attended a party at Kelly's on Monday. Let's stop by there and see what we can learn."

Zack picked me up in the convertible, and we headed toward Old Town. I looked over my shoulder, but I didn't see anyone I thought might be following us. Reaching for my purse, I dug out a few quarters, and we'd driven almost to the Little White House before we found a parking slot on Whitehead. Zack's parking karma must have taken a holiday. Backtracking toward Kelly's, I watched a gardener trimming the hedge behind one of the wrought iron security fences that protected all the mansions along that side of the street.

"Wonder who lives in those houses," I murmured. "Special people?"

"I know some of the families. Most of them are retired couples. A few widows. They're just ordinary people."

"Yeah. Ordinary people with megabucks." We crossed the street to the sidewalk in front of The Banyan guesthouse. Zack guided me around spots where huge banyan roots had broken through the concrete. When we reached Kelly's Caribbean, I took a long look before I snapped some pictures. The upscale restaurant is advertised as an exotic bar, grill, and brewery, and I liked the old whitewashed building on sight. I also liked the medley of exotic fragrances drifting from its kitchen.

"Caribbean charisma, Bailey. Drink it in. All the brochures say Kelly's is the reason you came to Key West."

"Hope it's open and someone's willing to talk to us." I peered behind us, checking for followers, before we climbed a few steps to a waiting area.

"They're open for lunch, so let's have a bite to eat and work from there. Want to sit at the bar or outside under the palms and figs?"

"Let's go outside, okay?" I glanced around, enjoying the aviation-oriented decorations — airplane photos, propellers from an old seaplane, and a sculpture of a helicopter. We followed a waiter between two touch-the-sky strangler figs that guarded steps down to an open-air dining room. Miniature hibiscus and glossy-leaved ivies in terra cotta planters decorated the perimeter of the area.

Once seated, in the sun-dappled shade of a palm, we studied the menu briefly before ordering conch chowder, Cuban bread, and beer.

"We'll be enjoying some history along with the great food," Zack said once the waiter left. "Kelly's once housed the original offices of the first international airline — Pan American. And now the new owners are making their own history."

"You'll be disappointed if I don't ask how, won't you?"

Zack grinned. "Of course. I planned to tell you all along. The actress Kelly McGillis and her husband, Fred Tillman, have created a unique microbrewery on the premises. It's one of a kind. Their all-natural beers are as special as the food they serve."

Before Zack could download more facts, the waiter returned with our order. The beer came as advertised — smooth on the tongue, delicious, and memorable, and it enhanced the flavor of capers, bay leaf, and leeks in the chowder. I wished we'd come here for the fun of it instead of for business.

"Who do you think will talk to us about the party on Monday?" I asked.

"Leave that to me. And put your mind and memory to work. Try to remember everything that's said."

"No note taking?"

"That'd be too obvious, don't you agree? We don't want to give anyone the idea we're prying into Gravely's private affairs."

I rolled my eyes. But when Zack motioned to a waiter, I listened to every word.

"I'm interested in knowing more about

the luncheon party Winton Gravely attended here last Monday. Do you know Dr. Gravely?"

The waiter shrugged. "I know him by sight only — not personally."

"Could you give me names of some of the people at that party?"

The waiter backed off a step. "Why are you asking, sir?"

"I heard that the party concerned creating an addition to the Conch Republic's annual celebration. Island history interests me. In fact, I've been doing some special research on the Conch Republic flag. I thought some of the people in attendance at last Monday's get-together might have some esoteric information to offer. I'd like to contact them."

Zack's long-winded approach sounded weak to me, but the waiter bit on it. "I'm a fan of the Conch Republic myself. Read a lot about it. You might want to look for information upstairs in our writer's library. The Key West Writer's Guild meets here on Saturday mornings. They maintain a few shelves of books pertaining to the island."

"Thank you, sir. I'll check up there before we leave, but could you give me a few names of the guests here last Monday? I'd ask Winton himself, but he's off-island today."

The waiter drew his lips into a tight O-shape and stared thoughtfully into the distance before he spoke. "Well, I remember Ben Bahama."

"Was his wife, Quinn, with him?"

"No."

Again, I watched the waiter's O-shaped lips and his gaze into space. Zack slipped him a twenty. He nodded his thanks and pocketed the bill.

"There was a lady who volunteers at the Hospitality House near Mallory. Ann Chaffey. And I remember a secretary from Pier House. Sue somebody. She stops here now and then. I think there were others in the group, too, but I can't remember any more names."

"How long did that party last? Remember that?"

"Oh sure. I was their waiter. It ran from about four until five-thirty or so."

"Dr. Gravely present all that time?"

The waiter shrugged. "Can't answer that one. It was a very informal get-together. Some people arrived late and others left early. I can't rightly say if Dr. Gravely stayed beginning to end. Being a doctor, he may have been called away."

"That's possible," Zack agreed. "Well, thank you for your help, sir. I appreciate it."

"You're welcome, Mr. — Mr. . . . I don't believe I caught your name."

"Not important. Not important at all. Give your cook our thanks for the delicious chowder."

"I'll do that, sir. He'll be pleased. You be sure to take a look at our books upstairs."

"Thank you. I'll do that." Zack paid our bill. We left Kelly's and hurried to our parking slot, happy to see we still had a smidgen of time on the meter. Sitting in the car we considered our options.

"We need to find one of the guests who stayed at the affair from beginning to end," I said.

Zack started the car and eased into traffic. "Let's find out what we can about Winton's whereabouts."

"That's not going to be easy. Nor is getting info from Quinn Bahama. Don't count on me to talk to Quinn. She probably has me on an I'll-never-speak-to-her-again list."

"Okay. Let's drive to the shrimp docks. I help Ben out now and then. Shouldn't have any trouble asking him a few questions and getting some straight answers."

We reversed our direction and headed for Land's End Village and the shrimp docks. Of course all the parking places were taken, so Zack drove to the city parking ramp.

Even though the ramp's an open-air structure, the trade wind failed to blow away the stench of exhaust fumes. We walked to the shrimp docks from the ramp, once again enjoying the salt scent of the sea.

Tourists crowded the area, window shopping the unique boutiques, pausing for hot dogs at the food stands, or drifting toward the raw bar for oysters on the half shell. Once we stepped onto the shrimp dock, I felt the sway of the wooden planks underfoot, and Zack took my hand to steady me. In the distance, several shrimp boats bobbed at anchor, their rigging silhouetted like jackstraws tossed against the sky. Closer at hand, pelicans perched on the dock pilings, and gulls screamed and swooped while kids flung the remains of their sandwiches into the air.

"Where can I find Ben Bahama?" Zack called to a deckhand standing on a rusty boat that looked as if it would rather sink than float.

"He's out on a run." The guy swabbed his neck with a red bandana. "Probably won't be in for a few days."

"Thanks, buddy." Zack nodded to the sailor, and we retraced our steps to the parking ramp.

"So forget Ben Bahama," I said. "Not that

I mind too much. I'm in no mood to talk to either of the Bahamas today."

"We might try to find Ann Chaffey at Hospitality House," Zack suggested.

"Why don't we walk there, Zack? It's not far, and it'd be easier than finding another parking place."

"Okay by me."

We headed toward Front Street and Mallory dock on foot. Zack circled his arm around my waist, pulling me close, so we could walk abreast along the narrow sidewalk. I didn't mind. I liked the feeling of being protected — a feeling I'd never needed until I discovered this morning's note on my door. Sometimes overhanging palm fronds tangled in our hair, and now and then we had to break apart to let pedestrians pass, but it took us only a few moments to reach Hospitality House and learn that Lucy wasn't there. Ann Chaffey had little to say about the Conch Republic party.

"I only stayed a short time." She pointed to a rack of brochures across the room. "We have folders with information about the Conch Republic. Freebies. Take one if you care to."

Zack cared to. He picked up a brochure for me as well as one for himself, and he pretended to scan it as we left the building.

It seemed like a long walk back to the car, and we said little until we were heading back toward Eden Palms.

"We've learned nothing, Zack. Most of the people that we know who attended that party didn't stay from beginning to end. Maybe Winton Gravely arrived late or left early, too. Just because he said he attended the party doesn't mean that he did. He could have paid the waiter to say he attended in case anyone came snooping around."

"Winton said he attended, and I believe him."

"Why? According to you, he had strong motive to protest the disturbance of his neighborhood — his and yours."

"I can't see him as a murderer, Bailey. I've known Winton almost all my life. We've been friends and fishing buddies. I can't believe he'd harm my mother for any reason in the world."

I scowled. "As an outsider, a newcomer to the neighborhood, I see Winton Gravely as totally weird. Who knows what goes on in his so-called clinic? Who knows his reasons for operating a pseudo-hospital in a residential neighborhood?"

"I know, Bailey. Winton has a brilliant

mind, and he attended med school to please his parents, who wanted to boast of a professional in the family. He had no deep desire to be a doctor, but to please them he added the clinic to their mansion and worked there on a small scale. His family had money. At that time Winton didn't have to earn a living."

"At that time?"

"Right. At that time. Then the family business went down the tubes due to bad investments. His parents both died — heart attacks. Probably died from the shock of losing the business. Luckily, Winton had his M.D. to fall back on."

"I understand that he doesn't offer his services for free. Francine told me it takes a fortune to be admitted to his clinic. I think he's weird and so is Tucker Tisdale."

Zack sighed. "Your personal feelings about the neighbors isn't helping our investigation, Bailey. Maybe we should drive back to Mallory and talk to the guy with the reptiles."

"And ask him what? I'm not eager to tangle with him again. But it wouldn't hurt to mention our encounter with him to the police."

Zack and I were at an impasse that could easily escalate into a full-blown argument.

When we reached the cottage, we made no plans for more private investigating tomorrow. I left the car, slammed the door, and strode toward the cottage. Zack hurried to join me.

"Will you have supper with me, Bailey? I hate ending today on a sour note. Maybe we should forget private investigating. How about finding some quiet spot for supper and forgetting our snoop plans?"

Zack's invitation tempted me until I remembered the threat note. I wasn't eager to spend the evening alone. But neither was I eager to spend it with Zack. After our activities and our near arguments today, Zack seemed almost as weird as Gravely or Tisdale or Courtney Lusk. Or maybe I was the weird one of the group — weird for sticking around at Murder Central.

"Thanks for the invitation, Zack. But I really need to spend time alone tonight. Perhaps in the morning we'll both feel differently about both our personal investigation and about the police and their activities."

"Perhaps."

And with that one word, Zack turned and left. That's what I wanted, wasn't it? How could I feel so strongly attracted to a man that I didn't completely trust, a man who might have murdered his mother? I wanted to trust him, but I faced reality. Zack Shipton had no airtight alibi for his actions on last Monday evening.

20

Gathering clouds precluded a candent sunset this evening. I waited until I felt sure Zack had gone inside before I walked to a paper box and bought today's *Citizen.* Once back home, I scanned every column for any latent news of Francine's murder. Nothing. Laying the paper aside, I sat at my desk, turned on my computer, and pulled my song-in-progress onto the screen. I'd worried about having no time to write, and now that a free evening stretched ahead of me, my mind refused to click into a fast-forward mode that made blues improvisations a possibility.

After a frustrating half hour of staring at the computer screen, I gave up creating anything new and started reviewing pages in my idea notebook. I paused. What title would give my album the impetus to fly off the shelves? Would blues aficionados as well as music critics like it? Titles could be all-important to the sale of a CD. But . . . plenty of time to jot down potential titles later.

I started considering first lines. Nothing new and fresh popped into mind. Still searching for a first line, I strolled to the living room and snapped on the TV before I wandered to the kitchen. I didn't feel hungry, but I tossed myself a salad, made a sandwich, and tried to eat while I watched the early news. Bad thinking. Who could enjoy eating while dead bodies and terrorist attacks dominated the screen? I ordered myself to stop stalling and start writing. I headed toward the computer again, but when I glanced out the window, I saw Zack's convertible stopping across the street at Courtney's home. Hmmm. Maybe more sparks were flying between Zack and Courtney than I realized.

Zack left the car, strode to the porch, lifted the brass knocker. Courtney appeared immediately, her long auburn hair flowing around her bare shoulders and almost touching the top of her sea-green sarong. She wobbled on her spike-heeled sandals, and Zack took her elbow to steady her. They walked hand-in-hand to the car where he helped her into the passenger seat. After they drove off, I felt like a fool for gawking.

What did I care whom Zack chose to dine with? Yet, if it was of no importance to me, why did I wish Courtney knew she'd been second choice this evening? I refused to admit jealousy, but I couldn't help wondering where they were going, how they'd spend the evening. I remembered the care Zack had taken to avoid being seen dining with me. Or maybe I'd been the one worrying about that. Evidently Zack felt unconcerned about being seen with Courtney.

Maybe Zack had asked Courtney to help in his covert murder investigation. Or, on the other hand, maybe he suspected Courtney. I liked that thought best.

Follow them, Bailey. Follow them.

The thought titillated my mind, tempting me, prodding me to action. Maybe they were meeting someone that Zack suspected of murdering Francine — someone whose identity he hadn't shared with me. Zack's convertible would be easy to spot on this small island. But my green town car would be even easier to notice. How embarrassing if Zack were to discover me stalking him.

Why not follow them on Francine's bike? She told you to use it whenever you pleased.

I saw the flaw in that idea immediately. How I hated books in which the heroine played the fool and then later claimed, oh so innocently, that she'd no idea she might endanger herself by walking unaccompanied along that lonely beach in the dark of night. Don't go there. A woman alone on a bicycle at night would be placing herself in danger — from traffic if from nothing more sinister.

All the time my mind juggled crazy thoughts, I was looking up Mitch's cell number. What if he didn't have his phone turned on? I'd no idea where he spent his nights, since he didn't use his apartment. Wrong. I did have an idea, but I refused to accept it. One. Two. Three. On the fourth ring Mitch answered.

"Mitch here."

"Mitch. Are you busy tonight?"

"Hey, Sis. What's the buzz?"

"I want to go biking, and I need company."

"May I translate the word 'company' to mean protection?"

"Perhaps. Can you come here so we can talk about it?"

"Sure. Got no big thing going tonight. Princess and I are just sitting here worrying about Wizard."

I asked the question he expected. "What's going on in Wizard's life that worries you?"

"He's disappeared. Gone. Nobody's seen him all day."

"Maybe he got tired of sleeping in a tent and found a more comfortable spot."

"Don't think so. I think he's in trouble and I want to help him."

I wanted to say, *Forget Wizard and help me instead.* "Have you reported his disappearance to the police?"

"Hah! Double hah! You think the cops are about to spend time searching for a homeless guy?"

"Maybe not. Have you tried the social services office?"

"No thanks, Sis. If they found him, they'd want to reform him."

"Well I have a plan of sorts. If you'll go biking with me tonight, we'll take time out from my mission to look for Wizard."

"Your mission?"

"Tell you when you get here. Ride over ASAP, okay?"

"May I bring my laundry? Got some duds that need a little swish and suds."

"Fair exchange. Bring them along. I'll run the washer while we're riding."

"Great, Sis. No need to separate whites from darks."

I tried not to imagine the state of Mitch's laundry. "Can you come right away?"

"Sure. You in danger?"

"No danger. But come as soon as you

can." I held back telling him about the threat note.

Mitch broke the connection, and I changed into a black jumpsuit, although I knew black clothes put riders in danger — hard for motorists to see. Well, that's what I wanted to be — hard to see. I wanted to leave the porch light on while I jogged to the carport for the bike, but no. Mustn't attract neighborly attention. Francine had been an avid early-morning biker, so I knew the bike tires would be up. And they were. I rode around the cul-de-sac twice to be sure I had the feel of it. Clouds still masked the sky. I felt nobody had seen me.

The night was so black that Mitch spoke before I saw him.

"Made you jump, didn't I?"

I could imagine his grin. "Okay, you did. But that's all right. You need a little victory in your life now and then."

"Let's go inside and get my laundry started. Your put-down bugs me."

"What a surprise! When did clean laundry become relevant to your present lifestyle?"

"It's not. I'm humoring you. Don't be such a wonk."

I led him into the laundry room without giving him the satisfaction of asking what a wonk might be. Once the laundry started swishing, I presented my case.

"So you intend to try to find Zack and then spy on him and Courtney? Hey, she's some dish, right? Don't blame you for being green-eyed."

"Don't be ridiculous. I'm not jealous."

"Then, what's the buzz? You afraid of those two? Think they did Francine in? That why you've called on a person of such negative social status to protect you?"

"Don't joke, Mitch. I'm jittery. Don't know who I can trust."

"And it bothers the hell out of you, to admit Zack might be guilty. Right? That the problem? And you'd like to blame the murder on someone else if possible?"

"What makes you think you're so smart?"

"Talked you into doing my laundry, didn't I?"

"Touché. Let's forget my motives for finding Zack and Courtney. Let's get going. In some respects Key West's a small island, but when you start searching for somebody on a dark night, it can be a very big island."

"Where ya wanta start? Duval Street?"

"No. I doubt that they'd head for any place on Duval. Unless, maybe Pier House. Judging from Courtney's outfit, I'm guessing they might go to one of the other posh hotels. We can scope the parking lots. It

should be easy to spot Zack's convertible —
if it's nearby. But they may have gone off
island for more privacy."

"Like you and Zack did?"

"How'd you know that?"

Mitch shrugged and grinned. "I promised
Mom to look out for my sister."

Mounting our bikes and riding single file,
we pedaled along Eaton Street.

"Maybe we should check the parking
ramp on Grinnell," Mitch said. "Those two
might like the idea of parking, then walking
to some hole-in-the-wall eatery where their
car wouldn't be seen."

"Don't think either of them are hole-in-
the-wall types, but if they're trying to keep
a low profile, well . . ."

When we entered the ramp, the obese guy
in the ticket kiosk gave us the eye, but he
remained seated. Probably required too
much effort to hoist all that avoirdupois
upright. He shrugged when he saw us riding
up the ramp. I scrutinized every car we
passed, although this proved to be a tougher
ride than I'd anticipated. I huffed and
puffed long before we reached the top level.
Mitch wouldn't admit to any weakness of
lung or limb, but he didn't push on when I
stopped near the top to rest.

"Guess they avoided this convenient and

inexpensive ramp parking with shuttle bus service so thoughtfully provided by our city fathers." Mitch managed the lengthy spiel of sarcasm without gasping.

I couldn't hide my own thready breathing, but Mitch didn't comment. "Key West at night. Twinkling lights. The scent of night-blooming jasmine. The swish and sway of palm fronds. Even on a night without moonlight, I feel like I'm looking down on a city of excitement and enchantment."

"Try sleeping on the beach if you really want excitement and enchantment. That's what my buddies and I experience every night of the world."

"I've changed my mind about Duval Street," I said when we headed back down the ramp, braking now to keep from crashing into a car or a retaining wall. "Let's scope the parking lot at Pier House. I think it'd be upscale enough for Courtney's taste, and there are secluded tables where they might dine in privacy."

"You been there a lot?"

"Only once long ago. But we might see them dining at beachside, or perhaps in candlelight on the outdoor patio."

"Okay, Sis. Whatever you say. It's your

call. But if we could see them, they could see us."

"Right. We'll take care."

When we reached Pier House, we circled the shadowed parking lot, avoiding making eye contact with the security guard.

"No laws against tourists bicycling into a parking lot," Mitch whispered, riding by my side.

"Let's not push our luck. Look for the Thunderbird."

We saw several convertibles, but no red T-bird, and we left the area quickly. I felt the security guard's gaze following us.

"Where to now?" Mitch asked. "You rule out a lot of places when you rule out Duval."

"If you wanted to find a quiet spot, where would you go?" I rode ahead of him, hugging the curbing.

"The beach. Not too many folks seek the sand at night. Maybe some of my friends, but few of your friends. We might spot Wizard somewhere on the beach."

"Okay. We'll keep an eye out for him. There are some pricey restaurants out that way. Martha's. Benihanas. The Sheraton."

"Lead the way. This's your party."

I paused to wait for Mitch at the next corner. "Okay. If we're going to South Roo-

sevelt and the beach, why not ride along Simonton? They could be at Logun's or at
The Reach."

We rode past Logun's, and turned at the
seawall where wind whipped waves over the
concrete retaining wall, dampening our feet.

"Enough of that." Mitch turned his back
to the spray, and we headed toward The
Reach. I didn't know the exact location of
the restaurant inside the hotel, but many
guests had parked on ground level in a
covered lot. When we tried to enter the lot,
a guard stopped us.

"No admittance," he announced. "Butt
out."

We rode out of his sight before we stopped
again.

"Now what?" I asked. "I want to check
the cars back there. Maybe we could ask
the guard if he's seen a red T-bird."

"Oh, right." Mitch snorted. "Then he'd
want to see an I.D. and know the why
behind our request. I've got a better plan."

"Give."

"Follow me."

I followed Mitch as he rode in the street
beside the curbing, heading away from the
hotel. We'd gone only a short distance
before he dismounted and began pushing
his bike toward a large house. I followed.

Before we reached the house, Mitch turned abruptly and we stood ankle deep in sand. And darkness. Even in bright moonlight, I guessed this place would be dark, shadowy. And smelly. No scent of jasmine here, and I refused to identify the stench. A planked fence blocked vision on one side, and tropical shrubbery growing heavy and thick around the white house cut off vision on our other side. Ahead of us waves slapped against a shoreline.

"Where are we, Mitch? I've never seen this beach before."

"Few people have. My buddies and I call it Dog Beach. It's only a few feet of sand where people can walk their dogs and let them play in the sea. Cops seldom bother anyone here."

I could understand why. Even the cops wouldn't want any part of this nasty-smelling place.

"Let's leave, Mitch. This scene's not for me."

"Don't wimp out on me now. I'm still keeping an eye out for Wizard, and I'm almost as interested in learning what Zack's up to as you are. I lost an upscale customer when Francine died."

"Some attitude. A woman lies murdered, and you only see her as a lost customer.

Looking for Zack was a bad idea, Mitch. This place's too creepy. Someone could be spying on *us* right now. Maybe there's someone here we can't see."

"Bring your bike. Follow me. We won't be here long. We'll walk closer to the water, prop our bikes on kick stands, and prowl the hotel parking area on foot."

I was following Mitch slowly — reluctantly — when a light in the back yard of the white house caught my eye. I peered through the tropical greenery. Zack! Courtney! They sat at an on-the-beach bar, their backs partially toward us, the glow from a patio torch playing on Courtney's profile. I called to Mitch, who had ridden on ahead.

"Look at this, Mitch." He joined me and we peered at our prey.

"Louie's Back Yard," Mitch whispered. "Forgot about this beachside bar. Are they with anyone?"

"I think they're alone. They're talking only to each other. Wish I could hear what they're saying. Wish I could hear if they're talking about Francine."

"Don't kid yourself, Sis. I'm guessing he's whispering sweet nothings into her ear between sips of champagne and bites of coconut shrimp. That's what I'd be doing if I was dining with a dish like Courtney."

254

"Let's go, Mitch." I peered into the darkness behind us, and then grabbed his arm. "Wait. I hear someone."

Mitch waited and we both listened, hearing nothing but music drifting from the backyard bar.

"See anyone?" Mitch asked. "It's blacker than a cat's insides out here."

"I thought I heard footsteps gritting in sand. I think we're being watched."

"You've got a big imagination."

I faced the street. "Let's grab our bikes and go. Enough of this."

"Okay," Mitch said. "But don't blame me. It was your idea."

We jogged across the fragrant Dog Beach. I half expected our bikes to be gone, but they were right where we'd left them. And someone had slashed all four tires.

21

"Damn!" Mitch whispered. "What s.o.b. . . ." Mitch kicked at his slashed tire, and then examined my bike. "Who could have followed us? Someone may have been tailing us all evening. When I find out who . . ."

"Mitch." I grabbed his arm. "Hush. Someone may be listening. The who following us may be the same who that murdered Francine."

Mitch pulled the slashed tires from his bike and tossed them onto the sand.

"Right this minute the killer may be lurking — watching us."

Mitch kicked at my bike tires and swore under his breath. "Let's bug out of here. The guy's got a knife. That's for sure."

I pulled him toward the street. "Come on, let's go."

He jerked away. "I'm not leaving my bike here. Got no other transportation."

"Lives rate higher than bicycles." Again I grabbed his wrist and pulled him toward the street. "I feel someone watching us. Come on. Come on!"

"After we lock our bikes to a tree." Mitch jerked away again and pushed his bike toward a palm growing at the side of the beach. "Humor me. We'll lock the bikes to the tree and maybe they'll be here in the morning. Maybe. Someone with a cable cutter could . . ."

Mindlessly I followed Mitch, my hands shaking, my stomach churning like a bowl of cold eels. "I've got money, Mitch. Let's go to The Reach and call a cab. Right now."

Once Mitch finished locking the bikes, he followed me. I hailed a cabbie, who stopped and drove us toward Eden Palms. He felt in the mood to talk. We didn't.

"Tourists?" he asked.

"Yes," I lied, unwilling to reveal we were locals.

"Welcome to our island."

We didn't reply, but our silence didn't forefend his chatter.

"Have you heard there's been a suspicious death at the mansion? Maybe murder." He chattered on with no encouragement from us, spilling out stale newspaper info along with tidbits of gossip he either made up or had heard from other sources. My nerves were frayed wires shooting silent sparks long before he let us out at the cottage. I paid him, tipped him well, and hurried toward the door.

Once inside, I closed every shade and drapery, and Mitch, seeing my consternation, pulled out my coffee maker, filled it with water, and began searching the cupboard for coffee as calmly as if he'd lived here all his life.

"I don't know what to do, Mitch."

"Begin by finding the coffee."

I opened the coffee tin, did some measuring, and started the pot. "Our lives were in danger on that stinking beach. Probably still are."

"Want me to spend the night?"

I choked back a yes. That's exactly what I wanted — someone here with me. "No, of course not, Mitch. I can take care of myself."

"Okay. Okay. Never let it be said that I forced myself on a woman. And don't worry about Francine's bike. I'll get a pal to go with me to claim both bikes in the morning. We'll get new tires on them. My friends have many talents. We'll get your bike back to you in good condition."

I'd forgotten about our bikes in my concern for our lives. Opening my purse, I thrust twenty dollars at Mich. "I'm not a charity case — yet. I'll be grateful if you and your . . . friends can get the bikes rolling again."

We sat at the snack bar waiting for our coffee to cool. I burned my tongue on the first sip and soothed the pain with an M&M. After several minutes I began to relax and shake off the feeling of foreboding that threatened to take up permanent residence in my mind.

"I actually learned some things tonight, Mitch. I apologize for taking you on a wild chase."

"No problem. I think you've learned a lot." He looked at me from under lowered lids. "You've learned Zack has an eye for the ladies."

"I already knew that. There's no romance between Zack and me — nothing but a strong friendship. I'm not concerned about his dinner partners."

"Yeah, right. That's why you wanted to follow him, wanted to see how cozy a relationship he has going with his near and — dear neighbor."

"Oh, hush! Zack had asked me to help him with a secret investigation of Francine's death. He hoped we might find evidence the police have no access to, or evidence they might overlook. Maybe he asked Courtney for that same kind of help. That's the sort of thing that interested me tonight."

"I think he wanted to spend the evening with a slick chick. Suppose you had no interest in that."

I ignored his implications. "I learned something big tonight, Mitch. Think about this. We were watching Zack and Courtney while someone, possibly Francine's killer, was watching us and slashing our bike tires. Go figure. That scares me, but it also tells me that neither Zack nor Courtney murdered Francine."

"You're willing to leap to the conclusion that the tire slasher is Francine's murderer? That's a stretch. A big stretch. Some kid who gets his jollies from tire slashing could have hit on our bikes. Happens all the time. You ever read the daily crime report?"

"You could be right, I suppose. Maybe I'm reaching the wrong answers." I remembered Mitch's laundry, went to the washer and shifted his clothes to the dryer. Maybe I couldn't eliminate Courtney and Zack from my suspect list yet.

"How about I pick up my duds tomorrow?"

"Fine — unless you prefer to tote them

along with you wet. I'll drive you home now if you're ready to go."

"Ready and willing." Mitch walked with me to the carport and checked inside the car before we got in. Then he nodded toward the T-bird parked in the dimness two stalls from mine. "Guess Zack's home, huh?"

Surprised, I noted the convertible and then the glow from Zack's kitchen window. As if by reflex, I glanced at a light in Courtney's upstairs hallway. "Guess they're both home."

"Sneaky, those two. I didn't hear any car doors slam."

"Where to?" I asked, backing from the carport.

"The bridle path, please, ma'am. Unless you've changed your mind and want me to stay the night."

"Not necessary, Mitch. But I appreciate your going bike riding with me tonight. I learned things I needed to know, and I wouldn't have gone out alone."

"Anytime, Sis. Anytime. But when you get home, watch your back while you're walking from the carport to the cottage. Some guy may be stalking you. You got a gun?"

"Mitch! Of course I don't have a gun."

"Then you'd better take mine. I'll be safe

enough with my friends tonight. Even Princess totes a gun. Says she's never had to use it — so far."

I shuddered, wondering how many armed vagrants walked Key West streets. On the way to the bridle path, Mitch pulled up a pant leg, and removed a silver pistol from a holster strapped above his ankle.

For an instant I forgot we were orphans. I came close to falling into my big sister mode and asking him if Mom knew he carried a gun. Catching myself in time I said, "Good grief, Mitch. Good holy grief!"

Mitch grinned. "Bought it myself and registered it in my new name. Some afternoons I do target practice with a retired cop at the shooting range. I'm a fair shot, but I want you to have the pistol tonight."

"No way. I don't know beans about guns."

"You don't have to know beans. The sight of a pistol scares the bejeesas out of most people. If anyone bothers you, flash the gun. That'll make the average joe back off fast."

Mitch laid the pistol on the car seat between us and the minute we stopped at the bridle path, he eased from the car, lingering a moment at the open window.

"I'll call tomorrow and give you the buzz on Wizard. He may have turned up by then."

Disinterested in any buzz he might hear

about Wizard, I watched until he disappeared into the thicket beside the path. Where would he sleep tonight? Tent? Under the cloudy sky?

All the way home I thought about Zack and Courtney. Does Zack suspect her of Francine's murder? Had he taken her to dinner to prod for clues? Or maybe, as Mitch said, maybe he'd merely wanted the company of a slick chick. I gloated, remembering again that he'd turned to Courtney only after I refused his invitation.

Upon entering the carport, I took care to drop Mitch's gun into my pocket and close the car door silently. For a moment I stood looking, listening. Believing I was alone, I started toward the cottage, my right hand clutching the pistol, my left hand gripping my house keys.

I stepped from the protection of the carport, quickening my pace, yet forcing myself to show no fear to anyone who might be watching.

"Bailey?"

For an instant I didn't recognize Zack's voice, and my whole body felt tense as a coiled spring. I relaxed when he called to me again.

"Bailey? That you?"

"Of course, Zack. Sorry to have wakened you."

"You didn't wake me. It's only a bit after ten. You okay? Everything all right at the cottage?"

"Everything's fine. I've been out on a few errands."

The next thing I knew a screen door slammed, and Zack stood at my side. The coiled spring feeling returned. My mind froze. Zack hadn't been the one following Mitch and me. Impossible. He'd been having dinner with Courtney. What if The Follower had been trailing Zack and Courtney and Mitch and I happened to get in his way — to interfere. Maybe Zack had been in as much danger as I.

"Bailey, what's the matter? Are you sure everything's okay?"

"No problem. No problem at all." Turning a bit away from him, I slid the gun up the sleeve of my jumpsuit.

"Good. Let me see you safely inside."

"Thanks for your concern, Zack. I'll be fine." He walked with me to the cottage, where I unlocked the door, entered, and bid him goodnight. Guilt feelings washed over me. Zack had been trying to protect me, hadn't he?

Hadn't he? I wished I knew for sure. What

if I'd shut the door on him, thinking only of my own safety and leaving him standing alone, leaving him as fair game for The Follower?

22

In my darkened bedroom, I pulled the window shade aside and watched Zack walk to Eden Palms and disappear inside. Was he afraid? Did he carry a gun? From my living room window, I peeked out. All looked dark at Courtney's house. Although I didn't know what difference that could make in my life, I felt relieved.

Using only the light in the laundry room, I slid Mitch's gun from my sleeve to my hand and considered a hiding place for it. Under a couch cushion? Under my mattress? In the refrigerator? I liked that idea. I dropped the pistol into a plastic bag and crowded it into the produce drawer beside the iceberg lettuce.

I jumped when the phone rang, wishing I could let it go unanswered. But curiosity outranked apprehension.

"You okay, Sis?" Static crackled around Mitch's voice.

"I'm fine." *Probably a lot safer than you are.* "Thanks for your concern, but don't worry about me."

The connection spluttered and broke, and I assumed that already he had started not worrying. I'd slipped into my nightshirt before I remembered Mitch's clothes in the dryer. After pulling them out, I gave each garment a shake before I folded it. Frayed jeans. Faded tank tops. Tattered boxer shorts that Fruit of the Loom would deny. I stuffed the garments into a plastic bag, all except a sweat suit that still felt damp. I slid it onto a hanger and hung it on the garment rack near the washer. The cuffs dragged on the floor but they'd be dry by morning.

Lights out. 'Fraidy cat. Feeling my way to the bathroom, I snapped on a night light and left the door cracked so the beam shone into my bedroom. Once in bed, my imagination magnified every sound. Was the rustling of palm fronds outside my window nature-made or man-made? Was there a native bird that chirped at night? Rising, I padded to the refrigerator, gave the lettuce ample space, and tucked the pistol under my pillow.

I dialed an all-night station on my radio. Although I thought I wouldn't sleep, the sunshine pouring through my window forced me from bed to turn on the air conditioner and plug in the coffee pot. Friday. Had nothing on my agenda today, and I vowed to settle at my computer and get to work on some lyrics. I'd blot out thoughts about real-life murders, slashed tires, gun under pillow, and relax in a world of music.

My long-ago goal had been to write an eight-measure theme a day, revise those measures, and proceed to the next eight measures. At that pace I could finish the rough draft of a tune in a week or so, if all went well. Then I'd be ready to begin a second revision. That plan worked when I wrote lyrics in Iowa, but it wasn't working for me in Key West. At least not yet. Lately, I couldn't move the melody forward no matter how many pictures I looked at, how many people I talked to. This morning the reason was Zack. He called, saying he was coming to talk to me. Not asking, telling. Had he noticed Francine's bicycle missing? *Bailey, think. Think. Have some answers ready if he starts asking questions.*

I left my computer on, hoping he would notice the bright screen and cut his visit short. When he arrived I offered him a stool at the snack bar, poured mugs of coffee, and set peanut butter cups, cookies, and, new to my junk-food list, sour-cream-and-onion Pringles.

I needn't have worried about explanations for the missing bicycle. When I glanced from my coffee, Zack sat staring into the laundry room at Mitch's sweat suit.

"Who is he? Bailey? It's none of my business, but I'm concerned about your safety. I've seen some guy hanging around the cottage."

"Oh, he's a friend. No need to worry."

"A friend for whom you do laundry?"

His questions unnerved me. Who was he to pry into my private life?

"Doesn't your *friend* know about Laundromats?"

"I owed him a favor, Zack. Have another Pringle? An Oreo?" I tried to change the subject, but when I pushed the snack plate toward him, my hand shook so, I hit my cup and sloshed coffee onto the floor. Zack grabbed a paper towel and helped mop up the mess.

"Look, Bailey." He waited until I met his gaze. "There's been one murder here, and I don't want there to be another one. This morning the police officially called Mother's death a homicide."

"We guessed all along they'd do that, right?"

"Right. Homicide. One death already, and I think you're in danger."

I willed my hands to stop shaking, my voice to sound firm. But it didn't work. My hands shook and my voice wavered. "Who'd want to murder me? And why? What motive —"

"Hold the questions. I don't have answers. Maybe we're both in danger. I may sound like your Dutch uncle, but I want to know about this guy you're seeing, doing favors for. He might be . . ."

Lying's a talent I've never perfected — especially that of lying to friends. I took a deep breath and faced Zack. "The man is Mitch Mitchell — my brother."

Zack stood and walked toward the sweat suit as if he might jerk it from the hanger and rip it to shreds. "Bailey Green has a brother named Mitch Mitchell? You expect me to believe that?"

"I expect you to believe it because it's true. And it's a long story."

Mitch sat down again at the snack bar, his fists clenched, his gaze boring into mine. "So make it a short story, or this guy's going to be on my hit list if the police don't get to him first."

"I'll be risking Mitch's life if I answer your questions."

"You may be risking his life if you don't. Once the police learn of his relationship to you, they'll demand answers. I refuse to protect him unless you give me a strong reason."

"You have to promise to keep what I tell you top secret."

Zack hesitated, clenching and unclenching his fists. "Okay. I'll keep it between the two of us as long as I can — legally."

I knew that was as good an answer as I'd get. I poured Zack another mug of coffee and began my story. When I finished, Zack remained silent for a few moments before he spoke.

"Your brother's on the hot seat for sure. If the Iowa druggies don't get him before he testifies in Des Moines, our local police may nab him."

My throat felt so tight I could hardly speak. "Why?" I slapped the snack bar so hard Zack jumped. "Why would the Key West cops suspect Mitch of being anything but what he says he is — a drifter looking for work to support himself here in Paradise?"

"A drifter who just happened to be inside Mother's house looking for snakes? Be real,

Bailey. Nobody's going to believe him — or you."

"If Mitch were guilty, don't you think he'd have been too smart to mention snakes?"

"Maybe. Maybe not. But you needn't worry that I'll tell the police anything about him — anything you've revealed. Seems dumb that he relocated here where he had a relative. Surprises me that the feds let him get by with that. I'm guessing they don't know about you."

"That's how it is, and I hate being the one who revealed Mitch's true identity."

"I'll keep his secret — and yours — as long as I can. But I'll need your help."

"Maybe we need each other, Zack."

Zack looked at me in a way that told me I'd said too much — or that he'd taken my words the wrong way.

"When the police officially called Mother's death a homicide, they funneled parts of the truth to the media."

"They mentioned the . . . the snake?"

"No. Not yet. They think withholding that information may work in their favor while they continue their investigation. But the snake facts will come out sooner or later. Now that the police have released Mother's body, I'm concerned with her funeral. You can help me with the arrangements if you will. I want to hold the service this afternoon."

"Of course, Zack. What can I do?"

"Her body will be cremated. That was her wish. She also wished to have her ashes scattered at sea on a moonlit night. I've decided that's going to happen tonight. Weatherman predicts fair skies and a full moon."

As if to argue with Zack, the TV announcer's voice that had been background noise, suddenly caught our attention. "Small craft warnings are now in effect for the rest of the day and evening."

"Nothing you can do about that, Zack. Can't the burial wait until tomorrow?"

"Small craft warnings won't matter. Nobody can depend on good boating weather — especially not in the winter. I've hired a pilot and chartered his helicopter. We'll fly to the waters beyond the reef, scatter the ashes there. Mother always loved fishing and snorkeling near the reef."

I hid my surprise. "What about the funeral? You expect to have a service today — on this short notice?"

"Yes, of course. It's been in my thinking all week, but it'll be a private service. I've talked with Tisdale and Reverend Walters and made the arrangements. We'll hold the service on the mansion grounds."

"Outdoors?"

"Yes. Near the pool and beneath the palms and sea grapes Mother planted years ago. I think she'd like that setting."

"Yes, I believe she would. You've taken care of everything, Zack. What's left for me to do?"

"The media will announce her private services, and I'd like you to telephone close friends and associates, invite them and tell them the time and place. Four-thirty this afternoon."

Zack pulled a list from his pocket and slid it in my direction. "Detectives Cassidy and Burgundy insist on being present. Looking for clues, of course. Can you do the telephoning this morning?"

"Yes, Zack. I'll start right away."

"Thank you, Bailey." He gave my hand a squeeze. "I'm counting on you."

Zack left the cottage without mentioning the missing bicycle. And of course I never told him about the slashed tires, never hinted that I saw him having dinner with Courtney. It surprised me that he hadn't asked Courtney to do his telephoning for him.

Then I sighed. Courtney had a work schedule. Nobody believed songwriters worked or considered anything that resembled a work schedule.

Breakfast. Mom's words replayed in my mind. *Start your morning with a good breakfast and the whole day will go well.* I hoped she was right. I hid the snacks from myself and downed a bowl of granola and bran flakes doused with skim milk, an English muffin with a dab of butter, a glass of guava juice. Then I contemplated Zack's calling list.

Courtney Lusk. Winton Gravely. Detective Cassidy. Detective Burgundy. Ben and Quinn Bahama. Mitch's name appeared, too. No doubt Zack and the detectives wanted to keep him under surveillance. Those were the only familiar names on the list. The rest were Francine's club members and bridge friends and Zack's business associates. The list totaled twenty people. I reached many of them quickly. I guessed that Miss Manners would disapprove of funeral invitations left on answering machines, but that's how I handled some of them. I saw no other way. Since I asked the ones away from their phones to return my call, I had to stick close to home.

I couldn't get my mind on music and lyrics, so I consoled myself with junk food — soul food — washed it down with a Coke. I expected Mitch to phone his response to my funeral invitation, but instead he appeared in person, unaware that I'd tried to get in touch.

"Don't like funerals," Mitch said after I gave him the news.

"Right. How well I remember."

"Come on, Bailey. You know I wouldn't have skipped Mom's funeral if I could have gone without risking my life."

"Sure, Mitch. Sure." Now, while I had him on the defensive, I decided to give him the word. "I had to tell Zack you're my brother."

Mitch whirled to face me with fire in his eyes. "What do you mean you *had to?* You may have risked my life! Don't you realize . . . ?" His face flushed crimson and he pounded on the snack bar with his open palm. "Bailey! How could you!"

"Take it easy, Mitch. Zack said he wouldn't tell anyone, that he'd keep your identity a secret as long as he could."

"You're soft on that guy, aren't you?" Mitch began pacing. "You got a thing going with him, right?"

"Wrong. He'd seen you skulking around the cottage, and he's worried about my safety. I had to tell him, Mitch. He was going to check on you. Thought I might be seeing someone dangerous."

"Which you are — Zack Shipton! I don't

276

trust that guy, Bailey. Once this funeral's over, I wish you'd cut out of this place. Move. Get clear away from him."

"Move to where? You got a spare garret?"

"Matter of fact, I do. You can have my apartment. I'm not living there, as long as my friends will put up with me. And by the way. No sign of Wizard — yet. I may go to the police again."

"Maybe he'll turn up today. Have you asked around on Stock Island?"

"Don't try to change the subject. No sense in my apartment going to waste. I want you out of this cottage — and soon."

"We'll talk about it after the funeral, Mitch. Why don't you take your clothes and go? I don't know where Zack is right now, but I do know he wouldn't be happy to see you here. Go."

Mitch left. I hoped he'd find his gun. I'd tucked it into the pocket of his laundered jeans. I can't bear the thought of having a gun in the house. Once he was out of sight, I stayed beside the telephone, telling callers of the funeral plans.

Somehow I got through the rest of the day, and then donned my best green silk for Francine's service. Shortly before four I stood with keys in hand, preparing to leave the cottage, when Zack arrived. I'd never seen him in a white suit. The word "debonair" flashed to my mind. Yet the suit, along with his black silk shirt and tie, gave him a cramped appearance, as if he needed a larger size to accommodate his broad shoulders.

"I'll escort you, Bailey. And don't worry. I'll be at your side throughout the service."

I tried not to sigh. "Do you think someone might rise up from that group of twenty souls and shoot me on the spot?"

"No, of course not. I need you by my side this afternoon."

"I'll be there, Zack. You can depend on it."

Zack took my arm as we walked from the cottage to the mansion grounds. The day brought back memories of my mother's funeral, although there were few similarities between Iowa's austere First Methodist Church and the lush foliage on the grounds at Eden Palms.

Opposite the swimming pool, someone had set up a white-skirted table that held a portrait of Francine. White tapers in Lalique candlesticks glowed on either side of the picture, wafting jasmine-scent into the air. Waterford vases held bouquets of lavender bougainvillea at either end of the table. Someone had arranged a collage of snapshots of Francine receiving civic awards and prize ribbons. There was no music. I'd never experienced the drabness of a funeral without music. Only a pair of mourning doves cooed into the weak sunshine of late afternoon.

An usher led us to the first of several short rows of rattan chairs with jewel-toned cushions, which were set back a few feet from the table. I sat at the end of the row and Zack sat next to me.

Courtney arrived wearing black, head to toe. Dr. Gravely wore his usual navy blue and white. I supposed the yachting cap was okay for an outdoor service. Mitch. Mitch arrived in jeans, but they were new and he'd topped them with a white shirt that still bore creases from its plastic wrapping. I made sure our glances never met. When the usher seated Quinn Bahama in a row behind us, I swallowed a sigh of relief and averted my gaze. I imagined Quinn doing the same thing as she looked at me.

At first, I thought the service would never start. Then I thought it would never end. The minister's voice droned on until the final prayer. At last Zack rose, took my hand, then stood beside me. I felt hypnotized until I saw the guests moving forward to shake his hand and then mine and to offer words of consolation before leaving the grounds. Mitch never made eye contact with me, nor did he pause to speak to Zack. Quinn Bahama disappeared into the crowd after offering Zack only the briefest of condolences.

Once the last guest departed, the workers from Tisdale's began clearing away the accoutrements of the service. I'd turned and started to walk toward the cottage when Zack touched my elbow, leaned toward me, and spoke *sotto voce.*

"Bailey, I should have asked you earlier. I want you to go with me tonight to scatter Mother's ashes. You'll do that for me, won't you?"

How could I refuse? I couldn't.

"Of course, Zack. Where? What time?"

"Don't worry about the details. I'll pick you up at eight for dinner. Moon won't be at its brightest until midnight. After a leisurely dinner, we'll drive to the pilot's private helicopter pad."

I felt as if I were being carried along on a tide of activities over which I had no control. What does one wear to dinner that's also suitable for riding in a helicopter to release ashes? I tried to block my fear of the helicopter flight by thinking of mundane things. But why was I afraid? Zack wouldn't charter a helicopter that wasn't safe, and I felt sure, well almost sure, that Zack wasn't the person who'd been threatening me. Mitch and I had seen him with Courtney at the same time someone else had been slashing our bike tires. Surely I wouldn't be in danger from a killer tonight.

23

I had a couple of hours of free time —
enough to do some in-depth thinking about
my lyrics-in-progress. Before I warmed up
my computer, I thought again about what I
should wear this evening. I couldn't keep
my mind on composing. What did one wear
to a post-funeral dinner followed by a
helicopter ride? Dress? Slacks? Skirt and
shirt? I laid a white jumpsuit and a green
cardigan on my bed along with green skimmers and a green clutch. *Relax, Bailey.
Forget the fashion police.*

After all the decision making and closet
searching, I'd lost interest in composing lyrics. I refused to admit that I suffered from a
writer's block. I'd get going on the lyrics
tomorrow. I tried to relax and listen to the
TV news. Bad decision. Radio? I found a
station playing favorites from some past I
didn't remember. "Willow Weep for Me."
"My Funny Valentine." "Stardust." I gave

up listening and dressed for the evening before I strolled to a paper box, fed it quarters, and picked up the *Miami Herald*. I was back at the cottage perusing Burdine's sale ad without really seeing it when Zack arrived.

"Where would you like to eat?" he asked.

"Your choice. Anywhere's fine with me."

"Then let's get off the rock. We've plenty of time." He held my hand on the way to the convertible, and I didn't draw away. Where were Francine's ashes, I wondered. In the car with us? Pick them up from the funeral home later?

"Let's try the Square Grouper on Cudjoe, okay? I hear good things about the food there."

"The Square Grouper? Another joke?"

"No, it's a real restaurant — a good one, too."

"Sounds okay to me, but I'm not hungry." With Francine's funeral behind him and the releasing of her ashes ahead of him, I wondered how Zack could bear thinking of food.

We drove a few miles up Highway One to the restaurant. Traffic flowed lightly in our lane, but cars sped bumper-to-bumper in the Key West-or-Bust lane. So what else was new! Every night was bumper-to-bumper night in the Keys. Since so few cars followed us, Zack drove slowly and we arrived at the restaurant after most diners had finished eating and departed. A few customers hunched over a bar near the entryway. A waitress led us to the left, until we reached a table for two covered in white butcher paper.

"My name's Elaine and I'll be your waitress tonight." She grinned and picked up a blue crayon from a crystal bowl. With a flourish, she scrawled her name on the table cover. "Elaine. That's me. What may I bring you to drink?"

"Iced tea, okay?" Zack asked, and I nodded. He didn't open his menu or give Elaine opportunity to spiel her list of the day's specials. "Fondue sound good to you, Bailey?"

I nodded, and he placed our order for cheese fondue and sourdough bread cubes. My mind wasn't on food, and I guessed his wasn't either. While we waited, we studied the décor. Life-size fish replicas decorated the walls — shark, barracuda, manta rays. I'd never been in a restaurant where one could look up and, instead of seeing a ceiling, see exposed ductwork and electric wiring. Must make power outages and repairs easy to deal with. We dawdled over the tea and the fondue, then Zack stopped pretending we were here to enjoy ourselves.

"Let's cut out of here, Bailey. Let's get on with the evening."

And that's what we did. Zack slid into the bumper-to-bumper scene and drove to Key West, taking a left onto South Roosevelt. When he turned onto gravel, scrub palm brushed against the car's sides, and weeds thudded against the undercarriage until we reached an unpainted A-frame set on a clearing.

"Who lives here, Zack?"

"Ben Bahama — and Quinn."

"Zack! Quinn's probably still in a snit because I wouldn't —"

"No problem. Quinn's working in Old Town tonight. Ben came in from a shrimp run earlier this evening. That's why he missed Mother's service. Flying the helicopter's his hobby."

"Hmmm."

"Don't worry. He's good. Hasn't crashed yet."

A pole light flashed on and Ben stepped outside, a barrel-chested guy wearing cutoffs and tank top that displayed muscular biceps and thighs. He could have modeled as Atlas toting the world on his shoulders.

"Been waiting for you, Zack." The thatch

palm encroaching on the clearing muted Ben's stentorian voice. I could imagine him shouting orders to his shrimp boat crew. Zack introduced us, and if Ben recognized my name, he hid the fact. Performers notice stuff like that. It was clear that the Bahamas didn't spend their evenings discussing or listening to blues singers.

I glanced away from Ben and studied the helicopter parked beside the house, trying not to shudder. It looked like a giant insect from outer space. Its propellers and windows gleamed in the moonlight. Ben led us to the machine, and I put on a brave front as I followed him.

"Everything's ready, Zack." He looked toward the car. "Where're the . . . the ashes?"

"I'll get them." Zack strolled to the convertible, popped the trunk, and removed a box — small, white, gold handle on top. It might have been a designer hat box, but it wasn't. Ben took the box and stowed it on the floor inside the 'copter before he boarded and turned to offer me a hand.

"Have a seat." Ben nodded toward two folding chairs behind the pilot's wheel.

I took the nearest chair and Zack sat beside me. I felt the cracked leather of the seat cushion and tried to sit motionless and avoid snagging my jumpsuit. Twinges of guilt pricked my mind. *How petty can you get, Bailey Green!* I smelled gasoline and oil and chocolate. Of all things — chocolate. Was Ben a chocolaholic? Did he have a secret stash of Hershey kisses hidden aboard? I didn't ask, but the fragrance comforted me.

After Ben slid the door shut and revved the motor, I grabbed for a seatbelt and clutched air. No seatbelts. Then I heard the roar of the engine, the whir of the propeller, and felt us rising straight up. I had questions for Zack, but helicopter noise made talk impossible unless I wanted to shout. Didn't want to shout. Only wanted to live to see tomorrow.

Did Ben have official clearance to make this trip? Was he a legally qualified and certified helicopter pilot? Was he sure of the route to the reef? My palms began to sweat. My feet tingled from floorboard vibration. I tasted copper on my tongue. Fear? No. Terror. Then I sucked it up and tried to put a positive spin on the situation. Maybe I could write a song about this experience later, if I survived. Were there words that rhymed with moonlight? Or ashes? Or helicopter? I could think of none.

What if we crashed into the sea? What

would it feel like to drown? What if nobody found our bodies? What if the shore patrol arrested Zack for littering?

"The box is biodegradable," Zack shouted.

"Good," I shouted back, wondering if he could read my thoughts.

At last, I tried to relax and enjoy the panoramic scene around me. Moonlight shimmered on the ever-moving sea. Levin flashes from Key West were like bright pin-pricks fading into the distance. After a few minutes, Ben lowered the helicopter to a few feet above the water. Were we going to crash? I grabbed Zack's hand and we both stood and looked down. We hovered above two red and white buoys where boaters could moor their crafts instead of dropping an anchor directly onto the coral reef. Ben flew beyond the buoys before he nodded to Zack.

When Zack reached for the box of ashes, Ben slid the helicopter door open. The salt air engulfing us surprised me for a moment, then Zack bowed his head and mouthed a whispered prayer before he leaned forward and released the box into the waves. Now, I joined him at the open door, clinging to a safety strap. The box floated until drawers in all four sides opened, releasing rose pet-als into the sea as the container disappeared from sight. I brushed away tears, and then Ben closed the door and we sat again. Zack took my hand, and I squeezed his fingers. While we headed toward the lights of Key West I thought of Francine.

This evening would have pleased her.

Zack and I peered at the water when Ben increased our altitude. With moonlight glinting on the water, the ocean looked like an unending sheet of aluminum foil. It irritated me that I couldn't think of a more romantic simile.

After a few moments, Zack touched my elbow and pointed below. I looked down and saw it. A speedboat with no running lights looked like a black knife cutting through the brine. Bad news. Holding my hand in a steel grip, Zack leaned forward to tap Ben's shoulder and again point downward. Ben circled and studied the sea.

"Let's follow that guy," Ben shouted.

24

Zack and I held our positions at the window. Ben trailed the fast-moving boat for a few minutes before he dropped closer to it. The boat's poling platform aft told me the owner might be a flats fisherman and perhaps a fishing guide, but this boat would be as efficient knifing through deep water as easing into backcountry flats. Painted on the floor near the bow, a likeness of a sun surrounding a conch shell caught the moonlight. Ben dropped another notch lower. Someone had blacked out the boat's name and I.D. number, but we could see the captain. He couldn't help knowing we were following him. His hooded slicker concealed his head and face, and he didn't look up.

Zack grabbed my hand. Moonlight glinted on a gun in the captain's hand.

"Out of here!" Zack shouted. "Now! Go!"

Ben lifted us quickly. If the captain fired at us, other noises camouflaged the sound.

When we looked for the boat again, it had disappeared, probably into one of the mangrove coves that surrounded nearby islets. Ben circled the area for a few minutes, but the speedboat never reappeared. We returned to Ben's clearing.

"Wonder what that guy was up to?" Zack asked after we left the helicopter.

"Up to no good, that's for sure," Ben said. "I'll give the shore patrol a call."

Ben had landed the 'copter smoothly, and now I wondered what I should say. *Thanks for the ride. Thanks for not crashing. Give my regards to Quinn.* Zack spared me from having to say anything.

"Send me your bill, Ben. I appreciate your help."

"No bill," Ben said. "This one's a freebie — for Francine."

When Zack and I reached home, we both were exhausted, but Zack surprised me after he stopped in front of the cottage.

"How about a swim, Bailey. It's a lovely night, and we both need a break. The stress's getting to me. Whadda ya say?"

He gave me an option. I could have said no. I could have asked if the pool was heated. I could have laughed at the idea. I could have . . .

"Sure, Zack. Why not?"

"Great. While you change, I'll park the car and walk back for you."

Once inside the cottage, I skinned from my jumpsuit, pulled on my favorite green bikini, and grabbed a terrycloth robe. Were we crazy or what! The clock said two a.m. I forgot about warning notes and slashed tires. I'd just survived a helicopter ride, and I felt like a free spirit let out of jail.

I snapped on the TV while I waited for Zack to return. Did TV stations still broadcast in the wee hours? I flipped channels until I found a live one. *Marine Patrol Captain Michael Beaumont reports retrieving marijuana bales from the sea east off the reef. As yet, no one has been apprehended, but boats from the shore patrol are aiding in the search.*

When I turned toward the door, Zack stood there listening. "Guess that explains the speedboat we saw. Druggies must have been spotted trying to make a drop tonight."

"Didn't see bales of anything aboard that guy's boat." I grabbed a couple of Hershey kisses to nibble on the way to the pool. "Glad Ben's going to call in a report."

I shivered while we strolled to poolside and shivered even more after I shed my robe. The night air sent goose bumps prickling my skin.

We splashed into the pool. Ice water! Corking a scream, I recovered from shock while I did a crawl, racing Zack to the other end of the pool. Palms shaded the water from the moonlight, darkening it to match the deep shadows surrounding the mansion.

"Whew! That'll shake the cobwebs from your head," Zack said.

I clenched my teeth to stop their chattering, but I had no luck until Zack covered my lips with his. I returned his kiss, feeling an inner fire warm me. Zack pressed his body against mine until no water flowed between us. I clung to him, feeling tingles in my breasts, my thighs — places I'd almost forgotten. Zack's body throbbed against mine, and our lips parted, only to close again in an even deeper kiss. How had I let this happen? Zack stopped any mental questions with another kiss, and I welcomed his touch.

When we heard a splash at the other end of the pool, we broke apart like guilty kids.

"Who's there?" Zack called out, again pulling me toward him.

I held my breath. Who had followed us? Why? The note writer? The tire slasher? I clung to Zack. After a brief moment, Courtney broke the surface. Nude. She seemed as surprised as we were, and she ducked back under the water. Did she think submerging hid her voluptuous breasts, the curve of her waist and hips?

"Zack!" Courtney exclaimed, resurfacing. "I had no idea! I mean, please forgive my intrusion." She swam to poolside, climbed the ladder, and slipped into a robe. "I mean, Francine offered me the use of the pool whenever I cared to swim." She knotted the sash of her robe — loosely. "I couldn't sleep tonight. Had no idea you were here."

"It's okay, Courtney. No apology necessary. It's a wonderful night for a plunge. I guess we all needed a break."

Zack and I swam toward our robes, climbed the poolside ladder, then stood dripping while we donned our cover-ups. Zack didn't try to stop me when I turned and jogged toward the cottage. At first I'd been furious at Courtney for interrupting us. But she might have done me a favor, might have saved me from falling irretrievably in love.

I was still pacing about in my swimsuit and robe when Zack knocked.

"Bailey?" He rapped again and called out. "Bailey, we need to talk."

I opened the door. He stepped inside and covered my lips with his. I forgot about Courtney. Warmth surged through our bodies until our kiss blazed beyond our control.

I followed Zack willingly when he led me to the bedroom, doused the light and raised the window shade, allowing moonlight to fall across the bed — and moments later across our bodies. We made love until dawn, parting reluctantly to face the new day.

25

Zack kissed me and slipped from the cottage. For over an hour I lolled in bed reliving the moments we'd shared. Love? I tried to quash the idea. My eyes felt scratchy from lack of sleep, but I rose, dressed, and fortified myself with M&Ms and black coffee. Nothing stirred at Eden Palms, so Zack must have decided to try to get a couple of hours of sleep. Good. I wanted to leave without waking him.

The snatch of news I'd heard last night fired purpose into my plan. There had to be a link between the unlighted speedboat we'd seen and the TV report of jettisoned marijuana. I might be unable to help Zack solve Francine's murder, but I sensed a new mystery at hand and I itched to know more. Maybe I'd learn something that would help me come up with the idea for a new song. Maybe something like "Mack the Knife."

That boat captain we saw last night

couldn't hide forever. He had to moor his craft somewhere near. In a mangrove cove? No way could I check all those uncharted islets. Private dock? Perhaps. But off limits for me. Public marina? Maybe. The boat's name and registration had been blacked out last night. This morning? A boat with no I.D would be obvious as a beached whale. True, I didn't know the craft's name or registration number, but I could look for a boat with a sun and a conch shell decorating its floorboard.

I left the cottage, making no noise and locking the door behind me. Then I checked the screen door. No note this morning. I breathed easier. I'd be safe enough in my car with doors locked. Walking toward the carport, I saw no sign of life at the mansion. Good. I wanted to avoid Zack this morning. If he heard me and called to me, he might ask questions I'd rather avoid. But once I reached the shadowed carport I saw Francine's bicycle, its new tires air-filled and at the ready.

"Mitch," I whispered.

Maybe I could camouflage another beg for help with my need to thank him for the bike repair. Two tourists bicycling around a marina would attract less attention than one woman in a green Lincoln. I shuddered, remembering the slashed tires. I had no business bicycling alone on this early morning when so few people were out and about, but taking the bike would allow me to leave Eden Palms without waking Zack.

Pausing at the cottage only long enough to change into biking shoes, I pedaled to the bridle path, stopping at the lane leading into Mitch's chosen thicket. Now what?

"Mitch?" I called into the thicket. "Mitch, can you hear me?"

No response. Then I remembered a signal Mitch and I'd used as kids to alert each other. I puckered my lips and gave a whistle. No bobolinks in the Keys. If Mitch heard me, he'd come investigate.

I whistled again. An early-morning walker gave me the eye and broke into a jog. Scared? Feeling a need to put distance between him and the crazy lady?

Another call, and Mitch stepped into sight.

"Hey, Sis. What's the buzz?" We grinned at each other, but neither of us mentioned the years that had passed since we'd used our signal. "You haven't seen Wizard, have you?"

I shook my head. "Too bad, Mitch. Guess you'll have to call him AWOL."

"Fat lot you care."

I didn't argue that point. I thanked Mitch for the bike repair and told him what I'd done and seen last night before I asked him to go riding with me — again.

"Look, Sis. Your Key West audience wants to hear blues — tunes about moon and June or love and dove. The Sandbar crowd isn't likely to want to hear a song about marijuana. When you mess with druggies, you're messing with big-time crooks. I know. Count me out."

"I don't plan to mess with crooks, but I'm curious. There's no law against taking a look-see at boats docked at a marina. And if I see that certain boat —"

"Even looking could get you in deep do-do if the owner saw you nosey-poking around."

"Looking is not nosey-poking. But forget it, Mitch. Sorry I woke you up. I'll go alone."

"And leave me to feel guilty when you wind up dead. No way. Stay here. I'll get my bike."

Do people ever give themselves a high five? I stood grinning and congratulating myself for getting my way with Mitch — something I've seldom been able to do.

When he returned, I patted my new front tire. "Thanks again for the tires and the repair job, Mitch." I reached for my billfold.

"Got a bill for the repair? That twenty probably didn't cover it and I want to pay in full. I feel like a creep accepting help from the homeless."

"My pals want no money for their help. We look out for each other. However, if you find it deep in your heart to repay their kindness, you might bake us a pie sometime. Coconut cream would be good. Very good."

I scowled. "Sorry. Pie baking's never been in my job description. But I'll buy you a pie."

"Not the same thing. Not the same thing at all." Mitch grinned and we both knew he had one-upped me. Again.

We rode to Old Town, stopping at the first marina we reached, walking our bikes along the concrete in front of the ship's chandlery. Then, after locking our bikes to a dock piling, we walked onto one of the floating catwalks where we could get a close look at the moored boats.

The Sea Nymph. Mama O. Mindy." I read the names on boats bobbing in the bottle-green water. Gulls screamed. Cormorants soared, searching for an unwary shrimp or a squid. Mitch ducked and dodged, barely in time to avoid a pelican relieving itself. I laughed.

"Not funny," he called over his shoulder.

"You ever try washing pelican poop out of blue jeans?"

"Not lately." I stopped laughing.

"This's dumb, Bailey. You don't even know the name of that boat you're looking for."

"A black boat."

"Lots of boats look black at night. Might have been any dark color."

"But it had that sun and a conch painted on the floorboard near the bow. Fluorescent paint. Maybe. The image glowed. That's what I'm looking for. The name of that boat might give me an idea for a song title." We walked all the catwalks before returning to our bikes.

"Ready to give it up?" Mitch asked.

"Not yet. This's only one marina."

"You plan to check out all of them? And what about private docks? Lots of guys keep boats right on their property. Be real, Sis. This's a lost cause."

"Humor me. Let's ride to the Chitting marina where the Shiptons dock their boats. No black speedboat there? I'll go home."

We rode toward the marina, pulling to curbside when a Conch Train clanged its bell. The "engineer" playing tour guide told the oldie about the Key West hotel that offered free rooms — the jail. Mitch and I

301

sighed, but the tourists laughed. Sometimes tourists are easily entertained.

As we pedaled closer to Mallory Dock we saw a Costa cruise ship, its yellow smoke stacks bright against the sky. We watched passengers on an upper deck helping each other into orange jackets. Lifeboat drill. In an hour or so, thousands of cruisers would stream down the gangplank and into the streets and shops. If they happened to crowd a local off his own sidewalk, the local usually smiled and remembered the tinkle of his cash register. Ah, Paradise.

When we reached Chitting Marina, a few early-morning fishermen were checking their rods and reels, filling bait buckets with seawater, and readying chum bags in preparation for a day on the water. We locked our bikes in a rack and began touring the catwalks. Dozens of boats bobbed in their slips. We started with the catwalk where the Shiptons moored their runabouts. I pointed to Francine's boat.

"Key West Mama," I said. "Zack named it. Francine objected, but she couldn't come up with a better name."

"Sea Questered." Mitch read the name on Zack's backwater skiff. "If I owned a boat, I'd call it *Sea Cured.*"

"Clever, Mitch. Clever." We walked along,

observing the boats, feeling the gentle sway of the boards underfoot. I took pictures of a few yachts, and nobody stopped us or asked for an I.D.

"How about some coffee?" Mitch asked at last.

"I had coffee at home, but go ahead. I'm sure there's a pot brewing in the chandlery."

Mitch headed toward the main dock and called over his shoulder. "I'll bring ya a mug, too."

I prowled the catwalks a long time before I spotted a boat that demanded more than a casual glance. The craft shone in the sunlight, gleaming in its blackness. Why did the word "lethal" spring to mind? From where I stood, shadows shaded the floorboard near the bow. I leaned as far forward as possible without losing my balance. A picture of a sun encircling a queen conch gleamed from the floorboard — an image more easily seen from above than from the ground. Hairs stiffened and prickled the back of my neck.

This had to be the boat we'd watched from the 'copter. Surely, there wasn't another boat like it in Key West. I looked aft, searching for the boat's name. *Sea Date.* The name must have been blacked out last night. My heart raced and I almost choked on saliva before I could swallow. The captain aboard this boat had flashed a gun. Maybe he'd been involved in a drug deal gone wrong.

Run, Bailey. Run! I heard the warning in my mind, but I balked. Common sense told me I shouldn't mess around here trying to get a pic of this boat, but, on the other hand, what could it hurt? Nobody stood guarding any of the crafts. I saw no dockmaster. I continued to rationalize. Creators of lyrics needed inspiration. I *needed* to snap some pictures here for future reference. Right?

"Sea Date. Sea Date." No reason I couldn't show a snapshot to Zack and let him take it to the shore patrol if he thought it advisable. *Sea Date.* Where had I heard that name before? Who owned this speedboat? I stood there trying to memorize the I.D. numbers on the stern until I realized my craziness. Lifting my camera I focused on the registration number, clicking two shots in case one of them didn't turn out. Then I thought more about the floorboard painting. I wanted a picture of that sun and conch shell. "Conch Shell Blues." How was that for a song title?

I stood winding my film, readying the camera for the next shot, before I tried to sight through the lens and focus on the painting. For the first time I wished I had a new digital camera. I didn't have enough light. The gunwale shadowed the floorboard, and beside that, I stood at a poor angle. I saw only one way to get the shot I needed. After stepping from the catwalk onto the bow of *Sea Date,* I hopped onto the floorboard, focused on the picture, and snapped the shutter.

After I stepped back onto the catwalk, I felt it sag and sway and I turned, expecting to see Mitch approaching with coffee.

"Mitch! I found —" My voice trailed off when I saw the newcomer.

"You found what?" Dr. Gravely asked, his gaze boring into me.

Heat rushed to my face flush. "Why, hello, Dr. Gravely. You surprised me."

"Obviously."

"Please forgive me for trespassing." My throat went dry, blocking more apologies that I couldn't vocalize.

"Is there something special on my boat or *inside* it that interests you?" He stepped closer, and I backed off in spite of an inner vow to show no fear.

"No, nothing special," I lied. "I had no idea you owned this boat. I'm interested in all beautiful boats. Sea crafts have inspired lots of songs. 'The Good Ship Lollipop.' Remember that oldie? 'Red Sails in the Sunset'? I've always liked that one."

Gravely's voice dripped sarcasm. "If you've taken pictures of every beautiful boat you've seen, you must have quite a collection."

"Yes, I do. At least I'm starting one."

He smiled, taking another step toward me. I took another step away from him. Why did I feel threatened? What was going on here? The man was Zack's neighbor and friend. I certainly had no proof that he was involved with last night's drug problems. But if I kept on backing away from him, I'd soon reach the end of the catwalk and splash into the sea. I saw no way to sidle around Gravely, and his body language made it clear he had no intention of letting me pass.

"I do have quite a few boat pictures." I forced calmness into my voice. "But I need a variety of shots to draw from. When I'm composing at my computer, either lyrics or music, it distracts me and slows my progress if I have to leave my chair to find some item I'm trying to describe. It's much more practical to have a snapshot at hand for quick reference. That way I can get on with the composition without interruption and . . ."

I realized I was babbling and that Dr. Gravely realized it, too, and knew he had unnerved me. Were was Mitch? I felt desperate for that coffee he'd promised. But no. Forget that! I needed to warn Mitch away. I didn't want Gravely to see me with him or to realize Mitch and I had a bring-me-a-cup-of-coffee relationship.

"Thank you for letting me snap a shot of your boat, Dr. Gravely." I stepped forward and tried to ease past him on the catwalk, but he blocked my way and reached toward me. I gripped my camera strap and pressed my camera close to my body.

"Excuse me, please. May I get past?" My mouth felt so dry I could hardly speak.

"Winton?"

Caught off-guard by the sound of his name, Gravely turned and stepped back, giving me room to pass him. The voice had surprised me, too. I fought to keep my balance on the narrow catwalk.

26

Zack! Had Zack seen Gravely and me struggling over the camera? Was Zack coming to my rescue? But had Gravely and I really been struggling? Or had I blown the scene out of proportion? Gravely had made no threats, and his voice often sounded oily and sarcastic. I owed him an apology. I'd been out of line when I boarded his boat uninvited. Had I known it was his boat and that he stood so near, I'd have asked permission or waited for an invitation aboard.

"Good morning, mates." Zack's smile lingered longer on me than on Gravely, and when our eyes met, I knew we both were remembering last night's pleasures. Then Zack looked directly at Gravely. "Going fishing, Win?"

"Not today. Too choppy. Heard small-craft warnings earlier. I'm here to check on my boat. Cops have reported kids prowling the marina at night, and I'm afraid the dockmaster's being too lenient with security. You had any problems with your boat? Or Francine's?"

"No. Not that I've noticed. But I haven't had time to take either boat out lately."

I saw Zack study Gravely's boat, saw his gaze linger a moment on the floorboard before he scanned the rest of the craft. I was so glad to have Zack break up my encounter with Gravely that I almost forgot about Mitch.

"Yeah." Winton's voice jerked my mind back to the present. "Guess none of us have enjoyed much on-the-water time recently."

"Done any night fishing lately?" Zack asked. "I know that's not your thing, but Ben says the shrimp have been running the past week or so. Under the bridges. Especially under the Boca Chica. We might give that a try. Get our minds off the police investigation."

"Count me out, Zack. You know I hate night fishing." A tic pulled at Gravely's cheek when he continued. "Even using a compass and channel markers, I get disoriented in the dark."

"How about taking my boat and letting me play pilot? Bailey, maybe you'd like to join us. Some of Ben's friends working under the Boca Chica brought up a bucket full the other night in only an hour or so. Those shrimp make tasty eating."

"Thanks, Zack, but I'll pass." No way was I going shrimping at night.

Gravely laughed. "Why don't you let me treat you to a good shrimp dinner at Kelly's instead?"

Zack slapped him on the back. "I may take you up on that, Win. Later."

Zack and Gravely stopped talking, and when I looked toward the main dock, I saw Mitch heading our way with a mug of coffee. When he saw Zack and Dr. Gravely, he changed direction and disappeared around the end of the chandlery.

I knew Zack had not-so-subtly been maneuvering Gravely into talking about boats on the sea in the nighttime, but I was tired of pussy-footing around the subject. I stepped forward and looked Gravely in the eye.

"Dr. Gravely, there's something you need to know. Late last night while Zack and I were in a 'copter beyond the reef, releasing Francine's ashes, we saw your boat below us."

"Impossible. I stayed home all evening."

The tic began working his cheek again. "Don't get me wrong. I didn't say you were in the boat. I only said we saw your boat.

Anyone could have been at the wheel. Maybe some of the kids you mentioned. Maybe you're right about lax marina security."

"You sure it was *Sea Date*?"

Now Gravely looked directly at Zack, and I hoped Zack would forgive me for opening this discussion. But my words were true and I'd made no accusation. We had no proof that Gravely had been piloting *Sea Date* last night. None at all.

"Yes, Win. We saw *Sea Date*. It cut through the water with no running lights. Ben lowered the 'copter close enough to scare the pilot and he pulled a gun."

"That doesn't sound like a kid out joyriding to me," I said.

"Right," Gravely said. "And I heard about the marijuana drop." His cheek tic kicked in again. "If someone's using my boat for a drug pickup . . ." His voice trailed off. "Come with me. I'm going to report this to the dockmaster — going to demand more security. I may need you two and your story to back me up."

We followed Gravely along the catwalk and into the chandlery, where he beelined to the cashier's counter. The smell of hemp rope, diesel fuel, and past-their-prime fish permeated the air. A small countertop grill

311

with hot dogs turning on a spit caught my eye. A hot dog for breakfast? I toyed with the idea and then dismissed it when Gravely spoke to the cashier.

"I demand to speak to a dockmaster," he said. "In fact, I demand to speak to the dockmaster on duty last night. I'm Dr. Winton Gravely, a long-time patron of this marina."

"Has there been a problem, Dr. Gravely?" the cashier asked. "Perhaps I can help."

"I'd prefer to speak with the dockmaster."

The cashier pressed a buzzer and relayed Gravely's request.

"Send him up," a voice replied.

We took the stairs to the second floor and a dockmaster wearing white pants and a white t-shirt bearing the Chitting Marina logo stood waiting outside his office door.

"Please come inside." He motioned to two plastic chairs in front of a pine desk pock-marked with cigarette burns. "Have a seat."

Since there were only two chairs and three of us, we remained standing and waited while Gravely told his story, his suspicions. Zack and I related the facts of our helicopter ride. When the dockmaster reached for a phone to get in touch with the shore patrol, Zack eased me toward the door.

"Look, we've told you what we saw." Zack

nodded to me, and I moved closer to him. "If anyone needs more information from us, we'll be at Burger King — one of the few places open for early breakfast. Winton, when you're through here, why don't you join us for bacon and eggs?"

Gravely looked nonplussed at our leaving, and he ignored Zack's invitation. We managed to wedge my bicycle behind the bucket seats in the T-bird, and when Zack held my hand all the way to Burger King, it seemed a natural thing to do. Neither of us mentioned Courtney's splash into the pool or our lovemaking that followed. Zack didn't ask if I'd biked to the marina alone, and I never mentioned Mitch being with me.

"I hate to have you biking alone, Bailey. I don't want to scare you, but remember that note. The police are still hunting a murderer."

Zack didn't know about the slashed tires, and I didn't bring that up. Early morning parking places were common as seagulls. After Zack chose one and plugged the meter, we followed the scent of bacon and hash browns.

"Nothing better than breakfast under the sky," I said after we'd carried omelets and toast to the second-floor open-air porch and stood for a moment looking over the railing at the scene below.

Zack grinned and winked. "I can think of a few things. Moonlight. You in my arms." He held my chair for me.

After we sat and began eating, Zack's playful demeanor disappeared. "Bailey, please tell me exactly what was going on between you and Winton this morning at the marina. Had he done something to scare you? You acted frightened."

I chose my words carefully, remembering Gravely was Zack's friend. "I'm not sure what happened. I felt relieved to see you, that's for certain. I'd stepped aboard Dr. Gravely's boat to get a snapshot of the floorboard. I hadn't seen him approaching, but when I hopped back to the catwalk, there he stood. Then in moments you arrived."

"It looked to me like he was reaching for your camera."

"I thought so, too, Zack, but I'm not sure. He had me on the defensive. I should have apologized to him immediately. I'd no business stepping aboard his boat, but when I saw that likeness of the sun and the conch, I had to snap a picture of it. At that time, I didn't know Dr. Gravely owned the boat. I only knew that someone in that boat had been speeding in the nighttime without running lights. Violations like that should be reported. How did you happen to come to my rescue?"

"If you interpreted my arrival as a rescue, you must have felt frightened."

"But you were there for me. You'd come looking for me?"

"When you weren't at the cottage, I guessed what you were doing and where you might have come to do it. But, were you afraid of Winton?"

"Maybe I just felt guilty for trespassing."

"Someone else could have hijacked his boat last night. That's true. But highly unlikely. Those dockmasters are well trained. They know the comings and goings of the boats — especially the arrivals and departures at night. Most boaters like to be in before sundown."

"Then you think Dr. Gravely lied about being home last night, about suspecting someone else of using his boat?"

"I'm like you, Bailey, not exactly sure what I think. Win may have been out in his own boat. No law against that — just an important law against running at night without lights."

"And maybe it was coincidental that a drug drop went down last night. Zack, do you think your friend's involved in drug smuggling?"

"No. I can't believe that. We've been friends for years, and I've had no reason to distrust Win about anything. As far as I'm concerned he's a straight arrow. He doesn't need drug money. He has a thriving medical practice and clinic."

"Some people never reach a saturation point when it comes to money." I added salt and a dash of Tabasco to my omelet just as Gravely stepped off the elevator carrying coffee and a plate of bacon and grits. Zack rose and pulled up another chair.

"What did you learn from the dockmaster?" Zack asked.

"Nothing all-important to your story about last night. The dockmaster — he's the one who took my boat out last night, but only momentarily. Some marina patrons reported an oil slick and they thought oil was leaking from my boat."

"An oil slick is that important?" What kind of a weak story was this!

"Yes," Zack said. "Oil can pollute the water and cause a marina and its patrons a lot of problems."

"Well, the leak came from some other boat. Not mine."

"Does someone at the marina have keys to all the boats?" I asked.

"Not usually," Gravely said. "I'd left an extra key with them a few days ago so a mechanic could make some minor repairs."

"That doesn't solve the mystery of who used your boat last night," Zack said.

"True," Gravely agreed. "And that worries me. I've ordered the dockmasters to guard it more carefully in the future. Any more suspicious stuff and I'll change marinas."

Gravely finished his grits and bacon and rose. "Excuse me for rushing off, please. I need to get back to my clinic." He glanced at his watch. "Do keep in touch."

I waited until Gravely took the elevator down and disappeared from sight. "Zack, what do you think he was doing at the marina so early in the morning? Shouldn't he have been at his clinic doing the pill-and-bedpan routine?"

"I'm sure he has nurses to do those chores. Maybe marina officials called him about his boat repairs."

"On Saturday morning? Is that likely? Maybe he saw me take the bike out. Maybe he followed me here."

"I don't know why he'd do that."

"You did."

"I didn't know for sure you were here. I was guessing — and hoping. Are you afraid of Winton?"

"He's not my favorite person, but I trust him because you do." Before Zack could respond, I tossed him a new subject. "Zack, do you really think it surprised Courtney to see us in the pool last night?"

"Yes. Surprised and embarrassed. I don't think she was putting on an act."

"Realtors are masters of putting on acts, of making prospective buyers see what the realtor wants them to see. If they didn't have that talent, they'd soon be out of business."

"Perhaps. But what reason would Courtney have had for making such an intrusion?"

"You." The word hung between us for a few seconds.

"Me?"

"Yes, you." I lowered my voice although we were the only people around. "I think Courtney had strong motive for murdering Francine. I think she sees herself married to you, retiring from real estate, and living happily ever after at Eden Palms. Maybe she thought all that blocked her dream was Francine, who enjoyed good health and who loved being deeply involved in Key West activities — Francine who had no thought of leaving her family home."

Zack shook his head. "But Mother did have thoughts of leaving the mansion. She had lots of thoughts and lots of plans for making it a homeless shelter. I couldn't talk her out of that idea."

"I was almost ready to drop Courtney from our group of suspects, but I'll have to admit that may be another reason to keep her high on our list. Courtney probably hated the idea of having a homeless shelter near. Of all the suspects, she had the most to gain from Francine's death — you, Eden Palms, and a serene neighborhood."

"Bailey, I think you're jealous of Courtney. She's very low on my suspect list."

My face flushed at Zack's accusation. Why couldn't I drop the subject of Courtney? "She has no alibi for the time of the murder. Anyone could say they were at Mallory for the sunset celebration. And few people could actually provide proof. She chose a pseudo alibi that she knew would puzzle anyone who tried to make an in-depth effort to check it out."

"Well, that's true. She couldn't prove that she was at Mallory, and we couldn't prove that she wasn't."

"So to make up for her lack of a solid alibi, Courtney comes on to you. You might say she shows you all she's got in an effort to distract you from her lack of an alibi for last Monday." Zack's face flushed. From embarrassment? Anger? I wondered.

"I'd like to change the subject to the Tisdales." Zack shoved his plate aside. "I've been thinking more about Tucker. Just because he managed Mother's funeral arrangements doesn't prove he's innocent of murder. So he says he was working at his business at the time Mother died. I don't think he can prove that. Like most business owners, he had opportunity to be in and out of his office. I checked on that once when you weren't with me. At that time, several of his employees vouched for his presence, but a double check wouldn't hurt. And it might help."

"Might help to get Courtney off the hook?"

"I don't consider Courtney to be on a hook."

I added jam to my last piece of toast. "Do you think it strange that Mrs. Tisdale didn't attend Francine's funeral? Since the Tisdales were your neighbors and close friends I find her absence at the service strange."

"Not so. She was in North Carolina visiting her sister, and I announced the funeral service at the last minute. She had no chance to make travel arrangements."

I shrugged. "If my close friend had been murdered and I knew the police were doing an on-going investigation, I think I'd have returned home immediately. And I've been thinking more about the Tisdale koi pond — and that snake. Water along with the tropical growth around the pond might attract snakes."

"So might the water in the Eden Palms pool."

"No. Your pool water's chlorinated. I doubt snakes would like that."

"So now you know what snakes like and dislike?"

"Zack, honestly now, what were you doing out and about so early this morning? Were you also looking for that boat we saw from the 'copter?"

"No." Zack looked at me until I met his level gaze. "I came looking for you. I saw you leave alone by bicycle, and that worried me. I followed and saw you meet your brother, and again I smelled danger."

"You followed us!" Heat rose to my face. It irritated me to have been followed. On the other hand, I was pleased me that Zack cared about my safety — pleased me more than I wanted to admit.

"Have you ever checked your brother's whereabouts on last Monday afternoon? He presented a good story to the detectives."

"Not so. Had he presented a good story, he'd have avoided mentioning anything at all about snakes."

Zack finished his cup of coffee without commenting on my words.

"You suspect Mitch of murdering your mother, Zack? If so, your suspicions about him are totally off base."

"Perhaps so. For your sake I hope so. But I intend to do an in-depth check on Mitch's Monday activities."

27

My anger simmered like a kettle of chowder. Not only had Zack accused me of being jealous of Courtney, but he'd also insinuated that Mitch might have murdered Francine. How could he be such a twad! How could he make love to me one minute and make light of my feelings the next? The air between us on the drive to Eden Palms might have blown in from Iowa, it felt that frosty. When he braked in front of the cottage I slid from the passenger seat without thanking him, stomped inside, and banged the door.

Lover's quarrel? No way! I needed to put space between me and Zack Shipton, move somewhere safe where I could think clearly. Did Zack plan to use Mitch as a red herring to distract the detectives from digging into his own whereabouts last Monday? Maybe I had slept with a murderer. Mitch was right. I needed to get away from Eden Palms.

I hated this cottage, hated the whole neighborhood, hated Zack's trying to make a scapegoat of Mitch. Francine had been my only friend, and now she was gone. Nobody wanted me here. Nobody. And somebody wanted me dead.

Winton Gravely resented my boarding his boat. Courtney disliked me for living — and thwarting her pursuit of Zack. And now Zack! What were Zack's true feelings? I wanted to pick up my marbles and go home. But I no longer had a home. For a moment I identified with Mitch's friends. Where would I go if I left Francine's cottage? Mitch's one-room apartment? One room? Could I stand that? Yes. I'd endure anything in order to leave this cottage. Maybe I should have listened to Mom and stuck with my clerk's job in Iowa.

I keyed in Mitch's number. Five rings before he answered.

"It's me, Mitch. I need your help."

"Again? What's the buzz *this* time?"

"Is the offer to use your apartment still open?"

"Sure. You have a mega-spat with Zack? You want to move into my apartment for permanent?"

"I'm not sure exactly what I want."

"Better calm down. How about trying my place a few days for size? Wouldn't hurt my heart to see you dump Zack Shipton. That guy doesn't like me — probably hates my guts."

"Could I move in today?"

"Lusk's my realtor. Better run your plans by her. See if it's okay with the apartment owner if I take in a friend or sublet the place. Don't want to risk doing anything that might call undue attention to me and jinx the witness protection deal."

"Would you call her for me, Mitch?"

"No way. I gave you prime time this morning. Right now some pals are going with me on another search for Wizard. Got no time for phone chitchat. Just call Lusk and tell her I said the subletting deal's okay with me."

Mitch broke our connection. Just call Lusk. Ha. Just call Lusk. Mitch knew Courtney and I weren't close. He knew I'd hate calling her, especially calling to ask for housing info. *Bury your pride. Make the call.* My mind still steamed on slow simmer. I refused to think about my lifestyle if I left this cottage and moved into Mitch's sleazy apartment.

I looked up Courtney's number and

punched it onto the keypad before I changed my mind.

"Lusk Realty. How many I help you?"

Her throaty voice and honeyed tone made me want to bang the receiver down without answering. But no doubt she had Caller I.D. She'd know.

"Good morning, Courtney. Bailey here with a question."

"Glad to help you if I can."

"I'm considering leaving the cottage and subletting Mitch Mitchell's apartment on Caroline Street." I paused. Why hadn't I thought this scene through more carefully? Courtney knew nothing of my relationship to Mitch. "I'm wondering about the legal details. As a renter, can Mr. Mitchell sublet the place?"

"Mitchell? Sublet?" Courtney let the words hang between us like terms from a language she didn't understand.

"Yes, sublet. I've discussed it with Mr. Mitchell and he said it's okay with him if it's okay with you and the owner. He's found quarters . . . elsewhere and . . ."

"I guess Mr. Mitchell and I needed to have a better understanding. The property owner has strict rules against subletting. Mr. Mitchell and I both considered the apartment within his means."

"His plans have changed."

"Where does he intend to locate? And why would you be interested in such cramped quarters when you're ensconced in the Shipton cottage? I don't feel you'd find Mr. Mitchell's apartment comfortable."

Now vinegar laced her honeyed tones, and gut-level danger signals warned me to watch my words. "I'm unaware of Mr. Mitchell's future living arrangements, but I need a quieter spot, a less-expensive place where I can relax and work on creating new lyrics. My CD-in-progress has been in progress far too long."

The pause on the other end of the line made me wonder if she'd broken the connection. "Courtney — Courtney are you there?"

"I'm still on the line, Bailey. I'm in this business to help people find suitable housing, housing that meets their lifestyles as well as their budgets. Mr. Mitchell's apartment is suitable for him — a loner with a low budget and little need for larger accommodations. Have you seen inside his apartment?"

"No. Of course not. But I heard Mr. Mitchell and Zack discussing his place, and I thought . . ."

"You thought you'd *want* to make such a

move? On top of the fact that subletting the place would be a violation of Mitch's lease agreement, I think you'd find the apartment unsuitable. Bailey, why don't you drop over to my house for a few minutes? We'll share a pot of coffee while I show you some nicer apartments. I have videos of at least five places that you might want to consider. If you see one or two you like, we'll drive by and you can take a look."

Drat! I'd wanted this transaction to be an over-and-out deal, something I could latch onto before I changed my mind. Courtney had turned my request into a situation I might be unable to handle. She couldn't sublet Mitch's place, but she wanted to find me a place to live — a place far from Zack and Eden Palms. I'd played right into her hands. But so what! I wanted to get away from Zack, from my memories of the mansion, from the turmoil of the police investigation.

But wait. Would leaving the neighborhood make me look guilty? No. It couldn't. I'd been aboard a plane at the time of Francine's death. Nothing could change that fact.

"Bailey? Do come over and let me see how I can help you. Workers have torn up the sidewalk to my porch in preparation for laying flagstones, so cut across the grass under the palms. I'll be waiting for you on the side veranda, okay? I'm free now. If you're free, too, let's get started."

I knew her apartments would be beyond my financial reach, but if I refused her invitation, she'd think I wasn't serious about moving. Or she might think last night's pool scene had prompted my decision. And what if she began to wonder about my relationship to Mitch and began to question it? I couldn't risk letting that happen.

"Thanks, Courtney. I'll come right over."

I felt trapped. But I could handle it. So what if Courtney had a reputation for being a high-powered salesperson? I could show her a verbal stone wall cemented with the word "no."

Changing from my biking shoes into sandals, I slung my camera around my neck. If we drove around looking at apartments, I could snap a shot of any I liked. Leaving the cottage, I walked toward Courtney's home. The sun glinting on coral rock pillars and then on a pair of second-floor windows, gave them the look of mirrored sunglasses. Draperies masked the lower windows, and I wondered if Courtney stood inside watching my approach. Somebody in the area was frying bacon. Although I'd eaten earlier, the fragrance enticed me, whetting a second appetite that made my mouth water.

The grass under the palms still held night dew that dampened my feet. I thought I was watching where I stepped, but a movement overhead distracted me. I glanced up at an iguana perched on a palm frond, and in that instant, I slipped and fell. When questioned later, I couldn't remember if I felt pain in my leg and fell or if I fell and then felt the pain. I'd stepped on the handle of a machete some yardman had failed to return to the caretaker's shed. The curved blade had flipped up and cut my thigh. At first I felt nothing, then I clenched my teeth against hot daggers of pain.

Blood running from thigh to ankle soon covered my foot. When I tried to move, blood spurted everywhere.

"Help! Help!" I shouted, hoping that this time Courtney had been watching and that Zack had not. "Courtney! Courtney!"

The veranda door flew open, and Courtney rushed across the porch and down three steps to the lawn where I lay.

"What happened?" Her gaze met mine and then traveled to the wound in my leg. "How did you manage to do that?"

"Easy. You have a first aid kit?"

"Yes. Keep calm. I'll get it and be right back."

I was better at keeping calm than Courtney was. In spite of the pulsing pain, I managed to sit up and take a closer look at my injury. My movement caused greater bleeding and now the pain throbbed in rhythm with my pounding heart. It seemed like an hour passed before Courtney returned with a pan of water, tape, bandages.

"This isn't in my job description, Bailey, but I think I can clean the cut and apply a bandage. Then we'll get you to a doctor. You in great pain?"

"No," I lied, unwilling to admit weakness. Courtney's plan failed. After only a few moments we eyed a pan of red-tinged water. Blood continued to flow from the cut, preventing her from applying a bandage.

"Maybe a tourniquet higher on my leg would help."

"I don't know anything about tourniquets, Bailey. Can you stand?"

Courtney helped me to my feet, but when I stood, the blood flow increased. Seeing my own blood pooling around my feet made me woozy.

"Don't faint, Bailey. Don't faint. Be strong. Grit your teeth. We'll walk to Dr. Gravely's clinic. He'll know what to do.

Come on, now. Put your arm around my waist and let me take your arm. It's only a short distance."

Short distance! Hah! It looked like a mile. "Leave me here, Courtney. Go knock on Gravely's door. Tell him I need him."

"No. I'm not leaving you here in a pool of blood." She swathed the cut in several thicknesses of gauze. "Walk. Walk. You can make it."

I forced myself to put one foot ahead of the other and move forward. How could this have happened! Any pain that wasn't in my leg was in my mind — the pain of having to depend on Courtney Lusk for help. I didn't have strength to look behind us, but I knew I must be leaving a bloody trail across the lawn.

Foot by foot. Inch by inch. At last we made it to Gravely's door. Courtney opened the screen and lifted a brass knocker. Its falling rang like a gunshot in my head. Courtney made no move to knock a second time, so I found the strength to lift the knocker and drop it again. Was the man deaf? Why didn't he come to his door?

Blood began to pool on his doorstep, and I imagined its coppery taste at the base of my tongue. I slumped, thinking Courtney would keep me from falling, but no. Now I was lying in a puddle of my own blood, unable to rise, almost unable to speak or cry out.

Courtney dropped the brass knocker again. This time the door opened so quickly I wondered if Gravely had been watching my helplessness through his peephole.

"Ladies? What's going on here?"

"Bailey's had an accident." Courtney stood back as if Gravely couldn't see my leg dripping blood. My mind regressed to Girl Scout days. Didn't continued bleeding mean a severed artery? Again my thoughts flashed to tourniquets, to quick death from loss of blood.

"Do something, Dr. Gravely," Courtney demanded. "Let us in. She's already lost lots of blood. She may be going into shock."

"Take her to the hospital." Gravely helped me back to my feet and let me lean against him. "I can't have her coming in here like this."

"Why not?" My voice wavered.

"Yes," Courtney said. "Why on earth not? You do run a clinic, don't you? Can't you see she's in no condition to make a trip to the hospital? If you refuse to help, I'll have no compunction about reporting you to medical authorities."

Had her threat scared him? Dr. Gravely

transferred my weight to Courtney and stepped back into the clinic, returning in seconds with a wheelchair.

Courtney urged me into the chair and started to push me through the clinic doorway, but Gravely scowled and stepped in front of us.

"Bailey may come in and I'll treat her, but you may not enter, Ms. Lusk. I have a heart patient in residence who requires absolute quiet. Your presence is a detriment. Go. Leave at once."

28

Courtney backed off when Gravely all but slammed the door on her toes. Although she had tried to help me, I guessed she was glad to be relieved from giving further aid. I was as glad to be rid of her as she was of me, but I hated being alone with Gravely. Was he still upset with me for boarding his boat? Feeling dizzy, I clutched the arms of the chair and tried to focus on some piece of furniture, some picture that would stop the spinning sensation in my head.

"I th-think I'm g-going to vomit." Hot acrid fluid rose into my throat. I swallowed. I forced it back. I swallowed again. Gravely scowled and stepped toward another doorway.

"Don't try to get up, Bailey. I'll be right back."

My heart thudded when Gravely hurried away, but he soon returned carrying a stainless steel basin.

"Try to relax, Bailey. This cut isn't as bad as it may seem to you. Look away from it. Don't let the sight of blood sicken you. I'll have a tourniquet on that leg in no time. You're going to be okay."

Once he handed me the basin, my stomach calmed down. I lifted my head and glanced around his waiting room, remembering a few days ago when I'd asked to see it. Had patients ever waited here? The couch and chairs looked so show-room fresh I imagined I could smell the scent of new leather. Even when Gravely helped me into a larger wheelchair, his pristine waiting room made me wonder if I were the first person to use it. It looked more like a show piece than a functional room in a clinic.

Was Gravely really a doctor? At least Courtney knew where I was. She'd check on my well-being. Wouldn't she?

"After a few minutes in my operating room, you'll be feeling fine." Gravely turned the chair and began pushing me along a dimly lit hallway.

Operating room? I sat stiff and straight, and I counted the doors opening into the hallway. Was his heart patient in one of those rooms? Were we making enough noise to disturb her? To cause her to go into cardiac arrest? Did he really have a heart patient in residence? I tried to avoid such thoughts, and presently we reached a darkened room which came to life with the flick of a switch.

A gurney. Stainless steel sinks — three of them. Medicine cabinets. Surgical tools. Maybe Gravely *was* a doctor. But of course he was a doctor. Zack would have had no reason to lie to me about that.

"I want you on the gurney, Bailey. It'll help slow the bleeding to have your leg elevated rather than hanging down."

Turning, and leaning toward me, he placed his hands under my arms and legs, and lifted me onto the gurney in one swift movement. I could hardly believe his strength. He placed one pillow under my head and another under my leg.

"Now lie back and relax."

"Not much chance of that," I muttered. But I did manage to relax — at least a little.

He washed his hands before he donned surgical gloves, opened a cabinet drawer, and pulled out a length of rubber tubing.

"A tourniquet will slow the bleeding quickly." He wrapped the tubing around my leg a few inches above the cut and we waited. The blood pulsed and flowed, but it became less and less, until at last it stopped.

"Such profuse bleeding tends to scare accident victims and those around them half to death," Gravely explained, "and it is dangerous if it isn't stopped. But in reality, if a doctor treats a patient correctly, the bleeding performs a needed service. It cleans the wound."

He stopped talking, and bit by bit over the next minutes he loosened the tourniquet. "Now I'll leave you for a few moments," he said at last. "Remain quiet. I'll return quickly."

A new terror gripped me. What if he didn't return? Would I be able to get off this gurney and escape? If not, would Courtney worry if I didn't reappear this morning? Would she be aware of my absence and summon help? And if she did, who would she call? Zack? I doubted Zack would be her choice. She wouldn't want him empathizing with me or offering sympathy. Since she didn't know Mitch was my brother, she wouldn't call him. I could die here and nobody would know. Before I could worry more, Dr. Gravely returned carrying a tray.

"Tea and buttered toast," he announced, "and a couple of pills. Down the pills first. They'll help you feel better and recover your strength." Once I swallowed the pills, he assisted me from gurney to wheelchair, and then rested the tray on the chair's arms. I ate the snack, feeling surprised at a surge of returning strength. I did feel better.

"How soon may I leave?" I asked.

"You need to stay here for a while. Before I bandage your wound, I want to wait until I feel sure the bleeding won't start again. I'll wheel you to my waiting room and you can look at magazines."

"I already feel well enough to go home."

"And therein lies the reason for delay. I can't release a tourniquet too quickly. I'll continue to loosen it little by little. When the danger of more bleeding is past, I'll gift-wrap your wound in layers of gauze and tape."

"In the waiting room?" Again, suspicions flared in my mind.

"Yes. The waiting room. I told you about my heart patient. She's in a private room, and she needs absolute quiet until her family calls for her. I'm sorry if I appeared brusque to you and Courtney earlier. It unnerved me to face an emergency on a Saturday morning. An injured leg is more of a general hospital thing rather than a problem for a private clinic. Miss Jessica, my nurse, will return soon, but until then my heart patient is dependent on me."

"I understand." I said the words, but I didn't understand anything about this clinic. I remembered Gravely's concern for me began only after Courtney threatened him. Had he been reported to authorities before? Maybe his malpractice insurance had lapsed.

Gravely wheeled me to the waiting room, and again I had the feeling that the room seldom saw patients. Everything looked too spic-and-span new. He helped me from the wheelchair and onto the leather couch and elevated my injured leg on an ottoman.

"If you'll excuse me, I'll leave you for a few minutes." He checked his watch. "Ten minutes for starters. I'll check on my heart patient, then I'll return and loosen the tourniquet." He handed me the current copy of *Key West Travelhost.*

"Thank you, Doctor. I'll be fine."

"A few days ago you asked to see my waiting room, my Conch Republic memorabilia." He gestured toward the wall opposite the door. "I've framed many replicas of the Conch Republic flag. They're similar to the likeness painted on my boat. Perhaps you'll find them interesting."

"I'm sure I will. Thank you."

Gravely walked to one flag, dusting the top edge of the frame with his forefinger. "I've framed many of these flags myself."

"That's quite an art — matting and framing. I tried to frame a blow-up of the CD case for *Greentree Blues,* but I botched the job. After three tries, I gave up and took it to the Photo and Phrame Shop at Searstown. I hired Free Glockner to frame it. He's a pro."

"You're right. Framing's an art. Takes a lot of know-how. And patience. But I enjoy the hobby. It gives me a sense of satisfaction to see my picture finished and hanging on my wall."

Once Gravely left, I thumbed through the magazine he'd handed me, scanning the headline articles, the advertisements, then reading carefully an article on buying a new home and relocating in Key West. Not that I'd be interested in buying a home. I didn't let that thought enter my mind.

Laying the magazine aside, I looked more closely at Dr. Gravely's Conch Republic flags. I liked both the variety of sizes and the variety of frames he had chosen. When he returned to loosen the tourniquet, I forgot the flags for the moment and smiled to see that my leg no longer bled.

"Let's wait another few minutes," he said. "Then if all's well, I'll bandage the wound and you can go on your way — resting the remainder of the day, of course."

"Yes, of course." He turned to go, but I

called to him. "Dr. Gravely, would you mind if I took some pictures of your flags? You have a variety of unique ones."

"No, I'm flattered. Go right ahead. I apologize for our misunderstanding at the marina this morning."

"And I owe you an apology for boarding your boat without invitation."

"No apology needed. I took my anger at the marina officials out on you. I hate knowing that strangers sometimes have access to my boat."

"I understand. And I'm glad your boat wasn't the one leaking oil."

Remaining seated with my leg on the ottoman, I managed to snap flash shots of several of the framed flags. Blue was the regulation background color, but Gravely had framed red flags, yellow flags — even a purple one. I started to slide my camera into its case when I spotted a flag I'd overlooked. It hung unframed and loosely taped to the wall, as if Gravely still felt undecided on the exact spot to hang it. I grabbed a deep breath to steady myself.

Ignoring my injured leg, I rose and stepped closer to the flag. No doubt about it. I'd bought this flag from the airport vendor last Monday. It'd been my token gift to Wizard on Tuesday when Mitch had introduced us. No mistake. I touched the grease smear on the corner of the fabric. Perhaps Gravely had taped it to the wall until he had a chance to get it cleaned. *Snap a picture of it. Now. Before it's too late. No. Don't. He'll catch you.*

A chill feathered up my arms. I hurried back to the couch and eased my leg onto the ottoman. What was Wizard's scarf doing here? I forgot how many days had passed since Mitch told me Wizard was missing.

Why would a vagrant have business in a private clinic? Gravely's upscale practice wouldn't include indigent patients. My mind reeled with questions when Gravely returned to the waiting room. I could hardly sit still while he made a final inspection of my wound, applied some Steri-Strips and a bandage. This might be my last, my only, chance to get a picture of Wizard's scarf. I hadn't figured out why that was important, but a gut feeling told me it was. And maybe I could get one after all.

Standing to leave the office, I delayed.

"Dr. Gravely, thank you for caring for my leg. I expect to pay you for your services. Will a check be okay?"

"Let's not worry about that now," Gravely said. "My secretary will bill you later."

"That'll be fine, but I have one more favor to ask."

"What's that?"

"I'd like to take your picture along with some of your interesting flags. Would you pose for me?"

Gravely shrugged and acted embarrassed, but I felt sure my request flattered him. Maybe he remembered my words about using pictures to help me create lyrics. Maybe he imagined himself immortalized in a Bailey Green song.

"Where shall I stand?" He struck a pose beside the largest of the flags. "How's this?"

I pretended to focus the lens, then I stopped and looked up. "The overhead light casts a shadow on your face. Would you mind standing about a foot to your left?"

"Anywhere you prefer." He moved to his left. "Okay?"

Approaching him, I took his arm and pulled him into the exact position I needed, the position that would show him and Wizard's scarf in the same frame.

"Now smile and say cheese. People laugh at those instructions, but they work."

Dr. Gravely smiled and mouthed the word "cheese" as I snapped the picture. I thanked him again and headed for the door.

29

"Wait," Dr. Gravely said. "You mustn't leave afoot. I want you to pamper that leg for a day or two while the wound heals."

"My leg feels fine, and it's only a few steps to the cottage. I can make it. No problem."

"I'd drive you there, but I can't leave my patient."

Before I could protest, Gravely picked up a telephone and keyed in a number. My hands balled into fists when he spoke.

"Zack, I've a friend of yours at the clinic who needs a lift to her cottage. Could you oblige? She's had an accident, and I don't want her walking yet. No. No. Nothing life-threatening."

I could barely hide my irritation. "Oh, you shouldn't have bothered Zack. I'm sure he's busy."

"But not too busy." Gravely's voice dripped sarcasm. "Not too busy for his favorite lady." He opened the clinic door and glanced outside. "Here he is already."

There was nothing I could do but thank Gravely again for his help. Zack hurried toward us, leaving the car door open in his rush to offer me an arm to lean on.

"Bailey! What on earth happened?" He helped me into the car, then turned to Gravely. "Win, thanks for taking care of her — for calling me."

On the half-block drive to the cottage, I made light of my injury and corked my anger at Zack in my need to tell him about everything I'd seen.

"Something's going on in that clinic, Zack. Something — evil. I need to talk to the police."

Zack raised an eyebrow. "Evil? That's strong language, Bailey. What do you intend to tell the police? You've no evidence of wrongdoing. Many people know of Winton's interest in Conch Republic memorabilia."

"But that scarf, that *special* scarf with the stain, may belong to a dead man. Mitch says Wizard has disappeared. Mitch and his friends have been searching for him for several days — with no luck."

"Can you prove the scarf belonged to, to this person you call Wizard?"

"I gave it to him, Zack. It's as simple as that. I bought the scarf from an airport vendor. It became grease stained when the cabbie caught it in the taxi door. The cabbie may remember the incident, if I need corroboration. I gave the scarf to Wizard, and I took a picture of him wearing it. That scarf, grease stain and all, is hanging on Gravely's wall, and I have a picture of him standing beside it. If you won't drive me to police headquarters, I'll drive there myself."

"Easy, Bailey, easy. Remember your injured leg. I'll take you wherever you want to go."

"Thanks, Zack. Police headquarters. I'll call Mitch on the way." Again, I corked my anger at Zack — for the moment — and forced myself to calm down. "Mitch's tried to get the police to search for Wizard, but no go."

"I can understand why." Zack headed for the police station while I tried to call Mitch. Seven rings. Then he picked up. I breathed again. What if he hadn't answered?

"What's the buzz?" Mitch asked, as if he knew who was calling.

"Any luck in finding Wizard?"

"None. He's gone and nobody's seen him since Wednesday."

"So listen up." After I told Mitch of my experience at Courtney's and at Gravely's clinic, I suggested we stop by for him.

"You sure your leg's up to chasing around?"

"My leg's fine. No pain."

"You're probably on pain pills. Probably can't tell if there's pain."

"Mitch!" I used my big-sister voice. "This trip to the police's top priority. Where can we find you?"

"Nowhere, Bailey. I'll ride my bike. Meet you at headquarters. I need my own transportation." He broke the connection before I could argue. So he didn't want Zack to see where he'd been living. Couldn't blame him.

"He'll meet us there, Zack."

Zack drove to the station and let me out by the entryway fountain while he parked in a visitor's slot. I checked my bandage. Good. No blood showing. And the pain pills were doing their thing. I only felt a slight numbness in my leg. My opinion of Dr. Gravely rose when I remembered his careful treatment of my wound, then it ebbed like low tide when I thought about Wizard's scarf hanging on the clinic wall. Dr. Jekyll? Mr. Hyde?

When Zack returned we entered the station, sitting on plastic chairs near the elevator while we waited for Mitch. If second-hand smoke causes lung cancer, I wondered why all of Key West's finest weren't its victims. I practiced shallow breathing.

After a few minutes Mitch arrived wearing his uniform of cutoff jeans and tank top. He padlocked his bike in a rack and joined us. We stood, and after curt greetings, Zack punched two on the elevator panel. The second floor was a trifle less smoky than the entryway. Zack approached the desk of a red-haired woman wearing a police uniform and a badge.

"I'm Officer Alverez, sir. How may I help you?" The phone on her desk rang and she turned to answer.

"Why didn't you ask for Cassidy or Burgundy?" I whispered while Officer Alverez played with her phone buttons.

"We're under enough suspicion from those two already. Don't want to alert them to a new problem. If there is a problem. Probably an exercise in craziness."

Officer Alverez ended her conversation and turned to us again. Mitch spoke before Zack could say anything.

"I'd like to speak to Sergeant Dominick, please. I've talked to him before concerning my missing friend."

I thought Officer Alverez raised an eyebrow, but I wasn't sure. She pushed a button and announced our presence to Sergeant Dominick.

"Follow me, please." She stood and led us to a small cubicle at the end of a long hallway. Opening the door, she announced our presence and then left. Beefy. Barrel chested. Bald. Sergeant Dominick looked like the type who hated working on Saturday afternoons. On his desk, a cigar smoldered in an ashtray that looked as if it hadn't been emptied any time lately.

"Have seats, please, and state your business." His gaze bored into Mitch, and Mitch leaned forward.

"I've come here again to report a missing person."

Sergeant Dominick pulled a legal-size pad of yellow paper from his desk drawer and poised a ballpoint over the top line. "Your name, please."

"Mitch Mitchell." Mitch supplied his name and address, and then Dominick requested the same information from Zack and me.

"Mr. Mitchell, what's your business here today?"

Dominick deliberately blew cigar smoke in my direction. Even Zack had to stifle a cough.

Mitch cleared his throat. "I'm here to

350

report again that my friend's missing. I know him as Wizard. He's a good guy, and he has lots of pals in the homeless community. He's been missing since Wednesday, and I want to know that the police are trying to find him."

"Wizard." Dominick mouthed the name as if it were a dirty word. "Where's he been missing from? He got an address?"

"Nothing permanent," Mitch said. "Few of the homeless have permanent addresses. But he gets mail at a post office box. You might be able to trace him through that."

"Maybe." Dominick shrugged. "Little chance, though. Probably only drops around to collect his social security check."

"Then the people at the post office must know his legal name. They won't tell us — his friends — but surely they'd tell the police, if the police were trying to trace his whereabouts."

"Our department's short on men and money. My guess's this guy, this Wizard's probably taken it on the lam of his own accord. Probably doesn't want to be found."

Mitch jumped up, eyes blazing, hands clenched. "My guess's that he's missing his friends and that something bad's happened to him."

"Be seated, please." Dominick waited until

351

Mitch sat. "Now what's your take on this? Why do you think something's happened to this person?"

"Wizard and I had plans for this afternoon, sir. Wizard likes kites. They fascinate him. He likes to watch them floating over Smather's beach. He's seen kites shaped like bats and triangles and boxes, but he wanted one shaped like a pirate's flag. A Jolly Roger."

"Isn't kite flying rather childish for a grown man?"

"I've seen lots of grown men on the beach flying kites. Tourists. Locals. Anyone who's interested in kites. It's a Key West thing — a Key West beach thing. I promised to give Wizard a Jolly Roger this afternoon. Had to order it special from the kite shop in Old Town, and he'd been looking forward all week to flying it — up until Wednesday, that is. That's the last time anyone saw him."

"So because this person missed a kite-flying appointment, you think something bad's happened to him."

"Yes, sir. I do."

Sergeant Dominick turned to eyeball Zack and me, and I spoke up. "I agree with Mr. Mitchell. I think his friend, Wizard, may be injured — or dead."

Sergeant Dominick never batted an eyelid.

"On what do you base that belief?"

Dominick took another pull on his cigar, and I began my story about Gravely and the Conch Republic flag.

"I can vouch for Wizard's ownership of that stained flag. An airport cabbie saw me buy it last Monday night. Mitch saw me give it to Wizard on Tuesday." I tapped my camera. "And I have a snapshot of Dr. Gravely with that same flag that now hangs on his clinic wall."

"Sir," Dominick said, looking at Zack, "are you acquainted with Wizard?"

"No sir," Zack said. "I am not. But I vouch for both Mr. Mitchell and Bailey Green. You can depend on what they say concerning this man."

Sergeant Dominick nodded, and he said nothing for a few minutes while he wrote on his legal pad and then held it toward me.

"Please read this and sign it. It's your statement of the facts you've told me today. It might be enough to prod some officers into searching for — Wizard."

I read the statement, making sure all the details were correct before I signed the page. Sergeant Dominick scrutinized my signature before he folded the sheet and slipped it into an envelope.

"I thank you for taking time to make this

report. You may go now. You'll be hearing from us if we have any news of — Wizard."

"And if we don't hear from you, may we call for further information?" I asked.

"If you must." Dominick rose, ran a hand over his bald head, then left his cigar smoldering in the ashtray.

Once we were outside the station, I inhaled. What a neat thing to breathe fresh air!

"You wait here," Zack said to me. "I'll get the car and pick you up."

I didn't argue, knowing my words would make no difference.

"I want to talk to hear more about Gravely and his clinic," Mitch said. "May I stop by the cottage?"

"Of course." I looked at Zack's Thunderbird. "Why don't you bike over? We'll meet you there."

When Zack and I reached the cottage, he came inside, helped me to the couch, and pulled up a footstool for my leg. I felt as if I should apologize to him for my anger, for running to Courtney for help. But no. Not now. Plenty of time later for apologies — and making up.

"Any pain?"

"No." I examined the bandage. "No blood, either."

354

Maybe Zack was right. Maybe I was a little jealous of Courtney. But only a little. I'd decided not to let her rush me into searching for an apartment. But that had been my idea, not hers. Hadn't it? The day's happenings left me wondering about a lot of things.

By the time Mitch arrived, Zack had set out a pitcher of iced tea from my refrigerator and added a dish of M&Ms and a plate of chips. Soul food.

"I want to hear your story again," Mitch said. "I want to hear everything that happened at Gravely's clinic. And then I want to tell you something."

"You go first," I said. "As you might say — what's the buzz?"

"The buzz from me is that I realize I've been wrong about a lot of things. I thought I could help Wizard. I blamed the cops for his plight. I didn't think they gave a stuffed shrimp about him or about trying to help the homeless. Their attitude made me mad. I began trying to bargain with them and with Wizard. I thought that by letting him know he had a true friend, I could change him and help reunite him with his family. Wrong. The whole scene depresses me."

"You tried, Mitch. You gave it a good shot."

"But Wizard didn't want to be reunited with anyone, did he? I've driven him away. If he's hurt and in trouble, it's all my fault. I'm ready to go to social services, to local ministers and their charities, with my apologies and my offer to work with them, to help. They're the professionals. They're the ones who understand the homeless and their situation."

"I don't want to hear anymore about any of this," Zack said. "I'm outta here. Gravely's my friend. He overlooked Bailey's trespassing on his boat. He opened his private clinic to her when she needed help. I have no way of explaining his wall hangings. I'll admit the circumstances surrounding the scarf are unusual, but the police have that info now. It's out of our hands."

Zack had shoved his iced tea aside and headed for the door when Detectives Cassidy and Burgundy arrived, strode toward the cottage, and knocked. Zack let them in and before any of us could say anything, Cassidy spoke.

"Mr. Mitchell, we're here to ask you to come with us to headquarters for questioning concerning the Shipton murder."

Had I seen a momentary flash of satisfaction cross Zack's face? Had he tipped the police that they could find Mitch here? I bit my tongue to hold back my anger.

"I have a choice?" Mitch asked. "I can refuse?"

"We hope you'll come with us willingly," Cassidy said. "If you refuse we can get a court —"

"This can't be happening." I jumped to my feet, forgetting about my injured leg. "You can't take Mitch away against his will. You have no proof of his guilt. None at all." Then I turned to Mitch. "You need a lawyer. Don't say a word to these men without a lawyer present."

30

"We'll see that Mr. Mitchell has a lawyer," Detective Cassidy said, "if he wants one."

"I can't afford a lawyer," Mitch said.

"Then the court will appoint one," Cassidy said. "You'll have legal representation."

"Sure he will," I said. "You'll appoint some twad of a lawyer who's been unable to get a client on his own for years. This isn't fair! I want to go to the police station with you. Zack? Zack, you'll go along, too, won't you?"

Detective Cassidy gave me his full attention. "Miss Green, your behavior is highly unusual. What's your special interest in Mr. Mitchell?"

I dropped back onto the couch and elevated my leg on the footstool, realizing I'd said too much. It was bad enough that they intended to question Mitch. He'd be in even worse trouble if I gave away his witness-in-protection status.

"Miss Green?" Cassidy's gaze bored into me.

"My only interest in Mr. Mitchell lies in knowing Francine Shipton considered him a trusted employee. She read people well. She'd never have offered employment to a . . . a murderer."

"The court will be the judge of that," Cassidy said. Then he looked at Mitch. "Let's go."

I stood again, but Mitch avoided my gaze. Facing the door, he walked between the detectives to the police car. Cassidy opened the passenger door and nudged him onto the seat while Burgundy sat on the backseat behind him. Tears burned behind my eyelids, and my throat felt stiff as a steel gaff when I watched the car leave.

"This can't be happening, Zack. They can't take Mitch away like this. They can't."

"But they did. I'm sorry, Bailey." Zack wrapped his arms around me and kissed my forehead, my eyelids, my lips, and, forgetting my anger at him, I returned his kisses before we broke apart.

"Zack, we have to do something to help. What if they arrest him?"

Zack shook his head. "They didn't say anything about arresting him. I can understand why they want to question a guy who had both opportunity and motive to murder."

"Opportunity, yes. That's true. Mitch had the opportunity. Francine gave him the run of the house and the grounds. But motive? Mitch had no motive. No motive at all. He wanted to help the homeless and the helpless. Seems to me he'd have wanted Francine to live, to establish her shelter annex."

"You may be right, I suppose. I sympathize with you, but you'll have to admit that your brother's life and lifestyle are unique."

"Right. And if the police dig into his background, their snooping's going to put him in danger."

"I think he's already in danger — if not from the police here, then from the meth barons in Iowa. But maybe Mitch has an alibi for last Monday afternoon."

"He does. Airtight. He told me that. He spent the late Monday afternoon working at Two Friends Patio with Quinn Bahama. She'll vouch for him."

Zack smiled. "That's good news. If you feel up to it, maybe we should talk to Quinn right now. Maybe she'd be willing to go with us to the police station if it'd help Mitch out of a tight spot."

"You think they might release him?"

"That's a possibility. How's your leg?"

"No pain. No blood. Let's go." I started to get up, then I sank back onto the couch.

"What's the problem?"

"The last time I saw Quinn, she yelled at me and stormed off in a rage."

"Maybe she's softened up by now. It's worth a chance."

"Right. It is. But I'll feel rotten if she won't help us, if I've accidentally hurt Mitch."

"You're borrowing trouble. Shall we call Quinn at the restaurant, or take our chances and show up at her door?"

"Let's take our chances. I hate facing her, but a call would make it too easy for her to say no."

Zack helped me into the car and we drove to Old Town. Even with his good parking karma, we couldn't find a legal spot. We stopped in a tow-away zone, and he left the motor running.

"Hope the cops are too busy on Duval to notice." He turned on emergency blinkers. "Wait while I try to find Quinn? If the police give you a bad time, drive on. Circle the block."

"Will do."

Zack returned before I had time to worry about being towed.

"Her shift starts a little later. Think she'll

be at home?"

"Guess it's worth a try."

Zack threaded our way through Old Town and drove to the A-frame where we'd boarded the helicopter. Even in daylight tropical growth almost masked the house, which was set a short distance from the 'copter pad.

"Want me to go to the door first?" Zack asked.

I squelched a "yes." "Let's both go. It's harder to refuse two people, right?"

Zack opened the car door for me then offered his arm. I tried to avoid putting all my weight on my injured leg, and Zack slid his arm around my waist to offer support. I liked his nearness. When we reached the house, the door stood open. No doorbell. No knocker. Zack gave a sharp rap on the screen door. Quinn appeared almost immediately.

"Oh!"

She started to smile at Zack, but the smile faded when she saw me.

"We need to talk to you, Quinn," Zack said.

"What about?" She didn't open the door.

"About one of your coworkers at the restaurant — Mitch Mitchell. You know him, right?"

"Yes, of course I know him. The dish-washer."

"He's in trouble," Zack said. "And you can help him."

"What kind of trouble? And how can I help? I really know little about him other than that he's a good dishwasher. Dependable."

"May we come inside?" Zack asked.

Quinn sighed and opened the door. I knew she wanted to smile at Zack, but she couldn't without including me, whom she didn't want to smile at ever again. She led us into a room that served as living area, family area, dining area. The room with its white-paneled walls and wicker furniture padded with yellow cushions made a charming backdrop for Quinn's blondness.

"Okay," Quinn said once we were seated. "What's up?" She glanced at her watch. "I'm due at work in half an hour."

"We'll be brief," Zack said.

Quinn focused on Zack. I felt invisible. Zack explained Mitch's predicament and waited for Quinn's response.

"This guy could be a cold-blooded murderer and you're asking me to vouch for him?"

"That's right." I spoke up. "He's innocent, and you can help prove it by telling the police you were working together at the time of Francine's death."

I'd frequently read about heavy silences. Zack and I experienced one. In the distance, gulls screamed. Closer by, a kitchen clock ticked. The refrigerator clicked on. Quinn sat silent as a chunk of coral and gave me a withering look.

"Quinn," I pleaded. "Please come with us to police headquarters and tell the detectives you were working with Mitch last Monday."

"Why is Mitch Mitchell, a dishwasher, so important to you?" Quinn scowled. "You gonna immortalize him by writing a song about him or something?" She jutted her chin and looked in my direction without allowing her gaze to meet mine.

"Come on, Quinn," Zack said. "Here's your chance to help a guy — a guy without friends in Key West. The cops may be locking him in a cell as we speak. Your vouching for him could change his life."

"No."

"Why not?" I demanded.

"Because." Quinn glared at me again.

"Quinn, please do this for me. You're a journalist, a fair-minded person. Speak up for Mitch Mitchell. His plight may be one you can write about later. You could make banner headlines in the *Citizen*."

"No."

Zack leaned forward. "I've done several things to help your husband, Quinn."

"I know that. Ben and I appreciate your help and concern."

"So I'm calling in a marker or two," Zack said. "You can help this man. I don't understand why you're refusing."

"If it's because of my refusal to help you a few days ago . . ." I let my voice trail away, wondering what to say next.

"If this guy's so lily pure, his innocence will come out later. Surely, there'll be more than one person who'll testify in his behalf."

"We can't be sure of that," I said. "Think about this murder, Quinn. The police are tippy-toeing around it big time. They don't want to arrest one of the wealthy Shipton neighbors. They don't want to arrest Francine's son and heir. But now they've found a scapegoat. They won't have to ruffle any feathers. How easy it'll be to blame the murder on the itinerant yardman, the lowly dishwasher. Who do you think will stand up for this guy if you refuse?"

For a moment I thought Quinn might storm from the room and leave us sitting alone. Instead, she burst into tears. Wracking sobs. Zack rose and walked to her, took her hand in his.

"What's wrong, Quinn? We didn't come here to cause you grief."

Quinn sobbed until she ran out of sobs. I studied her. She's the kind who can weep without her face getting red as a channel marker, without her nose running like high tide, without her eyes swelling like a puffer fish. How does she manage that?

Zack patted her shoulder. "Come on, Quinn. If you've a problem with Mitch, maybe we can help you."

Quinn sighed and leaned back in her chair. "Excuse the cliché, but I'm between a dock piling and a boat hull. I can't vouch for Mitch last Monday without putting my marriage at risk."

"Your marriage?" I leaned forward. "You're having an affair with Mitch?"

"No. No, of course not. But that's what Ben might suspect. Ben seems like an easygoing shrimper to most people. Not so. He hides his insecurity well."

"Are you saying Ben's jealous of Mitch?" I asked.

Quinn shrugged. "I hope not. But that's why I told him I was working with Mazie Younkers last Monday. A little white lie, right? I thought it'd put Ben at ease. There's nothing going on between Mitch and me."

"But Ben tends to be jealous," Zack guessed. "And I can understand that, Quinn. With a pretty wife like you . . ."

"I really want to do the right thing," Quinn said. "But yes, Ben's jealous of the people I associate with while he's out shrimping. I love the guy and I love my marriage."

"Quinn," Zack said. "If I promise you the police will never reveal your vouching for Mitch, will you tell them your story?"

"Can you make that promise and make it stick?" Quinn asked.

"Yes," Zack said. "It'll stick for today at least. But if you should be called upon to testify in court later, will you do that?"

Quinn hesitated and I spoke. "Quinn, if you'll do that for me, I'll make a deal with you."

"What sort of a deal?"

"I'll give you the lead to a story about a missing person. I won't do any investigating for you. Digging for details will be up to you. But I can tell you for sure that there's a homeless person missing from this city, a person who already may be dead. And Mitch Mitchell may have important information about that person."

"That's a lot of mays," Quinn said.

"Right, but isn't that how good stories

start? You handle this material well and it'll make headlines. You could find yourself on the staff at the *Citizen.*"

"I have a few friends at the newspaper," Zack said. "You write that story, and I'll see that it gets into the right hands."

The clock ticked thirty long seconds before Quinn made up her mind.

31

"All right," Quinn said at last. "I'll do what I can for Mitch, and I'll expect you to keep my secret. No squealing to Ben. As far as Ben knows, I was working with Mazie Younkers."

"Right," Zack agreed. "That's the way it'll be. Can you come with us to the station now?"

Quinn glanced at her watch. "I have a little time before I need to report at Two Friends, but I have to get dressed — in uniform and ready to work. Who knows how long I'll have to be at the station! Why don't I drive and meet you there?"

"Fine with me." Zack stood and made a show of helping me up. If Quinn noticed my limp, she didn't mention it. "See you at the station in about fifteen minutes, okay?"

"I'll be there."

Quinn watched from her doorway until we passed the helicopter pad and turned from her driveway.

"Don't worry," Zack said, reading my mind. "She'll show. She and Ben are decent people. Dependable people." Zack grinned. "That's important on an island, where 'I'll be there' usually means I'll be there if it isn't a good fishing day and I decide to drown a few bait shrimp."

"Zack, please take me home. I have an important errand and I need my own car. I'll be at the station as soon as I can."

"Well . . . okay. But you need to give your leg plenty of rest. Don't want the wound to open."

"Ever feel a need to be two places at the same time? I want to be at headquarters to speak up for Mitch, but I need to go to the Phrame Shop to have some film developed, film that may help prove his innocence."

"Maybe Mitch would be better off without you vouching for him. You heard Cassidy question your interest in a gardener. Your relationship with Mitch looks strange to those out of the loop."

"Right. I don't want to have to explain to the detectives. But, soon as I'm finished at the Phrame Shop, I'll come to the police station."

"Fine. You have the film with you?"

I pulled my camera from around my neck

and opened it, sorry to have to ruin the rest of the unexposed film. "Some shots here might help Mitch prove that Wizard is missing and may need help."

"Go easy, Bailey. If Wizard's missing, there's a good reason for his absence. If he's involved in illegal activities, the cops may be on his trail. There are lots of authorities besides the police. Marine patrol. Shore patrol."

We had reached Eden Palms, and Zack drove me to the carport. "Got your keys? Sure you feel up to making this trip alone? I could drive us to the station then take you to the photo shop later."

"My leg feels fine. No pain at all. Don't worry about me. I feel fine. I'll do my errand and then meet you and Quinn as we planned." I left the convertible before he could come around and open the door for me.

"Easy, Bailey. Easy."

"Thanks, Zack. 'Bye and thanks for everything." I tried not to limp when I walked to the Lincoln and slid under the wheel.

"I hate goodbyes," Zack called. "Don't make our parting sound so final. I'll see you in a few minutes."

Thank goodness it was my left leg I'd injured. Driving was no biggie. Even so,

Zack waited for me to leave the carport, watched while I turned toward the Searstown mall, and followed me until he reached his turnoff.

One great thing about Searstown is the plethora of unmetered parking spaces. I claimed a slot right in front of the Photo and Phrame Shop. It sat tucked between a pawn shop and an ice-cream bar. I smiled at Free, short for "Free Throw," Glockner behind the counter. All the locals know Free, a former basketball star for the high school Conchs. Tall, black, and handsome, he towered over me when I pulled the film from my purse.

"And I suppose you're in a hurry — as usual?" His velvet-smooth voice matched the smile that flashed easily from his lips to his eyes. In the few times I'd visited Key West, I'd called on Free to help me out now and then. He was one of the few people who understood that when I needed a picture to help me write a descriptive ballad, I needed it yesterday.

"This time I'm in a *big* hurry, Free. How soon can you get this roll developed and printed?"

Free looked around his empty shop and gave a shrug along with a palms-up gesture. "Got nobody breathing down my neck. It's been a snail-pace afternoon. You watch the counter while I do the dark room thing, and I'll have your pics out in a few minutes."

"Deal. Anyone comes in, I'll call you."

"You might consider investing in a digital camera, Bailey. I carry several brands."

"No way." I patted the camera hanging around my neck. "At least no way as long as my old camera still works."

Nobody came in. It seemed like hours, but it was only minutes, until Free opened the darkroom door and beckoned. "Want to see? Got the pics out of solution hanging to dry."

I rushed to look at the pictures dangling from a thin line stretched above a work counter. The room smelled of lotions and potions I couldn't identify, but I was interested in the film, not the smells.

"How they look to you?" Free asked. "Get the ones you wanted?"

I studied the shots one by one, my heart pounding when I realized the one with Gravely and the flag looked clear and well defined. And so did the one with Wizard wearing his scarf. I grinned my approval.

"How long before I can take them with me?"

"Very shortly. Give me a few more minutes. Need extra copies?"

I selected two shots. "Three each of these, please, and only one of the others."

I watched until Free was almost finished making the prints before I dashed to the ice-cream bar next door and ordered him a triple chocolate malt. I'd been planning to resist, but temptation won out. I ordered a triple for myself, too. Free and I weren't into worrying about cholesterol, and the malts paved my path to a friendly business relationship with him.

While Free slurped his malt, I set mine aside and selected the prints I wanted. "I need three envelopes, please."

Free stopped slurping long enough to find the envelopes.

I placed copies of Wizard wearing the scarf and copies of Gravely beside the flag into three separate envelopes. After labeling one envelope for me, one for the police, and the third for Zack, I left Zack's envelope with Free.

"Please take special care of that special envelope, Free. Give it to nobody except Zack Shipton. You know Zack, right?"

"Right. Everyone knows Zack."

I paid Free, adding a mega-tip in addition to the malt. Picking up my own treat, I left the shop and headed for the Lincoln. I keyed in my combination on the lock pad.

Nothing. My hands shook. What a rotten time for mechanical failure! I set my malt on the hood while I dug in my purse for the door key, the ignition key.

"Having trouble?" Dr. Gravely drove up beside me and called through his open window.

Drat! Was he going to scold me for ignoring his proper-care rules for my leg? My stomach tightened when he left his car and stood beside me smiling, while I continued to fumble for my car keys.

"Bailey, it's good you're able to be out and about with that leg. Has it been giving you any problem? Any additional bleeding?"

I hesitated, trying to find words more adequate and time-consuming than "no." I sensed Gravely hadn't come to check on my leg or to pass the time of day. What was he doing here? What could he want?

"My leg's doing great, Dr. Gravely. You've done an excellent repair job." As soon as I managed to unlock my car door, I started to get inside. Gravely put a hand on my arm.

"Wait, Bailey."

"What is it? I'm really in a rush. Zack's waiting —"

"Yes, Zack's waiting. That's why I'm here. Zack's worried about your trying to drive with that injured leg. He asked me to pick you up, take you to Eden Palms. He promised to send someone for your car later."

Liar! My thoughts whirled in a maze of fear and anger. I knew Gravely was lying when a tic contorted his cheek. Zack wasn't at home. He'd watched me leave. He knew I wasn't having driving problems. I glanced at the photo shop, hoping Free might be watching. But no. He was nowhere in sight. In fact there was nobody in sight, nobody out and about at the moment. But a blast on my car horn might bring someone.

I reached toward the steering wheel, but Gravely caught my arm and jerked me toward him.

"Let me go!" I shouted. "Right now! Let me go!"

I jerked my arm from his grasp, but he reached into his jacket pocket. When I looked down, he was aiming a gun at my heart.

"Shut up. Get into my car."

His words numbed me, and he nudged me toward his car with the gun barrel. Would he shoot me in the Searstown lot? I remembered words from a long-ago lecture on women's safety. *Run! Don't get in that car!* But running wasn't an option. Terror paralyzed me.

32

I couldn't see through his car's tinted windows, but when Gravely opened the door behind the driver's seat and shoved me toward it, I smelled the cloying scent that traveled with Tucker Tisdale. Funeral flowers? Embalming fluid? No long sleeves hid his arms today, and the sight of his peeling skin sickened me. I shuddered in fear and revulsion. In the next moment, I saw the gun in his right hand, the duct tape in his left hand, a coil of clothesline on the floor.

"Good afternoon, Bailey." Tisdale's falsetto voice chilled me. "How about a pleasure ride?"

I clenched my teeth and backed away until I felt the prod of Gravely's gun. *Run! Run!* My mind screamed the order, but my legs balked. Three kids on mopeds zoomed into the parking lot. I shouted. Their boom box blared hard rock. They didn't hear me. Free approached his shop window to watch the mopeders, but before I could call again for help, Gravely jabbed me with his gun.

"Get in the car. Now."

"Where are you taking me?" Again, I tried to back away.

"Shut up. Get in." He pressed against me, shoved me.

I slid onto the seat beside Tisdale. Gravely slammed the door. *Once a captor forces you inside his car, you have little chance of escape. You're facing death — a violent death.* The safety lecture replayed through my mind, but if it had contained a solution for surviving, I couldn't remember it.

"Shall I tie her up?" Tisdale's voice squeaked. He kicked the rope with his toe.

"Not yet," Gravely said. "Too risky. We need privacy. Keep your gun on her."

Gravely started the car, and the door locks clicked as we moved forward. He inched toward an exit. I looked over my shoulder at the Phrame Shop. No one in sight. Pausing only a moment at a stop sign, Gravely eased closer to the highway, waiting to nose the car into the stream of traffic.

My last chance of escape. Go! Now! I leaned forward. But no. Tisdale dropped the duct tape onto the coiled rope and grabbed my arm, restraining me. I eyed the door lock. Could I jerk free and yank up that button? Open the door? Run? Tisdale's grip tightened.

"Don't even think about it." He leered at me, following my gaze. "You're not going anywhere, Bailey. We've too much to lose to let you escape."

Too much to lose? What was he talking about! "Where are you taking me?"

"Be patient and all will soon be revealed to you," Tisdale squeaked.

A kind motorist slowed enough to allow Gravely to enter the stream of traffic. We were on our way.

"Where are we going?" I demanded. "Where are you taking me? You're not getting away with this. My friends will miss me and come searching."

Silence.

"Zack's waiting for me. We have an appointment. He's expecting me and I'm already late. He'll be looking for me."

"Save your breath, babe." Tisdale's laugh carried menace and now that we were moving in heavy traffic, he released my arm. "We're whisking you to a secret place, a place where Zack'll never find you. Zack nor anyone else."

Suddenly, car horns blared. Brakes screamed. Drivers shouted and flipped road-rage salutes to a mopeder who cut in front of a Bone Island Shuttle, narrowly escaping injury. A wreck, I thought. Please God, let there be a wreck. Let traffic back up for miles and stop us. But traffic paused only an instant and then flowed ahead.

Gravely drove beside the bay, where white-sailed boats skimmed across the water. Closer at hand joggers ran along the sidewalk two abreast. Three kids on skateboards defied the law of gravity, jumping over cracks in the concrete. When we arrived at the turnoff to Old Town, Gravely hung a right and we passed Garrison Bight and the docks where fishing party boats would soon be arriving with their day's catch.

I guessed Gravely's destination — the marina. What better way to get rid of me than to force me aboard his boat, bind me, and drop me overboard? Would he tie a concrete block to my feet to be sure my body would sink quickly? I imagined the scene, imagined sharks and 'cudas snapping off my toes and fingers, arms and legs.

Could these men get by with *another* murder? Now I felt sure they had murdered Francine to keep her from opening a homeless shelter in their elegant neighborhood. I felt sure they had murdered Wizard. But why? I couldn't figure out the why of that one. And me? Why did they need to get rid of me? None of this made sense.

Gravely turned onto Grinnell Street, where a motorist braked suddenly, undecided about making a left turn into the parking ramp. Behind us horns blared. Tisdale leaned forward.

"Pass him. Pass him!"

Gravely had no room to pass and traffic behind us screeched to a stop.

Now! Now's your chance!

Catching Tisdale by surprise, I yanked up on the lock button, opened the car door, jumped into the street. The jolt from car to concrete made my leg throb. So what! Better a bum leg than a dead body. I ran, expecting a bullet to slam into my back.

Run! Run! Now what? Clear thinking eluded me, yet I knew I couldn't depend on the goodness of a stranger for help. If I stopped running to approach a car, Gravely would be on my tail. *Doctor* Gravely. I imagined him identifying himself in sonorous tones and flashing his medical I.D., confident that strangers would give it immediate respect.

How easy for Gravely to call me a crazy who had wandered from his clinic, a mentally ill patient in need — a creature to be pitied. How easy for him to lovingly tuck me into the safety of his car. Few people argue with a doctor. Parents ingrain such deference in their offspring from childhood.

I ran in the only direction open to me — into the parking ramp. I dashed past the elevator on my right. If Gravely left his car and gave chase, he could follow me, trap me in there. Ha! I wouldn't give him that chance. The throbbing in my leg worsened and my lungs burned. I gasped for air, ignoring all pain. I ran for my life.

"Stop!" Gravely shouted. "I see you. Make it easy on yourself. Give yourself up."

Where was he? I needed time. I'd hoped it'd take him longer to escape the traffic snarl. Did he really see me? Could he? His voice echoed eerily, bouncing off the concrete walls. Had he shouted through his open car window? Or had he given chase on foot? My heart revved to a hard tom-tom thumping. I had to rest. I needed to recover my sense of direction and place — to recover my sense of *his* direction and place.

I ducked behind a salt-encrusted SUV, panting for breath. For a few moments I heard only my own breathing, the street traffic, the screech of distant gulls. Where had my captors gone? Then, peeking around the back of the SUV, I saw Gravely's car nose up the parking ramp, turn into an empty slot a few cars below me, and stop. I ducked from sight. Two car doors slammed and footsteps grated against concrete. Both men pounded toward my hiding place.

"Come on out, Bailey," Tisdale tried to entice me from behind the SUV.

"Save us all a lot of time and trouble," Gravely added. "Speak up. Where are you?"

Where, I wondered, was the parking attendant? Coffee break? Or maybe the kiosk where he sat was soundproof. I waited. The only way to run was up and I heard Gravely and Tisdale coming closer. If I stayed put, they'd soon see me. If I ran, they'd soon see me. I'd been a fool to jump to freedom. I'd have been a fool to stay in their car.

Trying for silence, I eased around to the hood of the SUV, slumped down, and crammed my body between the car's grill and the retaining wall. I raised my feet in case they looked beneath the cars, and for a few moments I suspended myself between SUV and concrete. My breath came in thready gasps, noisy gasps. I held my breath when I heard them approaching.

"Bailey," Gravely called again. "We see you. Come on out."

I knew neither captor had seen me, and I inhaled again once they passed the SUV. I had a few moments of respite while they trudged on toward the top of the ramp. Would I have extra moments of freedom while they paused to enjoy a panoramic view of their surroundings? Not. A view of the city would be last on their current list of things to see and do in Paradise.

I toyed with the idea of retreating back down the ramp and hiding nearby until they left the area. I'd noticed scrub palms, crotons, hibiscus bushes. Then I had a better idea. At least it seemed better at the moment. I walked down the ramp to Gravely's car, unscrewed the valve cap from his right front tire, pressed the stem. Some child-like urge made me want to giggle while the air hissed out. I squelched that urge. Had they heard me? Detecting no noise from them, I scurried around the car and began flattening the other front tire.

"Hey!" Tisdale shouted. "Listen! She's letting the air out of our tires! Hear it?"

"She won't get away from us," Gravely said. "She has to be close."

Right. Too close. I hunched over, too near to them for my own well being. Then I saw an open convertible only three slots from Gravely's car. In a moment I jumped inside it and ducked from sight, silently thanking a person so trusting he'd left his convertible top down.

"I saw her," Gravely shouted. "She's in that rag-top."

In moments they held me captive again.

"You bitch!" Gravely spat the words at me. "Come with us if you want to live."

"Can it," Tisdale said to Gravely. "Someone's coming."

True. Someone was coming, but by the time they took their parking ticket from the machine and reached us, Gravely had shoved me at gunpoint back into his car, and Tisdale sat smiling at me as if we were long-lost friends. The car passed us without its occupants looking in our direction.

"What do we do about the tires?" Tisdale asked.

"I'll call Monroe Tire & Auto," Gravely said. "You take her for a walk. Keep her out of sight until we're mobile again."

"No way," Tisdale said. "She said Zack's looking for her. I'm not going to be the one he catches holding her captive."

"Okay," Gravely said. "Bad thinking on my part. Stay here. Keep your pistol trained on her and don't say a word."

Capture. Escape. Recapture. Exhaustion and terror left me limp and my leg throbbed. I wished Tisdale had agreed to take me for a walk. I might have yelled for help if Gravely hadn't been present to call me insane. But now Gravely pulled out his cell phone and keyed in the service garage. After a long wait, a tow truck arrived. Even with the windows rolled up, I could hear Gravely explaining to the serviceman that kids had let the air out of the tires.

"Yeah, kids." The mechanic shrugged and inflated the tires. "Lucky they didn't slash them. Slashing's one of their favorite tricks."

Gravely signed some papers, the serviceman left, and we were off again. Gravely paid the parking attendant and we left the ramp.

"Think you're smart, don't you?" Gravely glanced over his shoulder at me. "Well, all you did was cause yourself a lot of trouble. You're no better off than you were."

Tisdale scowled and nudged me with his gun. "And now you've made us mad."

I wondered if Zack had missed me. Maybe he was searching for me right this minute. I live in possibility.

"Where are you taking me?" I didn't expect an answer, but there was a remote chance they might reveal something. There was a slight chance that if I knew our destination, I could do something to change it, to thwart their plans. I felt almost sure they were heading toward the marina where

Gravely kept his speedboat, but instead of turning in that direction, he drove to White-head Street, turned on Eaton and drove slowly until we reached the turnoff to Eden Palms. What a round-about route they'd taken. Maybe they'd been making sure they weren't followed.

33

Gravely passed Eden Palms, drove to his clinic, and rolled the car into the attached garage behind it. A dim bulb barely lighted the area, and when he opened the rear door, I smelled an odor of gasoline.

"Out." Gravely pushed a button and the garage door began to close. Although I had little chance of escaping, I lunged forward, pushed around him, and ran toward the closing door.

Both men sprang into action. Gravely grabbed me, pinning my arms to my sides while Tisdale wrapped duct tape around my legs.

"Do her arms, too," Gravely ordered. "Now."

Although my bound legs left me off balance, I flailed my arms, striking out against both men. Hopeless. Tisdale slammed me against the car and held me there with the pressure of his hip while he helped Gravely grab my arms and tape them together.

Although I could neither walk nor protect myself, Gravely wrapped more tape around my eyes. Tisdale laughed. They picked me up, one at my shoulders, the other at my feet. I could only guess they were taking me into the clinic.

"Easy," Gravely warned. "Don't want to damage her."

My spirits spiked for a moment. Maybe they were going to let me live!

"Where are you taking me?"

"Operating room," Gravely said. "You'll understand why soon enough."

Again, fear paralyzed me. Were these two mad scientists who experimented on unwilling patients, performing surgery that left the victim in a vegetative state? I could barely speak, but my voice was my only weapon. I mustered strength and screamed.

"Shall I tape her mouth?" Tisdale asked.

"No need. I dismissed my patient to her family earlier. We're alone."

I stopped screaming. I felt them carry me up a short staircase and heard them snap on some lights before they lifted me onto a bed — a hard bed — the gurney. I'd been here before.

"I'll ready the steamer while you untape her eyes," Gravely ordered. "Don't want to damage the eyes. Go easy with the tape."

Tisdale eased the tape from my eyelids fraction of an inch by fraction of an inch, lifting it carefully until I could open both eyes. I lay in the same room I'd occupied when Gravely treated my leg. Gravely clicked on an overhead spotlight that gleamed on surgical instruments lying on a table near the gurney as well as on many stainless steel pans and a stack of Styrofoam coolers.

"Loosen her feet."

Gravely had barely given the order when Tisdale began removing the duct tape from my ankles.

"Easy now," Gravely said. "Easy. Leg bones are valuable. Let me help you."

"What about her injured leg?" Tisdale asked.

Gravely checked the bandage. "No more bleeding. I did a good job. It looks fine. We may lose some tissue around the wound, but only a little. Bone's in good shape."

When my legs were free, I kicked at my captors, but they grabbed my ankles and used strips of terrycloth towels to tie both legs to the gurney. Then they untaped my arms. I struck out with enough force to knock off Tisdale's glasses. He swore as they clattered to the floor. But in the next minute they grabbed my arms and bound them to the gurney.

Walking to a closet, Gravely flung open the door and removed two white lab jackets. He thrust one at Tisdale and donned the other one himself. Both men washed their hands before they pulled on surgical gloves.

"Got to keep things sterile," Tisdale said, as if I'd asked.

"Off with her clothes." Gravely pulled two pair of scissors from the hissing steamer near the sink, handing Tisdale one pair and keeping the other pair. Both men clicked the scissor blades as if testing them for sharpness.

For a moment I thought I still had a chance of escape. When they unbound my arms and legs to undress me, I'd fight for my life. Whatever they intended to do, I'd flail and strike out. I'd make it difficult for them, if not impossible. But it didn't happen that way.

Both men began cutting my clothing away. Tisdale worked from the top. Shirt. Bra. He grinned at me, winked, and let his hand cup my right breast before he dropped the garments onto the floor. Gravely worked on the rest of my clothing. Slacks. Panties. After many snips, I lay nude. Gravely eased my sandals off and dropped them onto my mutilated clothes. Never before had I felt so violated. Anger flooded my body with pulsing heat at the same time terror chilled my being.

When I lay there naked, spread-eagled and helpless, Gravely ran his cool hands over each leg, ankle to crotch, and then nodded to Tisdale. Tisdale repeated a similar action on my arms, wrists to shoulders, winking when he let his fingers brush against my breast. My body broke out in goose bumps. When I tried to scream, no sound came.

"Perfect specimens," Tisdale said.

"Get the face cone while I prepare the solution," Gravely ordered.

For a moment, Tisdale disappeared from my sight, and I heard him open a cupboard behind me and begin moving pans. Metal scraped metal.

"It's right there in front of you," Gravely said. "Beside that stainless steel bowl."

"Right," Tisdale said. "I see it now."

Tisdale stepped into my view, carrying a mesh cone-shaped object. Frantically, I turned my head this way and that, trying to keep him from placing the cone over my nose and mouth.

"Ease up," Gravely ordered. "Back off. Don't hurt her. It'll take me a minute or so to ready the solution."

"What are you going to do to me?" Panic left my voice sounding thready and weak.

"We're going to make you a hero," Gravely laughed.

"Right." Tisdale winked at me. "You're going to make lots of people very, very happy. You're going to be one of the eight thousand body donors who leave their organs to science each year."

"How?" Horror was an icy balloon inflating inside me. "What are you getting ready to do?"

"Surely you've guessed by now." Gravely laughed again. "We'll put you in a coma — give you a knock-out drop or two while I harvest your body parts. Lungs. Liver. Kidneys. To be of value they must be taken from a living person. Rest assured we'll let nothing go to waste and you'll feel no pain."

"You can't do this to me." My shout escalated to a shriek. "No! No! No!"

Tisdale laughed. "A single heart valve might bring us ten thou. Knee cartilage, fourteen. Millions of people have arthritic knees. They'd pay almost any price for cartilage that might preclude knee surgery and ease their pain. You'll be an unknown hero in their eyes."

"There's a special demand for kidneys," Gravely said.

"Right," Tisdale agreed. "People in need spend hours on dialysis machines waiting for months, even years, for someone to donate a healthy kidney."

"Tucker and I have worked together for months now — surgeon and undertaker. When someone in my clinic dies, I have the equipment and the know-how to harvest body parts and deliver them to black-market dealers quickly and in prime condition. Tucker handles the funerals. I take only a few parts from each body, and his work disguises my mutilations from grieving families. You're a bonanza for us — all parts available and no family on scene."

"Too bad Francine's body went to waste," Tisdale said. "No way we could harvest any parts with the police around. There would have been many calls for her organs."

"Yes, there are many uses for a cadaver." Gravely stood out of my sight. I could hear him pouring liquid, mixing a solution. "Sometimes the army has used whole cadavers — blowing them up as they search for land-mine-resistant footwear. Your body might spare some soldier from losing a foot or a leg."

"That's a lie," Tisdale said. "We're not selling your body as a whole. It'd only bring us a pittance. The real money lies in harvesting your parts and selling them individually for use in hospitals or research labs. But cut the talk. You don't need to know so much."

"What does it matter?" Gravely snorted. "She's not going to live to reveal anything she's heard here. Nothing. Nada."

For the first time, I noticed a power saw lying on a counter top near the stainless steel sinks. I closed my eyes and gritted my teeth. I thought of my mother and how we'd spent weeks studying the body donor program before we'd decided to bequeath our remains to the University of Iowa's transplant program in the altruistic hope of helping others lead a better life.

We'd pictured our bodies being gently and carefully dissected by grateful teachers at medical schools, by respectful students. We certainly hadn't suspected that our body parts might be gleaned with a power saw and sold by hardened crooks for profit.

"You're making a huge mistake if you think no one will miss me," I warned. Where was Zack? Didn't he wonder why I hadn't returned to the police station?

"There's no way to stop us." Gravely continued to mix and stir. Metal scraped metal. I felt sick, humiliated. My stomach churned. What if I vomited? I'd heard of people choking on their own vomit.

"We have contacts." Tisdale tried to fit the cone over my face again, and again I fought it, turning my head from side to side until he called to Gravely in frustration.

"You'll have to help me with this one, Winton. Give her a shot before she damages her head and neck."

Gravely stopped stirring and Tisdale retreated with the face cone. Only a few more moments passed before Gravely stood at my side with a syringe, a drop of liquid hanging from the tip of its sharp needle. Sweat beaded on his forehead, and the tic contorted his cheek. He looked at me in disgust.

"You and Zack are lousy detectives, Bailey Green, or you'd have figured out that I use my speedboat for transporting body parts, not marijuana. You'd have figured out who left the note on your door — who slashed your bicycle tires."

Although I sensed death hovering near, I clung to life, using my only weapons, my brain and my voice. *Keep him talking. Give him a chance to brag.*

"Why? Why target me?" The fluid clinging to the needle felt icy as it dropped onto my breast.

"You and Francine Shipton were two of a kind — nosey do-gooder busybodies. Francine planned to destroy our neighborhood with her homeless shelter, and I knew you'd help Francine do whatever she wanted done. A surgeon in my business can't risk having snoopers nosing around his clinic. And if Francine had her way and enticed the homeless to an Eden Palms shelter, they'd soon be snooping. I had to kill her. She gave me no choice, and you sealed your fate when I caught you boarding my boat."

I tried to confuse Gravely by abruptly changing the subject. "What about Wizard?" By now my mouth was so dry I could hardly speak, but I croaked the words, afraid that he might ignore my question.

"What are you talking about?" His needle scratched at the skin on my arm as he searched for the best spot to plunge it in. "You'll only feel a prick. You'll calm down after that, calm down and let us get the face mask in place."

"I'm calm. And I want to know about Wizard — Mitch Mitchell's homeless friend. You were afraid of his snooping, too? I'd never seen him around here, but when I saw his Conch Republic scarf hanging on your wall, I guessed you'd murdered him."

"Oh, him!" Gravely rolled his eyes. "Yes. We made that scumbag a hero, too. Last Wednesday. Probably the first good thing he ever did for the world."

"Cut the talk." Tisdale stepped closer, face cone in his scaly hand. "Let's get on with it. Now."

Gravely stood pressing the hypo needle against my arm when a door splintered and feet pounded in the hallway.

34

With my scant remaining strength, I lifted my head and shoulders from the gurney and managed to knock the needle from Gravely's hand with my chin.

"Police!" a voice shouted.

In the next second Detectives Cassidy and Burgundy stormed into the room. Zack, Mitch, and Quinn followed.

"Hands up!" Cassidy ordered. "Both of you. You're under arrest."

Detective Burgundy grabbed scissors and cut my bonds, pulled me to my feet. He and Zack helped me into a lab jacket Burgundy jerked from the supply closet.

Zack held me close, and I managed to speak. "They're murderers," I said. "Gravely confessed to killing Francine and Wizard."

Cassidy read both men the Miranda warning. They said nothing. Tisdale made a break for the door, but Mitch tackled him, bringing him to the floor. Gravely and Tisdale rode to police headquarters in the detectives' car. Mitch drove Quinn in my car, which Mitch had claimed at the photo shop when he rushed there searching for me.

Zack and I stopped at the cottage long enough for me to get dressed again and give him a heartfelt kiss before we rode to police headquarters in his convertible.

"Thank you. Thank you, Zack. I'll always be in your debt."

"No debt accrued." Zack squeezed my hand. "Your sharp thinking saved you — connecting Wizard's scarf and Gravely's wall hanging, your taking those snapshots."

"How did you know where they were holding me?"

"After Quinn vouched for Mitch, the police released him. When you hadn't shown up, Quinn, Mitch, and I drove to Glockner's Photo and Phrame to check on you."

"But how did you know to come to Gravely's clinic?"

"Thank Free Glockner for that. When he checked to see what those noisy kids were doing in the parking lot, he saw Gravely urging you into his car. He knew you'd never willingly abandon the chocolate malt you'd set on your car hood. He called nine-one-one."

"So you made a lucky guess and drove to the clinic?"

"A lucky guess — maybe. But your negative feelings about Gravely influenced me — your intuition . . . I hate to admit I've been so wrong about him."

By the time we reached the police station, officers had put Gravely and Tisdale in holding cells. The detectives listened to each of us as we told our stories and signed statements. Then they released us.

In the parking lot, I drew Quinn aside. "When you write Wizard's grisly story, Quinn, it'll help alert the public and law authorities to a dark side of the organ donor program. Mom and I were naïve, seeing only the bright side."

"I'll do my best. That's a promise."

I gave Quinn a hug. "You do that, and Wizard won't have died in vain. Guys like Gravely and Tisdale — I almost choked on their names. They're sociopaths — scum. Your article can help put readers on guard."

Quinn nodded and smiled and when I left her, I knew we were friends again.

Zack and I started to drive Mitch to the bridle path, but he stopped us.

"Drop me off at my apartment, okay? I've

had it with sleeping under the stars."

"Any special future plans?" Zack asked.

"I've been reading online at the library about the Homeless Management Information System. Lots of information on their website. I've applied for a job."

"Where?" I asked.

"At the Neighborhood Improvement Association. Their office's on Emma Street. While I'm waiting to hear about a permanent job, I'll go to work there as a volunteer." He lowered his head. "That's the least I can do for Wizard."

I understood his grief. I didn't say a word. If I sounded too approving of his plans, he might change his mind.

"Good thinking, Mitch," Zack said, stopping at Mitch's apartment. "Go for it."

"See you later, guys. Thanks for the lift."

"Where are we going?" I asked as Zack headed toward the highway.

"It's a surprise. Something I want to show you — if you feel up to it."

"Strange, but I feel great. Guess the adrenalin's still pumping. But I'm warning you. After a day like today, it's going to be hard to surprise me."

Zack drove to Stock Island. We passed marinas and mobile home courts, slowed for kids skateboarding in the street, then stopped beside the dock at Shipton Boats & Salvage. Zack led the way to a small sailboat bobbing on the water. Gulls perched on the stern, screamed outrage as Zack shooed them away.

"This is *my* work-in-progress and today, although I still have some finishing details to complete, we'll take it on its maiden voyage. I've bought a bottle of champagne for the christening." Zack stepped aboard, pulled a bottle from a storage compartment, then joined me on the dock again.

I gasped, surprised. I'd only seen this sort of thing in movies, but I took the bottle he offered and faced the bow of the sailboat.

"Here's to calm seas and gentle breezes." Using strength I didn't know I had, I slammed the bottle against the steel tip of the bow, laughing as champagne splashed onto my legs and shattered glass dropped into the sea.

"Now we'll go for a sail." Zack helped me aboard the boat. "It's getting dark, but there'll be a moon."

We rigged the green sails, and after we motored from the dock and under the Boca Chica bridge, Zack cut the engine and we sailed in peaceful silence while we watched the moon rise like a golden globe. I enjoyed the gentle roll of the boat, and we skimmed across the water until Zack anchored near a tiny islet. He carried a blanket and we splashed to shore, reaching dry sand where we spread the blanket.

There were things I wanted to say to Zack about all that had happened to me this day, but he stopped my words with long slow kisses until our bodies joined in a feverish embrace, and we released our pent-up emotions.

"Bailey, you must know by now that I love you."

I stopped his flow of words with another kiss. Was I really ready for love? Love called for a commitment. What about my career?

"Bailey, do you love me?"

I hesitated only a moment before I answered. "Yes, Zack. I love you with all my heart."

"We can blend our careers and create a wonderful life together, Bailey, if you'll be my wife. Will you marry me? Will you spend the rest of your life with me?"

I pulled Zack close. "I live in possibility."

ABOUT THE AUTHOR

Dorothy Francis, an award-winning author, works from her home studios in Iowa and Florida, writing books and short stories for adults and children. She is a member of Mystery Writers of America, Sisters in Crime, Short Mystery Fiction Society, and the Society for Children's Book Writers and Illustrators. Her first three novels for adults, *Conch Shell Murder, Pier Pressure,* and *Cold-Case Killer* received critical acclaim from *Booklist, Publishers Weekly,* and *Crime Scene Magazine.* She lives with her husband, Richard, a jazz musician and avid fisherman.

For more information, visit her Web site at www.dorothyfrancis.com or send her an e-mail: dorothy@dorothyfrancis.com.

The employees of Thorndike Press hope you have enjoyed this Large Print book. All our Thorndike and Wheeler Large Print titles are designed for easy reading, and all our books are made to last. Other Thorndike Press Large Print books are available at your library, through selected bookstores, or directly from us.

For information about titles, please call:
(800) 223-1244

or visit our Web site at:
http://gale.cengage.com/thorndike

To share your comments, please write:
Publisher
Thorndike Press
295 Kennedy Memorial Drive
Waterville, ME 04901